Island Fire

Island Fire

An Anthology of Literature from Hawai'i

Edited by

Cheryl A. Harstad

and

James R. Harstad

Curriculum Research & Development Group
UNIVERSITY OF HAWAI'I
and
University of Hawai'i Press
HONOLULU

07 06 05 04 03 02   6 5 4 3 2 1

Library of Congress Cataloging-in-Publication Data

Island fire : an anthology of literature from Hawaii / edited by Cheryl A.
Harstad and James R. Harstad
     p. cm.
  ISBN 0–8248–2628–0 (pbk. : acid-free paper)
     1. American literature—Hawaii.   2. Hawaii—Literary collections.
  I. Harstad, Cheryl A.   II. Harstad, James R.
PS571.H3 I85 2002
810.8″09969—dc21

                                                                          2002018079

Cover design by Santos B. Barbasa

Curriculum Research & Development Group Staff
Arthur R. King, Jr., Director
Donald B. Young, Jr., Associate Director
James R. Harstad, Director, Performance English Project
Edith K. Kleinjans, Managing Editor
Gayle Y. Hamasaki, Publications Coordinator

Book design and layout by Lorina L. Modelski and Darrell T. Asato
Cover photo from the Blues Alley collection of Denny and
    Lynda Lou McPhee

Distributed by the Performance English Project
Curriculum Research & Development Group
University of Hawai'i
1776 University Avenue
Honolulu, Hawai'i 96822–2463

E-mail: crdg@hawaii.edu
On the Web: http://www.hawaii.edu/crdg

Printed by Versa Press, Inc.

We were backing from our parking spot and were slowly leaving when, from out of the blue, I saw an image of a lady in the smoke coming from the volcano. She looked like a very powerful woman with a beautiful imposing figure and pretty bushy hair.

"What's that?" I asked, pointing to the smoke.

"It's Pele's figure. She has come to welcome us to her volcano," replied Auntie Vicky, giving me chills and chicken skin.

I hid under my blanket the whole ride back, afraid she would approach our car and sit by me. I will never forget this scary and exciting experience. Seeing Pele in the fire? It could happen to you, too.

—Excerpted from "The Lady in the Smoke"
by Johanna Javier

(Johanna Javier was an 8th-grader at University Laboratory School when she wrote "The Lady in the Smoke.")

Contents

A Foreword

This anthology starts with a fire chant to King Kalakaua. And that's a fitting place to start. It's true to the nature of these islands, which began in fire. It's true to the literature of these islands, which begins with the chanted poetry of a centuries-old tradition.

Not all literary editors have seen it this way, of course. The first popular anthology of modern times, still available and still being read, is *A Hawaiian Reader,* edited by A. Grove Day and Carl Stroven. Judging by the way that volume is organized, the literature of Hawai'i begins in the log of an English sea captain. In his original introduction to this 1961 collection, James Michener said, "The present editors have been wise to save to the end of their volume the five selections dealing with the folklore of the islands, for the language of these passages is so alien to the modern world that it might have alienated the casual reader. It was advisable to start with some selection more in the modern world, like that written by Captain Cook . . ."

Among those strange and "alienating" selections relegated to the back of the book is an excerpt from Martha Beckwith's translation of the venerable creation chant, "The Kumulipo." Here are the opening lines:

> At the time when the earth became hot
> At the time when the heavens turned about
> At the time when the sun was darkened
> To cause the moon to shine . . .

I have a lot of respect for James Michener as one of the major story tellers of our era. But you have to wonder what he had in mind there. Why should the Genesis-like ring of such epic lines be somehow less engaging than the matter-of-fact journal entry that opens *A Hawaiian Reader:*

> In the morning of the 18th, an island made its
> appearance, bearing northeast by east; and soon
> after we saw more land bearing north and entirely
> detached from the former . . .

Needless to say, both of these works are enormously important for a full understanding of Hawai'i's past and present. But in the years since Day and Stroven put their anthology together, a profound change has taken place. Which is not to say that "The Kumulipo" or Cook's journals have changed. Their content remains the same. What has changed is the perception that one is superior to the other. What has changed is the perception that anything indigenous to these islands does not deserve to be at the beginning of a literary collection, or even somewhere in the middle, but belongs at the end, as an afterthought, as an "alien" presence.

What has changed is the idea—stated elsewhere in Michener's introduction—that writers of Asian ancestry have no voice at all in such an anthology, since "these Orientals did not produce a literature of their own." What has changed is the chorus of voices that now have a recognized place in the literature of the Hawaiian islands, a literature that reflects the complex history of a unique crossroads culture.

The collection now called *Island Fire* was among the earliest to convey this cross-cultural legacy. And it is still remarkable for its mix of voices and ethnicities, as well as for its variety of work. There are short stories here, novel excerpts, memoirs, poems, songs, chants, a contemporary one-act play, and a shape-shifter legend from ancient times. Student voices from local schools are heard, side by side with award-winning writers such as Maxine Hong Kingston and Oswald Bushnell, whose *Moloka'i* is regarded by many as "the great Hawaiian novel."

The islands are here, both in body and in spirit, with their many layers of settlement and terrain, the cities, the plantation towns, the rain forests and rural valleys, the waterways, the caves and craters of volcano country. Hawai'i has always been a place where nature and culture continually intertwine. This book contains a world where an island itself can have a voice and sing, where a sacred rock has the power to draw fish toward shore, where sharks are ancestors, and the dead often speak to the living.

Island Fire had its origins as part of a larger work, the landmark anthology, *Asian-Pacific Literature.* In the twenty years since it first appeared, the two-hundred page section called "Hawai'i" has quietly achieved a kind of classic status, as one of those pioneer collections that helped awaken a new generation of readers to the range and richness of what has been emerging here. Finally available as a single volume, the revised and expanded edition still has about it that air of discovery, still shining its own fresh light.

—James D. Houston
July 2001

Preface

> *Hillary had one of her millennium dinners and*
> *we had this very distinguished scientist there, who*
> *is an expert in this whole work in the human*
> *genome. And he said that we are all, regardless of*
> *race, 99.9 percent the same.*
>
> *Now you may find that uncomfortable when*
> *you look around here. (Laughter.) But it is worth*
> *remembering. We can laugh about this, but you*
> *think about it. Modern science has confirmed what*
> *ancient faiths have always taught: the most*
> *important fact of life is our common humanity.*
> *Therefore, we should do more than just tolerate our*
> *diversity—we should honor it and celebrate it.*
> *(Applause.)*
>
> —William Jefferson Clinton
> State of the Union, January 27, 2000

In 1981 we published the three-volume *Asian-Pacific Literature* text, a sampling of outstanding writing from twenty-four countries and island groups. With Hawai'i as our primary audience, we were not surprised that the most popular of the three volumes was the first, the one presenting a generous collection of works *about* Hawai'i. (By no coincidence, none of the authors was named Twain, London, Maugham, Stevenson—or Michener!) In those days, with Bamboo Ridge Press and its followers just getting started, our volume was probably the single best source of what has come to be called "local literature," writing both by and about people of all ethnicities who have lived most of their lives in Hawai'i.

Over the years, both the students who learned about their literary heritage from *Asian-Pacific Literature* and their teachers have told us how much they valued that unique experience. And, often, they have asked whether replacement copies are available. Regrettably, the first printing of our groundbreaking set was the last, and replacement copies of Volume One have not been available for about fifteen years. The success of *Growing Up Local*, co-published with Bamboo Ridge Press in 1998, led us to revisit the earlier work with an eye to republishing "Hawai'i," this time in a volume complete unto itself.

We liked what we saw, and this book is the result. No, it is not exactly what we published in 1981. By adding a few selections, dropping a few, and slightly reorganizing the mix, we hope to have made *Island Fire* more appealing, accessible, and representative than the original.

Because *Asian-Pacific Literature* was a textbook intended for classroom use, each of its reading selections was accompanied by a set of student activities. We have dropped those activities in hopes of giving this book a more universal audience, both inside and outside the classroom. For those wanting to use *Island Fire* as a textbook, we publish a teacher's manual of classroom-tested activities and strategies for each selection. It is available from the Curriculum Research & Development Group (CRDG) at the University of Hawai'i, Mānoa.

What has not changed in any way is our belief in the power of stories to bring diverse people together through a sense of shared community. Here's what we said in the Introduction way back then:

> Storytelling, whatever form it takes, is one of
> the most important bridges to understanding
> between human beings. It gives us the opportunity
> to express our most exciting experiences and our
> most important beliefs in ways that invite friend-
> ship and good will. And it is through the stories we

exchange between friends that we communicate our truest theology, mythology, and philosophy; our history, psychology, sociology, and language. We communicate our shared humanity through our stories.

Perhaps that is why many thoughtful, well-educated people believe that creative literature is the best source of disciplined knowledge about what makes us the way we are. Finely crafted creative literature is, after all, nothing more than an extension of the art of talking story, and its best examples tell us as much about ourselves as they tell about the characters they depict. When we read, we actually become the characters we are reading about, and when we are finished reading we have necessarily received, evaluated, and incorporated many of the attitudes and perceptions of those same characters. By as much as any literary experience changes us, we become that much more under-standing of the people that literary experience represents. The more understanding of other people we become, the closer we are to being members of their cultural communities.

In short, friends, welcome to the *'ohana,* the family.

—Cheryl and Jim Harstad

Acknowledgments

We extend our aloha to Eric Chock and Darrell Lum of
Bamboo Ridge Press and to Grace Fujita and the Hawai'i
Education Association for their nurture of writing in
Hawai'i. Our gratitude to Art King, Don Young, and Loretta
Krause of CRDG and the University Laboratory School for
supporting this publication and to Linda Kumasaki of James
Campbell High School for supporting *us.* Special thanks to
Ann Baldwin Taylor for allowing us to reprint the Big Island
photographs by her late husband, architect Robert S. Taylor.
And a heartfelt *mahalo nui loa* to Alfons L. Korn, whose
memory and legacy live on.

Alert readers will notice that some selections use diacritical
marks in Hawaiian words and some do not. We chose to
follow each author's usage.

Fire Chant for King Ka-lā-kaua
from *The Echo of Our Song*
Translated and edited by Mary K. Pukui & Alfons L. Korn

During the opening decades of the nineteenth century, the fire-burning *kapu* was one of the rights handed down from ruler to ruler among the Hawaiian kings descended from Ka-mehameha I and his ancestors. Later when David Ka-lā-kaua was elected king of Hawai'i in 1874, he wanted especially to strengthen the belief that his claim to the throne rested on more than man-made agencies and mere constitutional procedures. To burn torches by day became under Ka-lā-kaua again a highly significant symbolic act expressive of the king's sacred power, his *mana.*

Ka-lā-kaua's first royal tour through his kingdom began in the second half of March, with a visit to Kaua'i as stately prelude, and continued through a good part of April, culminating in ever more and more popular visits to rural O'ahu. He was loyally welcomed on all three main outlying islands with the customary speech-making in Hawaiian and English, hymn-singing, traditional chanting, presenting of leis and other offerings, interspersed with frequent feasts and bouts of liquid refreshment. (The visit to the leper settlement at Ka-laupapa on Moloka'i had important political overtones, but it was not made a festal occasion.) A marked feature of several of the public demonstrations, especially on Maui, was an elaborate fireworks display, not only in the familiar form of rockets and Roman candles, but enhanced by grand bonfires blazing simultaneously from beach and headland and by torches burning both night and day.

The *Fire Chant for King Ka-lā-kaua* commemorates the civic welcome given Ka-lā-kaua by his people on O'ahu upon the *Kilauea's* return to Honolulu on April 14. The chant was doubtless performed on later occasions during his torch-lit reign.

He Inoa Ahi nō Ka-lā-kaua

Lamalama i Maka-puʻu ke ahi o Hilo.
Hanohano molale ke ahi o Ka-wai-hoa.
ʻOaka ʻōniʻo ʻula kāoʻo ke ahi i Wai-ʻalae.
Hoʻoluehu iluna ke ahi o Lēʻahi.
Hoʻonohonoho i muliwaʻa ke ahi o Ka-imu-kī.
Me he uahi koaiʻe la ke ahi o Waʻahila.
Noho hiehie ke ahi i puʻu o Mānoa.
Oni e kele i luna ke ahi o ʻUala-kaʻa.

A me he ʻahi la ke ahi o Kaluʻ-āhole.
Me he maka-ihu-waʻa la ke ahi o Helu-moa.
Me he moa-lawakea la ke ahi o Kālia.
Me he pāpahi lei la ke ahi o Ka-wai-a-Haʻo.

ʻO mai ke Liʻi nona ia inoa ahi!

Kauluwela i Pū-o-waina ke ahi hōʻike inoa,
Uluwehiwehi ke ahi hoʻokele Hawaiʻi.
Heaha la ia ka pāniʻo o ke ahi? O ka Helu ʻElua.
Pū-ʻulu hōkū-lani ke ahi o Mālia-ka-malu.

A maʻamau pinepine ke ahi o Kawa.
ʻAlua ʻole ke ahi o Moana-lua.
I puʻupuʻua ke ahi ka mauʻu nēnē.
Kaʻi haʻaheo ke ahi puoko ʻula i ka moana.
ʻĀnuenue pipiʻo lua i ka lewa ke ahi o ke kaona.

'O mai ke Li'i nona ia inoa ahi!

Me he papa-kōnane la ke ahi o Alanui Pāpū.
Ahu kīnohinohi ke ahi i Alanui Ali'i.
Me he pōnaha mahina la ke ahi o Hale Ali'i.
Ku me he 'anu'u la ke ahi o ka pahu hae.
Wela ku'u 'āina i ke ahi o 'Ihi-kapu-lani.

'O mai ke Li'i nona ia inoa ahi!

Text by Mary Kawena Pukui

English Translation

Torchlight of Hilo lighted his way to Maka-puʻu.
Now Ka-wai-hoaʻs royal fire burns clear in the Oʻahu
   night.
A throng of red flashing fires of Wai-ʻalae swirls in
   the air.
Lēʻahiʻs fire scatters to the stars.
Coals banked at sterns of canoes glow in Ka-imu-kīʻs
   dusky fires.
Smoky fire of Waʻahila rises like scent of acacia,
   aroma of love.
A chieftain pillar of proud fire stands on a Mānoa
   hillside.
Springing fire of ʻUala-kaʻa embraces the sky.
Gleam of *ʻahi,* fish of yellow flame, shines in the fire
   of Kaluʻ-āhole.
Fire of Helu-moa shows phosphorescent, a mirage
   at sea.
White cock, head of white cock lifted in darkness,
   is fire of Kālia.
A great Aliʻi, fire of Ka-wai-a-Haʻo, stands wreathed
   in purest light.

Answer us, O Chief, whose fire chant we sing!

Intense fire spells out his name on Punchbowl Hill.
He is the Helmsman—*Ka Mōʻī*—revealed in flame
   and rockets' glare.
What is that portal of friendly lamplight? Fire
   Company Number Two.
Blessed fires of Mary of Peace shine like a congrega-
   tion of stars.

Fire of constancy is the fire of Kawa, unwavering
        fire.
Bonfires of Moana-lua burn unmatched for wild
        display.
Banks of *nēnē*-grass one after another burst into
        blaze.
So proud warriors tread by torchlight, their march-
        ing mirrored in the sea.
That double rainbow arching the sky is the reflected
        fire of the town.

Answer us, O Chief, whose fire chant we sing!

A checkered *kōnane*-board is Fort Street on fire.
Gay calico prints are the fires decorating King.
The fire at the Palace shines in a circle, a full moon.
Like a tower atop an ancient temple is the fire-ringed
        flagpole.
So lives my land heated everywhere by the sacred
        kapu-fire of 'Ihi-kapu-lani.

Answer us, O Chief, whose fire chant we sing!

The Queen's Prayer
Queen Lili'uokalani

Hawaiian Version

'0 kou aloha nō
Aia i ka lani,
A 'o kou 'oiā'i'o
Hemolele ho'i.

Ko'u noho mihi 'ana
A pa'ahao 'ia,
'O 'oe ku'u lama,
Kou nani, ko'u ko'o.

Mai nānā 'ino'ino
Nā hewa o kānaka,
Akā e huikala
A ma'ema'e nō.

Nō laila e ka Haku,
Ma lalo o kou 'ēheu
Kō mākou maluhia
A mau aku nō.

First English Translation

O Lord, Thy loving mercy
Is high as the heavens;
It tells us of Thy truth
And 'tis filled with holiness.

Whilst humbly meditating
Within these walls imprisoned,
Thou art my light, my haven
Thy glory my support.

Oh, look not on our failing,
Nor on the sins of men.
Forgive with loving kindness
That we might be made pure.

For Thy grace I beseech Thee;
Bring us 'neath Thy protection
And peace will be our portion,
Now and forevermore. Amen.

Second English Translation

Your love
Is in heaven,
And your truth
So perfect.

I live in sorrow
Imprisoned,
You are my light,
Your glory my support.

Behold not with malevolence
The sins of man,
But forgive
And cleanse.

And so, o Lord,
Beneath your wings
Be our peace
Forever more.

Pele's Own
Charles M. Kong

The road which battled its way across lava flats from the main highway leading to Mauna Kea and town was a desolate, dusty road. Farther on as it neared Winona's shack, the road twisted and squirmed its way along the craggy coasts, slowing to a pleasurable crawl only when it hit the sandy inlets which spreckled the barrens.

Shading her eyes, Winona spied the wastes ahead of her. The road was disgustingly empty. Angrily, Winona scratched her head. She shook her shoulders indifferently. She wished Julian would make it snappy. She was dreadfully anxious to see the new movie. Julian said it was a real hot love story.

That was typical of Julian. He knew so much about a lot of things. Maybe it was because he had gone to college. Anyway, he was different from the guys she knew. When she thought about that oaf, Kamaka, whom she had agreed to marry not a week ago, she wanted to scream. How could she have been so stupidly blind, so . . . so . . . so completely taken over by the scrubby fisherman whom her father employed. It made her shudder to think about it. If she hadn't met Julian at the county fair last Saturday, she would have been stuck forever. It was sure funny the way things happened.

Bending over, Winona lifted her skirt and wiped the dewy drops of sweat which glistened on her forehead. The air was a stagnant sea of heat. Delicately pursing her lips, Winona touched them with her tongue. She remembered that first night she had met Julian. He had kissed her, laughingly telling her that it was an old custom among civilized people. She wished she was as smart as Julian. Her lips suddenly felt full.

Ma called her. She went into the shack. Ma glanced at her, standing as she was over the sink savagely kneading the poi. "You going out tonight?"

"Yeah, Ma, I going out wid Julian."

Ma's dark forehead wrinkled as if she were trying to recall the name, "Who dis Julian?"

"Oh, Ma," Winona cried excitedly. "He da handsomest guy I eva meet. He going take me show tonight."

"And wat samatta wid Kamaka? I taught you going marry him." Ma put the bowl of poi on the table. "Wat you tink Kamaka going say wen him and Pa come in tomorrow? Wat he going say when he fine out you go fool aroun' wid dis guy?"

Winona pinched Ma's cheek gaily. "No worry. Wen Kamaka come in, I going tell him dat us pau. I not going marry him."

Ma swung around. "Wat you say?" she asked incredulously.

"I not going marry Kamaka, 'at's all."

"You mean because dis udda guy, dis . . . dis . . . wat you call him?"

"Julian."

"Yeah, dis Julian. You mean because you fall in luff wid him?"

Winona nodded her head. Sure she loved him. There was no use denying it. They were going to Honolulu where he would work. And they would have a big house, a hundred times bigger than the shack in which she was born. Julian would give her a lot of servants and a swanky car too. And they would have a lot of kids. And he would take her to the movies, like tonight. And she would love him. And he would love her. And maybe they would invite Ma and Pa and Kamaka to come—no, it would never work out if Kamaka came. Kamaka would try to lick Julian. Anyway, she and Julian would be happy forever and forever, and—

Ma was saying: "You dunno him, you sure you luff him? He luff you?"

Did he love her? Of all the silly questions to ask. Didn't he tell her the night he brought her home from the fair that she was as lovely as a Botticelli angel. Of course she had no idea what sort of an angel Botticelli was, but it really didn't matter. The way Julian's eyes had suddenly become hot and glassy told her everything she needed to know.

"Yeah, Ma," she answered, "he luff me."

Ma sighed heavily. "I dunno. I dunno, Winona."

"Dunno wat, Ma?"

"How dis going turn out."

Looking at Ma's mountainous body, Winona thought: How could you know what real love is, Ma? I mean the kind of love which I feel for Julian . . . the kind that eats away at your insides . . . the kind that gives you dreams which make you weak just thinking about them. Nature gave you a wrong deal, Ma. Maybe if you weren't built like a barrel, you would have had the luck to have someone like Julian fall in love with you. You never had the chance to love. You met Pa, and because he was a good fisherman, a good provider, and probably the only guy who ever paid you any attention, you married him. Well, Ma, it's different with me. I'm pretty.

"No worry, Ma, I know what I doing."

Ma shrugged as if she were too tired to go on. "I hope you right, Winona." Then in a burst of maternal indignation: "You betta go baiph. You sweat like Opunui's jackass."

"I went baiph dis aftanoon a'ready."

"Go baiph again." Winona knew it was useless to argue with Ma once she made up her mind. Ma was inflexible that way. Winona took another bath.

After bathing, Winona stood before the mirror admiring herself. Her hair was like a mass of black Spanish moss. She ran her hands over her hips, feeling a delicious tingle pulsate down her long, tan legs. Delightful, simply heavenly.

Ma came in, and watched Winona sort her clothes on the bed. She said, not without some pride in her voice, "I used to look like you befoa. Everybody in da village use to say I was pretty." And then, as if to offer further proof to her statement, she added, "Ask you fada. He tell you."

Winona smiled tolerantly. Let Ma rave. Let her dream. She wasn't fooling anyone. In a way Ma's self praise was a crying shame. Winona was sorry for Ma. Anybody who begins to relive the past is admitting that he has been defeated in the present.

"Ma," she asked, "how I going hide dis ugly mole on my neck?"

"Wat for you like hide 'em?" Ma came peering closely, " 'At's not'ing. In fact, 'at's look nice."

"Nah, Ma, you donno not'ing." Winona wrapped a forest-green scarf around her neck. "I tink I going use dis." Ma was silent.

Winona slipped on a purple blouse that had three-quarter sleeves lined with pink ruffles. Then she stepped into a dress which appeared as if it had been soaked in whale's blood. Pirouetting, like a ballet dancer with corns on her feet, Winona said, "Wat you tink?" She didn't really care whether Ma answered or not.

Ma didn't say anything. She looked at Winona, her face a blank mask, looking, just looking. Finally, Winona broke the spell. "Wat samatta, Ma?"

Ma put her hand on Winona. "You going wid dis guy all dressed up like dat?"

"Sure, Ma. Julian not like Kamaka, you know. When you go someplace wid somebody like Julian, you gotta dress up. You gotta be high tone. You gotta show 'em you not ignorant."

Sadly, Ma shook her head. "You can wear one feather dress but dat no mean you can fly. Dat no mean you one bird."

"You no need worry, Ma, I know wat I doing." Winona smeared her lips with strawberry red lipstick. She hoped Julian would like its taste. She admitted it was a cheap brand, but for texture and color you couldn't beat it. "By da way, Ma, I need some money."

"Foa wat?"

"I like buy Julian one box candy foa present."

"But Winona," Ma tried to protest, "You no . . ."

"If you no like give me no need," Winona interrupted. She flung her lipstick into her purse and slammed it shut. Ma quietly left the room. Presently she returned. "Winona, heah two dollars. You tink des nough?"

Winona threw her arms around Ma. "Ma, Ma, tank you, you so sweet." She squeezed Ma.

When Julian called for her, Winona invited him in. She introduced him to Ma. They shook hands. Ma was politely reserved, almost shy. Julian acted as if meeting Ma was the most important thing that could happen to him. His effusive behavior seemed to annoy Ma, for she fidgeted uncomfortably, as if she had the itch.

Turning to Winona, Julian said, "I see now where you inherit your beauty, Winona," he winked.

Winona grinned. Julian was the perfect gentleman. Only a gentleman would say such nice things about her mother. And he was considerate of her own feelings too, otherwise he wouldn't have tipped her off with a wink. Julian said, "You've got a swell place here, Ma. But aren't you afraid someday Mauna Kea will erupt? You people are living in the path of the lava flows."

"Pele take care o' us."

"You believe in Pele, the fire goddess? I mean . . . well . . . do you really believe in Pele?"

"Sure. Wat samatta wid dat?"

"Why, I . . . I . . . I don't know. I'm an Episcopalian myself." He fumbled for a cigarette. "Mind if I smoke?

Thanks." He took a deep drag and exhaled. Behind a cloud of smoke he said, "I'm a Hawaiian, you know."

Winona blinked in surprise. Julian's skin was as white as the clouds over Mauna Kea.

"Wat part you Hawaiian?" asked Ma innocently.

"My father's grandfather was half. I suppose that would make me, let me see . . ." he wrinkled his brows for a minute. "I guess it would make me about one-sixteenth, wouldn't it?"

"Yeah," Ma answered. "You Hawaiian a'right."

"Getting back to the Pele business, I thought good Queen Kapiolani proved to our people that Pele was a fraud? You remember the story. She went up to the rim of the volcano and dared Pele to harm her. Of course nothing happened."

"And wat dat proof?" Ma seemed to have come to life. Winona was embarrassed. Why didn't Ma keep her mouth closed? She was only showing her ignorance. Julian was smart. Ma couldn't hope to hold an argument with him.

"It proves," Julian explained patronizingly, "that Pele is only a myth, a fairy tale."

"You mean because Pele neva keel da Queen, she no live?" There was a strange light in Ma's eyes. Julian puffed leisurely. "Yes, that's right, Ma."

"Who you belief?"

"I'm a Christian. I believe in Christ."

Ma rolled her sleeves. Raising her fists, she hollered, "Hey, Christ, I like see you keel me. I dar' you! I dar' you!"

"Good God!" exclaimed Julian aghast. "It's blasphemy."

A deep stillness descended upon the room. Julian's mouth was agape. Winona was confused. Ma had done something terribly, terribly wrong. She didn't know what it was, but she sensed it. At last Ma spoke. "You God one fairytale, Julian. He no do not'ing."

"I . . . I . . ." Julian fumbled, "I don't know what to say, Ma." He appeared dumb-founded.

"Julian," Winona said hastily, "we betta go befoa we late foa da show."

"Yes, yes, Winona." Hurriedly he killed his cigarette as if glad for the chance to escape. "You go ahead and dress, Winona, and we'll leave."

"Dress! Wat samatta, you tink I naked?"

"But surely . . ."

"Den let's go." Winona grabbed his arm, at the same time talking over her shoulder, "No need wait foa me, Ma. Maybe I come home late."

It was the morning after. The sun was shining, a perverse sun that streaked through the window and splashed all over Winona. It got into her eyes, and soaked through the covers, steaming her as neatly as if she were in a sweat box. Desperately, Winona dug her head under a pillow splotched with lipstick stains.

Somebody was calling. She pushed the pillow away from her head. "Winona! Wen you going get up?" Ma was shaking her. "Late a'ready, and us get plenty wo'k foa do today."

"Oh Ma," she groaned, "lemme sleep five moa minutes."

"We get plenty foa do. Pa comin' in today." Ma pulled the covers off the bed. Sleepily, Winona sat rubbing her eyes.

Ma was grumbling. "You go have good time, no come home til da frogs go sleep. Den wen time foa get up, you like sleep."

Stretching, Winona yawned. "You always squawking, Ma."

Ma snorted. "Who going do all da wo'k?"

"Wo'k, wo'k, 'at's all you tink about, Ma. Take it easy. We get plenty time." Again she yawned. Ma noticed the clothes Winona had worn the night before strewn on the floor.

"Why you throw all you clothes on the floor, Winona? You moa worse den one baby." Groaning, Ma stooped over with an effort and began picking up the clothes. "Who going do dis foa you wen you get married? I pity you husband."

Grinning, Winona patted Ma on the cheek. "No worry, Ma. Wen I marry Julian I going get servants."

"You mean he wen ask you marry him a'ready?"

Winona slipped into her dress. "No, Ma, not exactly."

"Den wat you mean?"

"Jest wat I say. He going marry me."

"But he nevva tell you he going marry you."

Exasperated, Winona said, "He no need tell me. I jest know."

Ma shrugged. "I dunno. Maybe dis new style you get. Befoa, da boy use to ask da girl he like marry her. Now you tell me he no need."

"Look Ma," Winona said, trying to control herself, "you can tell if da boy luff you by da way he act, by da way he talk, by da way he look. If you know all dat, he no need tell you not'ing."

"I suppose," Ma replied sarcastically, "you fine all dis out last night wen Julian look at you, talk to you, and do something to you, eh?"

Winona felt herself blushing. She wished she hadn't introduced the subject. But it was true, every word of it. Somehow she felt she knew Julian much better after last night. She didn't enjoy the movie as much as she had thought she would, but that was because Julian didn't seem to be having a good time. He had appeared embarrassed, self-conscious, not his usual self. He had tried, however, to conceal it by grinning most of the time, but she had noticed. Of course, she hadn't said anything to him. That would have made him more uncomfortable. It was bad enough with all those people staring at them. Why they were so rude, she could never understand. She wondered if all town people behave that way. She must ask Julian about it when he came in the evening.

It was funny, thinking about it now, how fast Julian had recovered. The movie had no sooner been over, and they were driving home, when he had swerved to the side of the road, doused the lights, and in complete darkness began to tell her how much he loved her. A delicious sensation came over her as she recalled his amorous advances.

"Okay, Ma," Winona answered moving toward the door. "I go eat breakfast den I help you wo'k."

And work she did indeed. She was so fagged out at the end of the day that she had hardly enough strength to bathe and dress and pretty herself before Julian would arrive. But miraculously, by six-thirty she was ready. Pa had come home by then, bringing with him a sack of fish and Kamaka. She was thankful to Ma for not mentioning Julian to Pa and Kamaka. Sometimes she suspected Ma of having a little common sense.

After dinner and another hour had passed, Winona decided that the thing she detested most, of all the things in the world which she could possibly dislike, was waiting. In spite of Pa's long talk on politics and fishing, which he had carried on throughout dinner, Winona couldn't remember a word he had said. Her mind was a seething turmoil. She was worried about Julian, and oblivious in a vague way, to everything that went on around her. Once or twice Kamaka had tried in his shy, unobtrusive manner to speak to her, but she had cut him short. She was sorry. Poor Kamaka, she hadn't meant to hurt him. He was so sensitive with women, that a harsh word or cross look would immediately wilt him. Yet he was a regular bull with men.

Julian still didn't come. Kamaka had humbly said goodnight to her and had departed. Pa and Ma had retired to their bedroom; and she, left alone, had gone out into the inky night with the chirping crickets and the eternal jewels blinking in the sky. A thousand questions tumbled through her mind, and there were a million answers, but none would satisfy the question: Why hadn't Julian come? She wept for a while. And then she must have sobbed herself to sleep, for Pa came out and carried her in.

Julian never returned. For months after his disappearance Winona never stopped looking for him. Ma never spoke of Julian, even to Pa. And Kamaka never understood what was going on, but sometimes when he'd visit with Pa, he'd quietly go out and sit with Winona, saying nothing, respecting silence.

Winona was grateful to him and one day as they were sitting together, she said, "Kamaka, you betta no foaget dat you and me was going get married."

Excerpt from
The Mystery of the Ku'ula Rock
Joseph Keonona Chun Fat

My mother showed me a flat rock near the beach when the tide was high and just touched the rock. This was called the altar or papa mohai where the Ku'ula is placed. A Ku'ula was used for two purposes; for celebration by the chief of the village and the arrival of the royal family, and for the welfare of the people of the village. There was no monetary value received for getting the fish by using the Ku'ula rock. To violate these purposes meant the penalty of death to the one who tried to use it for his own gain or to his loved ones.

I asked my mother if the stone on the altar was a Ku'ula as I didn't see any fish. She explained that the rock I saw was just an ordinary rock which someone had left there. A real Ku'ula was not left alone. It was taken by the keeper either to his hut or to the cave. He guarded this Ku'ula like you take care of your money. She told me it was very dangerous to keep a Ku'ula because the rituals that went with it must be observed. If you failed you would be punished, usually by death. So, she advised me not to try and look for one.

I will explain to you a case where this had happened. A young man explored a cave that happened to be a burial cave. He found a small rock statue and thought it was a nice ordinary rock that meant nothing and he could take it home. He did not realize it was a Ku'ula rock. He put the rock in his living room on the book case and forgot all about it. As time passed, he forgot everything.

Then one day as he was in the kitchen, he heard someone call him. He answered and walked into the living room where the voice came from but saw no one. Then he called out, "Who wants me?" No one answered. He stepped into the bedroom and also saw no one. For a minute he thought maybe he was hearing voices and thought it was from the living room. He stepped outside of the building and walked around the house but still did not see anyone, so he came back into the house.

That night he woke up after midnight, got up, walked to the kitchen, opened the door, and stepped a few steps to the stone wall. He left the lantern inside the kitchen door. He stood at the wall and urinated as the house had no toilet facilities. The moon was out and there was a light haze. As he turned back to walk to the kitchen door, he stopped because he saw an object standing in the door. It was a small person about four feet high, wrapped in a white sheet. The face was black and it was hard to make out the features. For a minute he stood looking at the object. He pinched his arm twice to see if he really was awake. He made a mistake as, instead of talking, he advanced to see whether the object would move or not. In one move the object disappeared. He closed the door and walked to the bedroom but did not wake his wife until the next morning.

While she was making his breakfast, he told her about the incident of the night before. His wife was worried. She knew something was wrong in the house. She told him, "Since you brought that stone in the house, I have felt uneasy. I think the stone is a Kuʻula rock." The husband said, "It's nothing but an ordinary rock. That rock is just like any rock. The only thing I like about it is that it looks like a small statue." Then he told his wife what had happened the day before. He told her he was sure he heard someone call him. His wife told him that they must go to see a Kahuna. He asked, "Do you know any Kahuna who would know about this?"

She said, "I do not know any. All the old folks are dead. How about going to see the Elder of the Mormon Church? He is an old man and maybe he can help us."

They got into their little car and started for the next town about ten miles away. The Elder's little home was next to the church. They both walked to the house and were greeted by his wife who asked them to come in. The Elder was in the living room listening to his radio. He stood up and said, "Come right in and sit right next to me." He looked at both of them and said, "I know something is troubling you. Whatever it is, let me ask the Lord for His blessing." So, he prayed and when he finished he said, "Your trouble is that you have a Ku'ula in your home." Then the husband explained where he got the Ku'ula and he had brought it home because it looked like a little statue. The Elder said, "This Ku'ula is lonesome and wants you to return it to where you found it. You are a very lucky fellow. A Ku'ula is a dangerous weapon to have, since you do not understand. Return it and when you do, just say these words of appreciation. 'I am thankful to you. I am leaving you here because this is your home and you will be happy.' " So he left the Ku'ula in the cave and came home. This story is the true one. I just want you to know what you are in for.

There are two kinds of Ku'ula rock. One is the meteorite rock that comes from outer space. You see falling stars at night. This meteorite falls from space and lands on earth and burns for several days. The native would walk to find where the fire was and wait until the rock was cool before he tried to pick it up. All he wanted to pick was one piece and return home. He knew that the meteorite rock had the power to attract fish in schools such as ahole or mackerel. This is all the power that this rock possessed. The owner or the keeper of the rock had the supernatural power to set a taboo system. Whoever stole the fish Ku'ula was penalized by death to him or his loved ones.

The second Ku'ula is the ordinary porous rock that was hand chiseled to the keeper's image. A blue rock was used to chisel the Ku'ula porous rock. The owner of the Ku'ula rock was usually the head of the family. The purpose of this Ku'ula was to get more food for the family. It was used during the planting season in order to bring good harvesting and during harvest time the Ku'ula was brought out again and placed on the altar. This time a bounty of one of each kind of the crop harvested was placed at the altar to satisfy the Ku'ula. The rest the family could use and what was left was given to those who were in need. At night the owner would pick up the Ku'ula and return it to the house or the cave.

In the family circle, the ritual was taught to the older son. If no son, then to the oldest daughter. When she married, her husband took over the responsibility. A Ku'ula rock was never used for monetary reasons for the owner but only for the family and those in need.

In the process of getting this Ku'ula rock, the head of the family usually called a family Kahuna whom they came to with their troubles for advice. He received his training from his forefathers. He usually possessed the same supernatural power. That was the reason they listened to him.

The first sign in the making of an ordinary rock to become a Ku'ula rock, and the power to perform its duty or destiny by the Kahuna or keeper, always came from his dream. In this dream, he is destined to go to a certain valley to pick a rock. It also states in the dream what the object will be. With this in his mind he must chisel this rock with a blue rock by hand. As soon as the image of the rock is the same as in his dream, the work is done. He returns home and names the rock for the place from which he got it. This is how the Ku'ula is named Ku'ula o Kalaoa.

The next step occurs when all the family gathered at the home of the keeper for him to demonstrate how he talks to the Ku'ula. He brought the Ku'ula and laid it on the floor. They all sat around the Ku'ula. The keeper sat in front. He looked at the Ku'ula, concentrating on the eye of the image. In a few seconds he was in a trance. His body began to shake a little and his shoulders began to move from right to left. It seemed as if some force came into him. In a little while he began to talk. He was communicating with the Kuʻula through mental telepathy. It seemed as though he was asking questions and answering them at the same time. This is what the family saw, but he was actually talking to the Kuʻula and the Kuʻula was answering. This was one of the mysteries that only the keeper knew. Whatever instructions were given, the keeper would accept and carry out. The purpose was to bring more food during planting and harvesting. If this was carried out, the village would share in the prosperity.

But some keepers, knowing the power of the Kuʻula, used the Kuʻula for personal gain by extinction of the spirit or soul. This is what they called death by Hawaiian sickness without any cause. In these cases even the doctor claimed one died a natural death.

In that village there was another Kahuna who knew that a keeper had a good Kuʻula for planting and harvesting. He was going to try and steal the Kuʻula from him, but not in the sense that he would walk in his hut and take the Kuʻula. He would use his power when the keeper was sleeping. As soon as he made contact with this Kuʻula he would walk into the house and use it to kill the owner by extinguishing his spirits. This is why a Kuʻula is a dangerous weapon in the wrong hands because it gives the owner the power.

There are many rocks called Kuʻula that decorate the hotel roadway. Their purpose is for a marker or a reminder for others to see. Kuʻula, if it is literally translated, means a "red stand." The word "ula" means "red." The color red to a Kahuna is sacred. In speaking of Kuʻula, it is a sacred stand. If you happened to wander down the roadway around the hotel, especially in the Kona district, you will see all kinds of Kuʻula rocks and some will have names written on them. Whatever the purpose the hotel people have in mind is the same that the natives had in the years gone by. The Kuʻula you see is not different from the Ku'ula the keeper or owner had.

Sometimes the Ku'ula is buried as there is no one to take care of it. It happens that this kind of Ku'ula is unearthed and taken from a cave and sometimes found among other rocks. There are a few noticeable signs that the Ku'ula may have to call your attention. When you notice this, the next step is to find someone who knows how to interpret it. There are very few Hawaiians who know how to, and if they do, they will not tell. This is a dangerous thing to do. Once you interpret the Ku'ula, you probably will be the keeper. There are many restrictions, and if you fail them the penalty is too great. It is easy to refuse not to do anything. The best bet is to return it to any cave and leave it there. The next best thing to do is to go to one of the Buddhist temples and see the priest. He can help and tell whether the stone is a Ku'ula rock or not. If it is, the priest will bless it and put it away from harming anyone in the future.

There are symptoms that a real Ku'ula rock will cause and you wonder if it is coincidence or not. If you are planting you pick up this rock and put it alongside the plant. You may or may not notice that this plant will not grow. The same kind of plant not far from the rock will grow beautifully. Sometimes you see a rock and it takes your fancy because it looks almost human. You clean it and place it in the yard for decoration. Some children happen to ask you about it and you remark that it is a Ku'ula rock and has supernatural powers. Just be careful. You spoke without knowing. Children are funny. One looks and makes a funny face, thinking it is a joke. The next thing that happens is that this child becomes sick and the parent takes it to the doctor. The result there is that there is nothing wrong, the child is all right. Then the parents want to know what happened or if he ate at your place. Your answer will be no. You know he made faces at the rock. This is why he has a red face. There are many more incidents where you will see the real Ku'ula from the other rocks.

This incident happened in the district of Kau, Hawai'i. A Japanese woman owned a small store. The husband worked at the plantation and her son worked for the county to repair roads. She loved to plant flowers and vegetables around the back yard. She always kept a wooden barrel at the back where the family urinated. The urine was mixed with water and sprayed over the plants and they grew beautifully. She also was a barber and cut the hair of those who came to the store.

I met her several times and stopped at the store to have a haircut. I saw a little shrine on the shelf. In this shrine I saw a Ku'ula rock and a small fresh bowl of rice in front of the Ku'ula. I told her that the rock was in the wrong place. She told me the rock was Japanese now because he was eating rice. She said, "I talked to him in Japanese. He cured me of my sickness when the doctor said he could not cure me."

I asked her, "Did you go and see an Hawaiian Kahuna?"

The answer was, "No, I went to a Japanese temple and a priest came here and blessed the store and told me to keep the Ku'ula in the house. I did and I am well now." She told me her hands and feet were swollen and said, "You can see now I am all right and well."

I asked her how she came to get the Ku'ula rock. She told me, "My son found it while he was working on the road."

I asked, "Where is your son today?"

She replied, "He is at the back of the house building a small chicken coop. He loves to raise chicks after they are hatched from an incubator." I asked if I could see him. She said I could after she finished my haircut. I was interested in knowing how he got this Ku'ula. I paid the woman for my haircut and walked to the back to see the son. He was setting the coop near the fence. I asked him if he had a minute to spare. He told me to wait a few seconds until he was finished with the coop.

When he was through, I said, "I am interested to hear from you about the Ku'ula rock you got on the road while you were working." He sat down and began to tell me the exact story.

One morning after the tractor was removing the rocks from the road, he tried to shovel but a rock wouldn't come out, so he got a pick ax and dug around it. Then he tried to yank the rock away, but it wouldn't come, so he stopped and took a closer look. He thought it would come loose with the next try so he lifted the ax high and came down with a heavy stroke. All it did was to chip off the top of the rock. He tried once more by using his pick ax to yank the rock out. This time the point of the pick was caught. As he pulled and yanked, he broke the rock and he fell on the road. He stood up and picked up the loose piece of rock. To his amazement the broken piece was no longer an ordinary rock. This piece looked like the shape of a human arm. He started to dig around the rest of the rock and finally got it out. It was a rock with the form of a human and the broken piece of arm fit right in. He said he would take it home for his yard. All the men stood by and looked at the human form rock but no one said a word. He wrapped the rock in the gunny sack and left it in the hollow of the tree trunk with his lunch. During lunch one of the men told him that it must be a Ku'ula rock and if it was he had better leave it as it was too dangerous, but he said it was only a rock and no harm would come to him. Another one of the men told him to see a Kahuna as he could tell whether it was a Ku'ula rock or not. He replied, "I am going to leave it in the garden and when I have time I will see a Kahuna."

He continued, "That evening when I came home, I took the Ku'ula rock in the garden and left it with the plants. I did not tell anyone. During the weekend when I had time I could clean off the dirt and cement the arm to the body. After the second week I did the job and the Ku'ula rock looked good to me. I was satisfied so I left it between the plants. I wanted to make a concrete stool and place the Ku'ula rock on it like a small statue and put it in the middle of the garden. It would look beautiful. This was my idea but I did not get around to it.

"Then I noticed my mother's hands and feet were swollen. I told her to see the doctor. She did, but the medicine did not take effect. It did not dawn on me that it had something to do with the rock I brought home. My only idea was to beautify the garden. My mother went to see the Japanese priest at a nearby temple and he told her that since the medicine did not do anything, there must be something wrong in the house. He said, 'I am busy now, but I will be over to your place during the weekend.'"

The son said, "The day he arrived I was not home. This is what my mother told me."

"I met the priest at the door at the store. I invited him to come in so he came into the living room and sat down. I got a bowl of tea and offered it to him. He sipped the tea and talked to me.

"My sister was home so she kept the store while my mother took the priest around the house. He walked in every room of the house including the store and the barber shop. He blessed as he walked. When that was over he told my mother that there was nothing there and that the place was free from all evil. Then the priest and my mother walked in the garden. He then sensed that something was not right and he told my mother that there was something there of Hawaiian origin that was causing her sickness and he must find the object. Then my mother asked the priest what this object looked like. He said it was a small Hawaiian statue kept in an unclean place and asked if my mother had seen it.

"She said, 'I did not notice an Hawaiian statue in the vegetable garden. All I did was to water the plants and sometimes pour on the urine mixed with water as a fertilizer.'

" 'That's nothing wrong,' the priest said. 'I know the answer. This statue is clean and wants to be kept in a clean surrounding.'

"As they walked through the vegetable plants, they noticed a pile of rocks. The leaves had covered the rocks. They removed the leaves and among the pile of rocks was resting the little Ku'ula. The priest picked up the rock and told my mother to clean it and keep it in the house. The priest examined the rock and said, 'If I can only communicate through mental telepathy, maybe I can give you the answer of the duties of this Ku'ula rock. There is something about this rock. I can only feel and I cannot see. To me it is a good omen. You take good care of this rock and I can assure you, your trouble will be over.' She took the rock into the house. While it was sitting on the table he gave a blessing of thanksgiving and left the store."

The son told his mother, "I will make a small shrine and set the Ku'ula rock on it." The following week he did and it looked like a natural setting for the Ku'ula. His mother said, "If Buddha has his rice in the morning, the Ku'ula rock will have his."

He continued, "We did not give the rock any name and left it as is. If we did, it would complicate matters. This little Hawaiian statue became the main attraction in the store. To prove it my mother said, 'Look at my hands and feet. They are normal now thanks to the Ku'ula rock.'"

There is another incident that happened on the island of Maui. I was there when I was distributing film for the Royal Film Company, a business I owned. I had a picture that was showing at one of the plantations. I came to the theater to see it and asked the doorman about the crowd. He told me it was a full house. This picture had to do with rocks almost similar to the Ku'ula rock. Whoever owned this rock seemed to have everything come his way. The owner was puzzled and did not believe it was the rock. There is more to this story.

As I was standing outside the theater, an elderly Japanese man asked me if I believed the story about the rock. I told him that it might be true for whomever the story was written about, but that we had the same thing here in Hawai'i. I told him what I knew of the Ku'ula rock. Then he asked me if I could help him and I asked him in what way. He wanted me to find some Kahuna who could cure his son who was mentally unbalanced. I told him that I had never done this kind of work but after hearing his story I might be able to direct him to someone that could help him. I told him I would come to his house the next day to hear his whole story. I went to his home in Makawao, Maui, and met his wife and his only son who was mentally unbalanced. The wife prepared coffee for me and we sat down to talk. He asked me to stay at his home for the night. Then I listened to his story.

"I am a fish dealer. My place of business is in Wailuku town. I travel to the different districts and buy fish from individual fishermen who want to sell their catch. I met a Hawaiian fisherman who always catches a lot of fish. One day I was at the beach and watched him catching a school of fish. I stood at the edge of the beach as he was bringing the fish in. He stepped in front of me, picked up one fish, and placed it on a rock. Then he walked past me to his wagon to unload the fish. I stood and looked at the fish on the flat rock. Next to the fish was a small rock statue. Then I turned and walked to his car to see what deal I could make for the catch he had brought in. He gave me a figure and I paid him. Then the Hawaiian returned to pick up his rock and walked back to the car.

"I asked about the rock and, at first, the Hawaiian did not want to say. Then he said, 'This is a Ku'ula. All my catch is made with this Ku'ula.' "

The fish dealer told him he was interested in buying the rock. He said, "I am willing to pay you five hundred dollars. If you are interested, let me know."

So the Hawaiian said, ''I will speak to my wife. If she says yes, I will let you know.''

The dealer said, "All the time I am buying fish from the Hawaiian and if only I could get that rock my future would be well rewarded.''

I asked him if he knew that the rock had a ritual that had to be performed and to break one of the rituals meant death to the owner or his loved ones. He was not told of these things. He said, "Why do you ask, because I never asked. All I see is that he got lots of fish and only what I see I am interested in.

"One day the fisherman called me to see if I wanted to buy the Ku'ula. He said it would cost me five hundred dollars. I talked to my wife and she agreed to buy it. The next day I went to the bank and drew out the money. I went to his house and bought the rock. There was no receipt given. We agreed as gentlemen. I never asked what the duties were. He seemed to think I knew what to do like when I make a catch, I must leave one fish as a bounty at the altar. He never told me but I saw what he did. I was glad to get the rock and he was happy to have the money. I came home and showed the rock to my wife.

"After the week was over I took the family to the beach. I also took the rock with me. I had the throw net at the back of the fish wagon. I walked the beach and scouted for a place to set the Ku'ula on and scanned the ocean to see where the fish might be. I found the place and set the stone on it and waited to see the fish. In a second I saw the fish swimming toward the Ku'ula. I was amazed to see that an ordinary stone had such a force or power to lure the fish. I got my throw net ready and made one throw. The net was filled with fish. I had a hard time bringing the net together. My wife, seeing my predicament, brought a gunny sack and helped me pick the fish from the net. We both were surprised. We had two gunny sacks filled with fish.

"I picked up the Kuʻula and threw it to the back of the fish truck on one of the bags of fish we caught. We hurried to the fish market to unload the catch. My wife helped me bring the fish into the market while I was selling to the customers. Because it was fresh fish the sale was made in no time. When it was over I said to my wife, 'One more catch like this and I will have my money back and the rest is all gravy.' We were both happy with the results. The next week we were out at another part of the beach and we got the same results. As time went on I got all that I paid and still more and this was wonderful.

"Then one day I got a report from the school that my son had lost his memory. I came to the school to see the teacher who told me, 'This morning he was all right. After lunch I gave him a paper to fill in, answering some questions. All I saw was all kinds of marks such as this. Lots of fish sketches. I was puzzled and asked him and he did not know what I was saying. This is something I do not understand. It is best to take him to the doctor.'

"This I did. We arrived at the doctor's office and I had to wait as he was busy with other patients. When he was ready I took the boy in and he questioned him. He seemed to lose his thinking and repeated the same word over and over. He checked his health and nothing was wrong. The doctor said his mind was unbalanced and that we must keep him home and report to him every third day. This I did, but began to worry and thought it must be something to do with the Kuʻula rock. My wife was worried too and tried to look for help. She told me to return the Kuʻula to the owner and never mind about the money. Only if someone knew how to cure our son, we would pay whatever they asked."

So, both of them went to see the Hawaiian fisherman. They met him as he was returning from the beach. He told the fisherman that he was in trouble, that his boy was mentally unbalanced and he would return the Kuʻula rock to him and did not want any money in return. He said, "Only if you can help to cure my son. You probably know how to cure."

The fisherman listened and told them this sad story. "This Ku'ula rock doesn't belong to me. It was left in the house. I think my grandfather owned this Ku'ula. He forgot to bury it or give it to someone. I heard someone say that it was a fish Ku'ula rock. I tried and caught lots of fish. When I brought in my catch I always offered one fish to the Ku'ula. You were watching me do this the day you came and saw me bringing the fish in. Did you do exactly as I did? When you took the Ku'ula rock I thought you understood."

The father replied, "I forgot to do this."

The fisherman said, "So this is your trouble. Instead you are being punished. Your boy is being punished. There is no way I can help you because I do not know anything about the Hawaiian art in curing this kind of matter. Did you see a doctor?"

The father replied, "I did and the boy is the same. I came here hoping maybe you could help me, or you can tell me who can."

The fisherman said, "As I told you, I do not know. In this case I cannot help you. I am sorry. Also, I do not want the Ku'ula rock."

So, the father left the Hawaiian fisherman and came home with the Ku'ula rock. He said, "I told my wife it was my fault for being so greedy for money. Now I understand but it is too late. So I tried to see other Hawaiians but with no results. I was desperate when I looked at my son. Here was a young man and on account of me, his future was lost forever. After I tried for help with no results, I was mad and took the Ku'ula rock and threw it into the ocean, thinking this would help my son. It did not help a bit."

After listening to his story, I told him he should have found out all about the Ku'ula rock before he took it and said to him, "I have two things you can do. Have you got a good

Hawaiian friend that you have known well for a long time? Talk to him and he will tell you who to see. If he is a true friend he will do this. This ritual will be the Hooponopono seance. This is where you ask for forgiveness. You must listen to the person who does this and do what he tells you to do. I believe your boy will be well when he releases the taboo.

"The next thing, you go to your Japanese priest and ask him what he can do. Here is what I advise you. Never tell them you will pay if they cure your boy. Never bargain with money for him. After the boy is well you can send them a thanksgiving in a present from you and your wife. This is the only thing that I know.

"When you find someone to cure your boy, you must go in with a feeling that you are sorry this happened and you are ready to ask forgiveness This is the way to get help."

It was getting late and we all went to sleep. When I woke up breakfast was ready. After breakfast I asked them to take me to Wailuku town where I had some business to attend to. The husband drove me to town and during the trip in he thanked me for advising him. I told him it was not much help but whatever it was, it was a step in the right direction.

Three months later he wrote me, "It was a hard thing to try to get someone who knew how to help out but I am glad I did and the boy is well now." He thanked me again and told me that whenever I came to Maui to stop at his home as long as I wanted. He wrote, "I cannot repay you for what you advised me to do." I only did what I knew to help and that was all.

Three Island Images
David C. Farmer, Mudra, James N. Gusukuma

Summer's day hālau.
Transistor radio sings Aunty's
Favorite chant.

David C. Farmer

Shadows painted red
    against the night sky, beckon;
Pele—the temptress!

Mudra

'I'IWI
Fragile bird whose scarlet song
Radiates from branches of 'ōhi'a,
Flitting from flower to flower
Blown by the breeze;
I still blink with surprise
To see the blossom fly.

James N. Gusukuma

"Malie"

Excerpted from *Molokaʻi*
Oswald A. Bushnell

Not for long did we keep our school under the *kukui* tree. Father Damien soon heard of it and invited us to use the Infirmary in the afternoons. On the first day it held two pupils: Akala and Eleu. By the fifth day it held nine. When the second week was ended, twenty-one boys and girls sat in the schoolroom, learning to read and write and to do sums. Among them were Moki, and Joel, the *haole* boy who came to Kalawao when Tutu and I came. Because these two already could read and write a little, they became my helpers. But it was Eleu who was the monitor, who took care of the books and the papers and the pencils, who handed me the guava switch when I was in need of it.

I learned, alas, that I was as all other schoolteachers must be: sparing of freedom, jealous in my demands for the attention of my pupils, liberal in my use of the supple switch Eleu brought to me the second week of school. "Here," he said with a straight face, thrusting it into my hand, "a stick for teaching with." Given this permission from him, I did not shrink from using the stinging rod. How else was I to keep the discipline? *"E, hoopono loa he kumuao"*—I heard my pupils say one day when school was done— "Strict is the teacher." But not for a long time did I learn how, away from the schoolhouse, they called me "Miss Switch."

Inside the school there was good order. But it was not so outside the schoolhouse. When the men of Kalawao learned of it, they gathered around to see this new thing and to laugh at it. And when the school day was ended and my pupils dashed away to their play, and the men saw how I went alone along the road to my home, some of them tried to molest me.

This was one of the evil things in Kalawao. The other evils were drunkenness and gambling. But the lusts of the flesh were the most difficult to satisfy. For it is a part of the sickness, in certain of its stages, for the diseased flesh to burn with a rage for love. When this time comes upon a sufferer, it is said, there is no denying him his need, and no sating of it.

But I did not know of these things when I walked alone through the village to the school. Not even Tutu's plain-speaking, not even Emma's service to the Settlement, prepared me for them, or for the men who whistled at me, when I stepped forth from the schoolhouse, who called their evil thoughts to me, thinking to excite me, who offered me money to lie with them, thinking to buy me.

At first I was angered by their indecencies. With my head lowered, I hurried away from them, where they lounged against the stone walls on either side of the road, just as they do on some of the street corners in Honolulu. Dressed in their tight trousers and *palaka* shirts, with bright kerchiefs knotted at their throats, and brazen smiles fixed upon their faces, they sang their dirty songs or played at cards and dice, to while away the time. In Honolulu there are policemen to keep such loafers from molesting decent women, but in Kalawao there was no one to guard me from their intentions.

When, on the third day, they took to following me along the way, serenading me with their suggestive music, beseeching me with their calling, I grew frightened. When, on the day after that, one of them, bolder than the rest, called to me from a lane, entreating me to go to his house, I was terrified. Breathless from running, I asked Tutu for her counsel when I reached home.

"Filthy dogs!" she cried, *"pilau* bums!" and much more. I sat upon her bed, openmouthed at her language. "Wassamatta?" she laughed, "you think I do not know about life? Those loafers need horsewhipping. Let us talk with Makaio about this."

"No, Tutu, no! I—I don't want him to know about it."

"Malie, you *aku*-head. Do you think Makaio does not know about these things? Do you think his white hair makes him innocent? Come, we go now, for his advice."

Makaio listened to my plight, told more by Tutu's mouth than by my own. When we were finished he said sadly, "This is not a new thing to Kalawao. Sometimes, too, it is the other way, when a man is endangered by a woman. This sickness: it does strange things to the appetite of people. Perhaps I should have told you of these dangers, before you learned of them in the street. But it is better now than it used to be. The priest has made it so."

"Should we tell Kamiano?" asked Tutu.

"No, there is no need. To hear of it would make him unhappy. He thinks that since his coming the people of Kalawao have learned decency, if they have not learned goodness. He does not know how when his back is turned, some of them still show their evil ways. Let us spare him this disappointment."

"Well, then, will you be her bodyguard? Her policeman?" Tutu's voice was sour, like the taste of *poi* four days old.

Nothing disturbed Makaio, not even the impatience of Tutu. "No. No, there is a better way. I will speak to Ambrose about this. It is his business. He will take care of it."

The next morning Makaio walked to Kalaupapa to speak to the Superintendent. In the afternoon, at four o'clock, when school was ended and the hoodlums were gathered again outside the schoolhouse, as the men of Sodom were gathered outside the house of Lot, big Kewalo came into their midst. They knew him, they paid him no heed. From the window of the schoolroom, where I hid, I watched Kewalo take his stand on the schoolhouse steps. Still they did not think anything of his being there. Laughing among themselves, strumming their guitars, they waited lazily for me to come out. Fifteen or twenty of them, of all ages, from old to young, they were the wastrels of Kalawao.

From the pocket of his dirty work pants Kewalo drew a piece of crumpled paper. In a loud voice he called to the men: "Hear you the words of the King! Hear you: these are the words of the King!"

Startled by his summons, the men ceased their chatter. Mouths open, hands stopped upon the strings of their guitars, they looked up to Kewalo, where he glared down at them.

"These are the words of the King," he said, shaking the paper to smooth it for his reading. Profound was the silence when he began.

> "There is a kapu placed upon this schoolhouse, and upon all it holds. Books, papers, pencils, chairs, they are mine, the King's. Let them be preserved.
>
> "There is a kapu placed upon the pupils of this schoolhouse. They are as my children. Let them be protected and fostered, for the good of the land.
>
> "There is a kapu placed upon the teacher of this schoolhouse. She is as a daughter to me and to the Queen. Let her be honored and protected, for the good of the land.
>
> "Hearken to these words: they are the words of my mouth, the words of my heart. Surely, the life of the land is preserved in righteousness.
>
> KALAKAUA, THE KING."

Quickly did the men steal away. Without a sound, without a backward glance, they vanished.

No longer did they foregather at the schoolhouse door. No longer did they molest me. With the King's hand outstretched over me, I was safe. And thereafter I walked without fear in the paths of Kalawao and across the face of Kalaupapa's plain.

Song of the Chanter Ka-'ehu
(Mele a Ka-'ehu ka Haku Mele)
Translated by Mary Kawena Pukui & Alfons Korn

E aha 'ia ana o Hawai'i
I nei ma'i o ka lēpela,
Ma'i ho'okae a ka lehulehu
A ka 'ili 'ula'ula 'ili ke 'oke'o?

'Ano 'e mai ana nā hoa hui
Like 'ole ka pilina mamua.
He 'āhiu ke 'ike mai,
Ne'e a kāhi 'e noho mai,
Kuhikuhi mai ho'i ka lima,
He ma'i Pākē kō 'iā 'la.

Kūlou au a hō'oiā'i'io,
Komo ka hilahila i ka houpo.

Lohe ana kauka aupuni,
Ho'oūna ke koa māka'i.
Hopuhopu 'ia mai kohu moa,
Alaka'i i ke ala kohu pipi.
Ku ana imua o ka Papa Ola,
Papa ola 'ole o nei ma'i.
Ki'ei wale mai nā kauka,
Hālō ma'ō, ma'ane'i,
Kuhi a'e na lima i Lē'ahi,
"Hele 'oe ma Kalawao."

Lālau nā koa Aupuni,
Halihali iā kai ka uwapo.
Ho 'īli nā pio a pau,
Ka luahi i ka ma'i lēpela.
Hiki ke aloha kaumaha nō

I ka 'ike 'ole i ka 'ohana.
Ka waimaka ho'i ka 'elo'elo,
Ho'opulu i ka pāpālina.
Pau ka 'ikena i ka 'āina
I ka wehiwehi o ke kaona.
Hao wikiwiki iā lilo ho'i,
Kū ka huelo i ke kia mua,
E nonaho lua 'o *Keoni Pulu*
Kīpū i ka hoe mahope,
Ho'ohū ka helena o ke kai,
A he pipi'i wale mai nō.
'Ike iā Moloka'i mamua
Ua pōwehiwehi i ka noe.

Ha'ina mai ka puana
Nō nei ma'i o ke lēpela.

English Translation

What will become of Hawai'i?
What will leprosy do to our land—
disease of the despised, dreaded alike
by white or brown or darker-skinned?

Strange when a man's neighbors
become less than acquaintances.
Seeing me they drew away.
They moved to sit elsewhere, whispering,
and a friend pointed a finger:
"He is a leper."

I bowed my head.
I knew it was true.
In my heart I hugged my shame.

Word reached the medical authorities.
The doctors sent the military to fetch us.
We were caught like chickens, like cattle herded
along roadway and country lane.
Then they paraded us before the Board of Health
but there was no health in that Board for such as we.
Examining doctors eyed us, squinted this way and that.
More fingers pointed Diamond Head way:
"You go to Kala-wao!"

Again the militia took over.
Soldiers escorted us to the wharf for farewell.
Prisoners, we were marched aboard,
victims of leprosy, branded for exile.
Abandoned, cut off from family and dear ones,
we were left alone with our grief, with our love.

Rain of tears streamed from leper eyes.
Leper cheeks glistened with raindrops in the sun.
Never again would we look upon this land of ours,
this lovely harbor town.

Quickly the sails were hoisted.
Ropes dangled from the foremast,
tails of wild animals writhing,
whipping in the channel breeze.
The *John Bull* drew anchor.
In the stern the rudder turned.
So sailed we forth to dim Moloka'i Island,
enshrouded in fog.

So ends my song and this refrain.
What will leprosy do to my people?
What will become of our land?

Tearing Down a Plantation House
Vittorio Talerico

While working on the rafters,
real two-by-four
two-by-fours,
a car idles up to us,
an older man hesitates
then gets out to watch.
After pulling a dozen more nails
Richard asks if we can help him.
"No, no jus' stop to look.
You know fifty-eight years ago
dis house I was born."
Quietly we both lay down our hammers.
"Soon I hear all dis kine camps no mo', eh?"
A "Yeah" from Richard,
almost like it was his decision
to have this camp razed.
"You see dis one,"
pointing to the house next door.
"Da Japanee barber stay,
and whooo plenty nights
all da men come for haircut
and talk story
and drink da kine.
We kids alla time try stay wake
an watch from da window.
Good fun."
He pauses, picks up a bent nail
and points with it.
"And dat place ova der
is kine furo house.
Plenty big one, and whooo da hot.
For da first fifty guys, ten cents
after dat, nickel."

Hanapepe, Kaua'i
Geraldine Heng

january does not awaken this town.
this skin of stillness has lain quiet now
for gentle lifetimes.

the houses, like colored wooden make-believe
sit perennially charming in picture frames,
in the metal reflection of a family car.

sunlight, teeming with dusty life
warms the storefronts, yellowly.

in shadowy interiors, proprietors measure
condiments and words, their greeting a secret meaning

shy as deep water, the memories of this town,
dimly glimpsed in the glass jars.

and a modest dance studio waits down the road
now serene, once eager perhaps
with impatient feet quick for the new steps

perhaps the doctor in the clinic danced them.

perhaps once the two old friends
dreaming gently over ice-shop counter

waxed companionable moustaches
in steamy barbershop mirror,
while their wives, tired by children, softly complained.

holiday visitors come this warm afternoon
in bright voices, chasing weekend lives
they leave the sound of feet on bare boards.

in the evening the young gathered at jukebox and pooltables.
the movie house plays a lone feature.

soon, february passes unnoticed by the sodafountains.

The Luna of the Landing
Marshall M. Doi

On a gusty afternoon, a lone mynah bird was startled out
of a pine tree by the sound of footsteps rapidly approaching
the edge of the cliff. He chattered angrily, then flew away as
a youth with huge curious eyes stared up in his direction.

"Boy! Boy!" a voice called out hoarsely from the
distance. The youth continued staring even after the bird had
completely disappeared, until a wrinkled old man caught up
to him.

"I tell you, no run away like that," the old man scolded.
"You like fall down and get hurt?"

A gigantic smile spread over the boy's face. Then,
without a word, he turned and immediately started down a
winding trail which led across a sloped portion of the cliff
wall. The old man started to voice a second warning but
stopped because he knew that it would be of no avail. He
hitched up an old knapsack, faded and frayed from years of
constant use, and dropped out of sight after the youth.

The Hamakua coast on the island of Hawai'i is a string of
steep black lava cliffs dropping straight down into the sea. A
man on shore can stand directly over the turbulent water and
yet be hundreds of feet away from the surface, never being
touched by the sea except for the salty mists which drift inland
on days when the wind blows from the north.

Few are the coves which in past days allowed wary
steamers to deliver supplies to the sugar cane plantations
located at strategic spots along the coastline. Strong winches
constructed at the top of the cliff wall stood ready to lift the
cargo up to where mule trains waited. The job was long and
difficult as well as hazardous because of the temperamental
sea. Perhaps the ancient Hawaiian gods were alarmed at such
intrusions upon their sacred burial grounds, for many hidden

caves in the area contained the bones of kings and lords of old Hawai'i. Whatever the reason for the turbulence, the ships had to approach the shore with extreme caution since there was no way of telling when the sea would belch forth a swell capable of hurling the ships against the rocks. Many men vanished under the raging sea to be lain in submerged crypts or carried away by predatory sharks.

But when those days passed, the coves were forgotten and tangled underbrush covered the mule trains leading to them. No one visited the landings except for fishermen who told stories about hearing the rusty winches being operated again on dark nights when the sea was in a less angry mood.

One of the coves was even more isolated than the rest because the sugar mill which it formerly served had been abandoned many years ago. A wide grove of mournful pine trees circled along the cliff rim high above the sea. It was through this grove of trees that the old man and the youth had just passed.

The old man shuffled cautiously down the trail, sometimes gaining leverage by grabbing hold of the tough-stemmed grass growing on either side. He was still strong and healthy, his figure showing few of the physical impediments which usually accompany old age. But though his legs showed no signs of weariness, the old man was aware that his once-sharp reflexes were no longer suitable for the steep trail. Over places where the youth would have scampered heedlessly across, the man conveyed himself with all four limbs.

A length of manila rope was coiled around the old man's waist, serving to hold up an ancient pair of pants. Several holes in the seat were covered with crude patches while others remained exposed to provide ventilation. It was difficult to say whether his shirt was tan colored or just covered with dust, but it had the long sleeves which are common among the plantation laborers who work with the thorny leaves of the sugar cane. An obsolete safety helmet balanced precariously on his head. A piece of sheet metal was soldered around the side for added protection from the sun so that the helmet resembled a shiny metal bonnet. The metal bonnet completely hid the old man's white hairs but not the two huge ears which protruded from below it. The old man attributed his good health to his ears because of Japanese superstition which declared that large ears portended a long life.

At the bottom of the trail, the youth was waiting impatiently on an old concrete landing platform which was faded and covered with seaweed where it entered the water. In his stubby hands he grasped two bamboo fishing poles which he had retrieved from a crack in the cliff wall. As soon as the old man set foot on the landing, the boy ran to the water's edge where he laid the poles down and beckoned furiously with both of his hands. The old man smiled at the way the youth jumped up and down in gleeful anticipation while he attached hooks and lines to the poles.

When the old man had baited his hook, the boy dropped the line into the water and sat down on the edge of the landing. His face changed from one of anticipation to one of the most intense concentration. His huge eyes were focused deep into the water where he saw shadows gliding back and forth. When one of them approached the hook, he held his breath in expectation, his face frozen and his eyes piercing.

Suddenly, a small form moved where the water lapped against the slimy cement. The boy's attention was immediately directed to a black crab gathering seaweed with rapidly moving claws. How strange it looked with its eyes extended up into the air. The boy contorted his face into weird shapes, trying to extend his eyes into the air also. His face flushed and his eyes hurt but he could not get them to stand upright. A rage flashed through the boy. In anguish, he pulled at his hair and kicked his feet out wildly. He swung his pole viciously at the crab in bitter disappointment. With the crab's departure went the boy's rage. He turned his attention back to fishing and was soon hunched over with his former intense concentration, though he often paused to try to extend his eyes outward.

When the boy finally felt a twitch, he yanked the pole up hard enough for the fish to arch over him and land in back. With a triumphant cry, he jumped clumsily to his feet and fell on the fish as it squirmed furiously on the cement.

"Hooey," the old man chorused the boy's excitement. "As one nice size papio you catch, boy. Good eat, that one! We tell your mama cook'um for you tonight."

The youth danced a happy victory jig over the landing, trailing the fish behind him. When he tired, the old man unhooked the remains of the fish and placed it in the knapsack. After his hook was again baited, the boy hunched over his pole with the same intense concentration. Each time the boy caught a fish, he danced for joy. But after a while, the sea grew restless and he lost all interest in fishing. He wandered away to chase crabs on the rocks off to one side of the landing.

Taking out a bag of tobacco from the knapsack, the old man slowly and carefully rolled himself a cigarette. After running his wet tongue over the cigarette, he raised his head to see where the boy was, then lighted up and settled back to fish. But his mind was not on fishing as he sat there blowing out blue clouds from under his silver bonnet. He looked out toward the horizon where the dark sky was creeping landward. White-capped swells were already arriving at the cove, speeding heralds of the approaching storm. The old man watched the waves hurl themselves at the peninsula which protruded from the opposite side of the landing from where the boy had gone. Each wave hissed angrily as it rushed upon the rocks, exploding into white foam at the impact. How often the two of them had sat and examined the same scene from the top of the cliff. Under the wailing pine trees they sat, each enjoying the sea in his own way. Sometimes the boy screamed encouragement to the pounding waves, rising to his feet in his excitement. At other times he sat in a trance, open-mouthedly staring.

The waves brought different emotions for the old man. They brought memories of the days when he had been the luna of the landing. At those times, he explained to the boy how to judge the wind and the sea in order to determine whether or not it was safe for a ship to enter the cove. He had spent many cold nights on the landing waiting for tardy steamers to come in. Many times he had given the order to start the winches and many times had given the muleteers their instructions on where to deliver the supplies. The luna was in charge of all operations at the landing and few were more important than he.

Looking up once again, the old man saw that the boy was zealously pursuing crabs, hurling rocks away to his right and left as he attempted to corner the elusive creatures. He and the boy belonged together. They understood each other as no one else did. Or perhaps it was just he who understood, the boy only instinctively attaching himself to the old man. One thing was certain though, this little cove was their private world and no one had the right to disturb their bond with each other and with their friend, the sea. No, not even the boy's parents should be allowed to interfere.

Deep within himself, the old man sensed (though he was unwilling to admit it) that he depended on the boy just as much as the boy depended on him. It would be so very lonely to have to visit the little cove by himself again. It never occurred to him to ask himself why he still came to the landing. If he had asked himself that question, he could not have given an answer. Or else he might have answered simply, "Me the luna of the landing."

No other explanation was needed. The old man's life had never been one of expanding horizons. When he first came to work at the landing, he had set only one goal for himself, to wear the shiny hat of the luna. After he became the luna, the little cove became his world. Everything had changed since then, but not the old man. He was still the luna. This was still his world though he was long retired and the landing was long outmoded. He was content with his memories, except that he could not speak to memories.

Long after the old man resolved himself to being the solitary sentinel of the cove, the boy had come. At first, he brought the boy only out of sympathy toward his parents. The youth was an intruder who feared the powers of the sea. But the boy's intense curiosity was too strong to keep him afraid for long and now the boy loved the cove almost as much as the old man.

More important, however, the cove itself had accepted the boy. It had befriended him and it had washed away the impurities. The youth was all right here, with a place where he belonged. Nowhere else would he find an environment which suited him more. If he was kept in a cage, the dynamo of emotion and energy inside the boy was sure to explode, while here at the old man's side, the cove could absorb all of the outbursts. None of the complications, the confusions, and the restrictions of society existed here to bewilder him. All the boy needed was freedom, freedom to explore the strange world that existed within his disproportional head. Both the man and the youth were useless to the world beyond the pine trees, and it was useless to them.

The shock of cold water splashing over his feet awakened the old man from his reverie. The tide was coming in as well as the storm. Glancing over his shoulder, he saw that the boy was nowhere in sight. After packing his knapsacks and replacing the fishing poles in the crevice in the wall, the old man made his way over the moist rocks to the hidden spot where he knew he was most likely to find the boy. He walked until he came to the gaping mouth of an old lava tube which wormed its way into the cliff. Inside was the boy.

Lying very still on the floor, the youth was listening intensely to sounds coming out of a fissure. Apparently, the noises were produced by water rushing into a hollow chamber beneath the lava tube and somehow the fissure distorted the sound so that it resembled the clamor of distant voices. Whatever the voices were, they spoke intimate messages to the youth, for he never moved while he listened to them. They never spoke to the old man but it was obvious that the boy understood them so he was satisfied to sit and wait.

Having sat on the floor beside the boy, the old man said without looking at him, "Hey, boy. They sure making big noise today, hah? I think they talking about the big storm coming tonight."

The boy did not acknowledge the other's presence, which did not surprise the old man. He simply took out his tobacco and silently rolled himself another cigarette. His feet were folded under him and, with the boy close behind his back, he faced the entrance of the lava tube through which he watched the swells roll into the cove. The man and the youth sometimes spent hours here, the boy with his ear to the fissure and the man puffing on his hand-rolled cigarettes. For several minutes they continued as they were, man and boy together in comradeship, yet each engrossed in his own world. The old man knew that this was likely to be the last time he would ever share the silent bond with the boy. It marked the end of a phase of his life. As for the boy, perhaps occasionally a dim spark of remembrance would light in his mind, but for the most part, the old man and the voices would soon be forgotten.

Slowly, the old-timer turned toward his friend until he was staring directly at the prone figure, a great sadness shining in his eyes. He again spoke, more to himself than to the boy. "They telling you good-bye, boy. They know you not coming back no more. Your mama and papa sending you away to the city tomorrow." He had tried to convince them otherwise but they were sure of themselves and refused to be dissuaded. Each sentence was followed by a long pause, as though his words were intrusions within the silence. "You listen what they say and be good boy, okay?"

The youth still had his ear to the fissure, enthralled by the voices. "Get plenty nice things for see. You be real happy over there." He wished desperately that the boy could say, "No, I will not be happy." But the boy said nothing.

Tears trickled down the cracks on the old man's sunbaked cheeks. The fear and love poured out of his chest in one pleading sentence, "You no understand, boy?" The question was futile, merely a confirmation of fact. All self-control had left the old man. "How you can take care of yourself, boy? You almost one man but you no even talk yet. Nobody going to look out for you now."

Finally, the strange tone in the old man's voice caused the boy to look up at him. However, only curiosity appeared on the youth's face as he waited for his companion to give the usual sign that it was time to go. Two pairs of eyes met each other, one huge and waiting, the other moist and pitying. The old man looked deep into the other's eyes, trying to grab hold of just a little something inside the boy, but he could not see anything beyond the fog.

The eyes of the old man dropped first. He pushed himself to his feet and the youth quickly followed. From the landing, they watched the storm waves beating against the peninsula for the last time. One after another, as methodically as falling raindrops, the waves crashed onto the rocks. At regular intervals, an exceptionally large wave struck with such momentum that it hurled itself entirely over the piece of land.

After studying the sea for awhile, the old man looked thoughtfully at the boy's innocent face. No, it was not right for the boy to leave this place. It was unfair. He looked again at the peninsula as it was submerged by a giant wave, then he motioned toward it with his arm and said, "Come. We go catch some more crabs."

And together they set off.

Plantation Christmas
Vivian L. Thompson

It is December on the plantation and Christmas is just around the corner. Days are still warm, but mornings and evenings bring a cold wind down from the mountain. Mauna Kea is powdered with snow, while here at the lower altitude, poinsettia hedges are full bloom: single, double, scarlet, pink, even an occasional yellow or white. Tour buses stop at the Gomes' place in the village for visitors to take color shots of the solid bank of red poinsettia. Cardinals have returned to the mango tree. You hear their impudent whistle before daybreak, followed by the harsh chatter of the mynah birds.

Plantation roads are strangely quiet. No clumsy Kenworths, top-heavy with cane, go lumbering by. Hamakua Mill Company is having its annual "off season."

Holiday preparations begin early. The front of Paauilo Store is lined with Douglas firs. You sniff their nostalgic fragrance when you do your shopping, for the *Hawaiian Craftsman* just brought in a boatload of 10,000 trees. Folks who prefer the local Norfolk pine, arrange to have them cut "up mauka." Most homes have their Christmas trees up and decorated by the first or second week of December.

The mail trucks deliver bulging sacks of holiday mail with widely-scattered postmarks: Iran, Tokyo, Manila, Fresno, Anchorage, Maryland, British Columbia, Mississippi, New York City. There is a line at the Post Office no matter what time of day you stop there. People wait patiently with bulky packages, handfuls of Christmas cards, money order blanks, and customs declarations. The Post Office line becomes a favorite spot to meet neighbors and catch up on the latest gossip.

Gifts begin arriving: gaily-wrapped ones from Mainland family members and faraway friends . . . unwrapped neighborly ones from plantation friends: a jar of homemade mango chutney, a loaf of Tutu Jean's delicious fruitcake . . . a basket of limes, tangerines, and bananas . . . a beef roast from a nearby rancher . . . fat loaves of Portuguese sweet bread . . . a box of sweet red plums from the ranch . . . two fresh-caught fish wrapped in ti leaves . . . a cluster of butterfly orchids from the post mistress's prize collection . . . an armful of crisp red anthuriums with one or two "obakes" included.

Your days become a patchwork of card-writing, gift-wrapping, holiday planning, and tree-trimming. The calendar is filled with party invitations and rehearsal reminders. "Why the Chimes Rang" at Paauilo School . . . "The Littlest Angel" at Umikoa Ranch . . . "The First Noel" at Umikoa Ranch. From the Scout House you hear the high clear voices of Brownies, practicing "Away in a Manger" to sing for Dispensary patients. From the Buddhist Hall come the rattle of feather-trimmed gourds, the tap of split bamboo sticks, the click of river stones, as the hula classes practice for their holiday program. The six-year-olds are doing the "haole" hula, "Rudolph, the Red-Nosed Reindeer." The older girls follow, swaying to the strains of "Mele Kalikimaka" and "White Christmas."

Suddenly it is Christmas Eve, and somehow, everything that had to be done, is done. The cards and notes are written and mailed. The gifts are wrapped and delivered. The tree is trimmed and the party menus planned. You drive up to Umikoa Ranch for the annual Christmas Eve dinner and program.

The stars are bright above the pastures where Herefords graze. They lift their heads to watch you open the cattle gates, drive through, and close them. At the ranch manager's home you enjoy a delicious dinner of ranch beef stew over rice with crisp salad vegetables from the garden. Dessert is rhubarb shortcake—homegrown rhubarb topped with thick rich cream from the ranch dairy. You troop down with the other guests to the Hall, to see the Christmas play. Mary is a dark-eyed Portuguese girl and Joseph, a stalwart Hawaiian.

The shepherds wear garments made from feed sacks and carry staffs cut from nearby koa trees. One young shepherd cradles a baby lamb in his arms. It gives a plaintive "baa-a-a" as he comes onstage. A mischievous little Japanese angel, her tinsel halo slightly "kapakahi," calls out, "Hi. Mommy!" and gentle laughter sweeps the audience. The stately Wise Men come down the aisle, resplendent in blue, green and purple velvet—three ranch "paniolos," their weathered faces impressive beneath gold paper crowns and jeweled head cloths.

The curtains close, and the strains of "Jingle Bells" herald the coming of Santa. The crowd surges to the door.

Up the road from the stables comes an old-fashioned "sleigh" drawn by four reindeer whose antlers are trimmed with twinkling Christmas tree lights. Some enterprising ranch hand has designed the antlers from wire and tape, and fastened them to the horses' heads.

The "sleigh" pulls up in front of the door and a roly-poly Santa descends, carrying a bulging pack. He makes his way into the Hall with much ho-ho-ing and the children cluster about him. There is a gift for everyone and Santa calls each one by name. There are toys for each child and lengths of specially-printed Umikoa fabric for shirts and muumuus for ranch fathers and mothers.

Santa reaches the bottom of his pack, and invites some of the youngest children for a ride in his sleigh. In the excitement, you say your thank you's and slip out, for the clock says eleven-thirty and you don't want to miss the midnight service at the new little Episcopal church. You drive back down the ranch road, open and close the cattle gates carefully, and drive through the sleepy village. A procession of neighborhood worshipers with sleepy-eyed children clinging to their hands, moves towards the church. The organ is playing "O Come All Ye Faithful" as you enter.

It is Christmas . . . Christmas on the plantation . . . in the year 1957.

New Year
Gail Harada

This is the old way,
the whole clan gathered,
the rice steaming over the charcoal,
the women in the room, talking,
a layer of potato starch on the table.

This is the old way,
the father watching his son lift the mallet,
pound the rice, pound mochi,
the children watching or playing,
the run of the dough to the women,
the rolling of the round cakes.

This is the old way,
eating ozoni, new year's soup:
mochi for longevity,
daikon, long white radish
rooted firmly like families;
eating burdock, also deeply rooted,
fish for general good luck,
and lotus root, wheel of life.

This is the old way,
setting off firecrackers
to drive away evil spirits,
leaving the driveways red for good fortune.

The new year arrives,
deaf, smelling of gunpowder.

Comfort Woman
Nora Okja Keller

When I entered the world, bottom first, arrows impacted my body with such force that it took twelve years for them to work their way back to the surface of my skin. My mother said she tried to protect me from the barbs the doctors who delivered me let loose into the air with their male eyes and breath, but they tied her hands and put her to sleep. By the time my mother saw me, two days later, she said she knew the *sal* had embedded themselves deep into my body by the way my yellow eyes turned away from her breast. My mother spent two weeks in the hospital waiting, she said, to see how the arrows would harm me: so swift and deadly that she would never have time to fight their power, or slow detonating, festering for years, until I formed either an immunity or an addiction to its poison.

Years later, when the evil-energy arrows began to work their way from my body, I often wished the *sal* had killed me outright so that I would not have had to endure my mother's protection.

At the start of each Korean New Year, my mother would throw grains of rice and handfuls of brass coins onto a meal tray to see my luck for the coming year. In the year of the fire snake, I turned twelve, and my mother missed the divination tray completely.

"Mistake! Mistake!" my mother yelled toward our ceiling as she scooted on her hands and knees to pluck coins and rice from the carpet. As soon as she collected enough to fill both fists, she held her hands above the tray, closed her eyes, and chanted, calling down the Birth Grandmother to reveal my yearly fortune. When my mother cast for the second time, she poured the riches from her hands rather than threw them, hoping to fill the tray with a better reading.

When she opened her eyes and saw that she had again missed the tray, she cried. She wrapped her arms around her body and rocked. *"Aigu, aigu,"* she moaned. My mother chanted and swayed until she fell into a trance. Then she got up and, eyes sealed, danced through the apartment: on the sofa bed, around the black-lacquered coffee table, over dining room chairs, around me. And as she danced, my mother touched our possessions, feeling—she later explained—for the red. My mother held her hands in front of her, and like divining rods, they swung toward the color of blood. She ripped red-bordered good luck talismans from our walls and furniture, where they fluttered like price tags. She knocked over our altars, sending the towers of fruit and sticky rice crashing to the floor, and rummaged for the apples and plums. Clawing through the bedroom closets and drawers, she collected everything red, from T-shirts and running shorts to a library copy of *The Catcher in the Rye* to the bag of Red Hots I bought with my own money and stashed in my sock drawer.

When she was through piling the red things into a mountain in our living room, my mother said, "We need to burn the red from your life. Everything."

At first, I didn't understand what she meant to do; sometimes she said such things to her clients, then just waved a lit incense stick or a moxa ball over their heads. But when my mother took an armload of clothes to the kitchen sink and lit a match, I scrambled to the floor and rooted through my possessions, trying to save something.

When the material in the sink caught fire, my mother came and took the one thing of mine I had managed to find: the tie-dye T-shirt I had made with rubber bands, melted crayon, and Rit dye in Arts and Crafts the year before. "Beccah," she told me, *"honyaek,* the cloud of Red Disaster, is all around you. I am trying to weaken it so it won't trigger your *sal* and make you sick.

Red Disaster, the way my mother explained it, was like the bacteria we had learned about in health class: invisible and everywhere in the air around us, *honyaek* was contagious and sometimes deadly. Burning the red from our apartment was my mother's version of washing my hands.

The fire in the sink kept sputtering out, held in check by flame-resistant clothing, until my mother added her talismans and money envelopes and a dash of lighter fluid. When she held a match to this kindling, the fire licked, hesitant at first, and then devoured what was offered. Flames shot up amidst coils of thick smoke that blackened our kitchen walls and ceiling. When this first batch had almost burned down, the smoke alarm sputtered to life with grunts and whines and a final full-strength shriek before my mother whacked it with a broom. After she cracked open a window, my mother continued to burn our possessions, even the Red Hots, which melted like drops of blood-red wax, filling the apartment with the stench of burning cinnamon.

Since I was particularly susceptible to Red Disaster that year, my mother did not want me wandering about in unknown places, picking up foreign *honyaek* germs. I was not allowed to ride the bus without her or to swim at all. Consequently I was not supposed to attend school field trips. When my classmates went to Bishop Museum and to Foster Botanical Gardens and to Dole pineapple cannery, where they sampled fresh juice and fruit slices, I stayed behind in the school library, reading and helping Mrs. Okimoto shelve books according to the Dewey decimal system.

But when my sixth-grade social science teacher arranged a snorkeling expedition at Hanauma Bay, I signed my own permission slip after practicing my mother's signature for so long that even now I cannot write her name without my letters cramping into her small, painfully precise script. I remember my hands shook when I turned in this first forgery on the day of the excursion, but Miss Ching just shuffled the form and the fare I had stolen from the Wishing Bowl into her carryall folder. Pushing me into line with the rest of the class, she counted our heads and led us like ducklings onto the bus.

Since my mother had burned my red-heart bathing suit, I wore an olive-green leotard—not the sparkling Danskin kind with spaghetti straps, which might have passed, but one that was cap-sleeved and frayed in the butt. I knew I would catch stares and snickers from the Toots Entourage (led now by Tiffi Sugimoto, since Toots spent all field trips in detention hall for smuggling packs of cigarettes to school in her tall, frizzy rat-nest hair), but I also knew that this trip would be worth it. And even though I had to pair up with Miss Ching in the walk down the winding trail from parking lot to beach, and even though I sucked in water each time I tried to breathe through a snorkel, and my mask fogged no matter how many times I washed it with spit, the trip was worth the teasing and the lies. Because when I trudged across the network of coral reef to dive into pockets of water as deep and clear as God's blue eyeball, I felt perfect, seamless, and as whole as the water that closed over me.

Only afterward, on the hike back to the parking lot, did I begin to feel the sting of Red Disaster. With each step, I felt a prick against my heel. By the time we reached the top, what had started out as an irritation had turned into bolts of fire shooting jagged through my leg.

In the middle of that night, my mother said she woke up on the couch in a suffocating heat, the sheets clinging to her body, a damp second skin. She fought to take each breath, her throat and lungs burning, and worked her way toward the bedroom, where the waves of heat originated.

"I thought there was a fire in there, that you were burning to death," my mother told me when I woke the next morning, my feet bandaged in strips of bedsheet.

"I swam through heat so heavy the room rippled before my eyes, and when I touched the bedroom—*aigu!* Red hot!" My mother flung her hands into the air, showing off the raised welts on the palms. "I had to take my pajama, hold like this, then open."

The night of the terrible heat, sure that I was surrounded by a ring of fire, my mother wrapped the bottom of her nightgown around the doorknob and, waist bared, burst into the bedroom to rescue me. She was knocked immediately to the ground from the heat and enveloped in smoke that was not black but red. She pulled the collar of her nightgown over her nose and mouth to filter out the worst of the heat and the red smoke. "Just like a dust storm," she said. "Or like that plague curse in *The Ten Commandments* that killed off all the children—only red, not black.

"Red Death filled the room, thickening every breath I took, clouding my eyes so that I could barely see you—a motionless lump—on the bed. I called on the Birth Grand-mother to help me beat a path through the *honyaek* to the windows. I tried to push some of the poison out, but the wind blew in even more *honyaek.*"

My mother, who could not swim in water, would always pantomime the breast stroke when she told this part of the story. "I dove into red thick as blood pudding, fighting the tentacles of *honyaek* that tried to pull me under, and found you sweating and shivering under the blankets. I reached out to feel your forehead, but you burned so hot I could not touch you with my bare hands. I tucked the blankets underneath your body and carried you just like you were a baby again. But I could barely lift you; the Red Death sucked my energy, fed on my fear for you, so that I felt weak and unsure. I could barely force my legs forward as the fog of *honyaek* swirled around us, trying to trip my feet into missteps. I knew one wrong turn would lead us into the land of homeless hobo ghosts, *yongson* where we could wander for ten thousand years without even one person knowing we were gone.

"I closed my eyes and told the Birth Grandmother to guide my feet, and when I opened them, she had led us to the bathroom. I placed you in the bathtub and turned on the water. At first the water evaporated as soon as it left the faucet, turning into red steam when it hit your body. I turned the cold on full blast, and finally enough trickled out to dampen the blankets and cool you off."

When I was out of immediate danger of "burning to ash," my mother said she needed to leave me in order to prepare her weapons. She opened the hallway closet, shook out our extra bedsheet, and after studying it briefly, tore it into seven long strips. Then, with a felt marker, over and over again, she wrote my name, birth date, and genealogy—what she referred to as my "spiritual address." When I first looked at my feet in the morning, I thought they were bound in black-and-white striped material, so densely written were my mother's words.

"You needed to be tied into your body," she told me when I asked her about the linen around my feet. "And in case you slipped out, these words would have led you back." She pointed to one of the lines. "Look here—this character means you. This is me, this is the Birth Grandmother, this is each of her sisters. I linked us all together, a chain to fight the Red Death."

My mother said she forced the Birth Grandmother to call upon her sisters, the Seven Stars—each of them named Soon-something, which my mother said meant "pure"—to come protect me. "I didn't want to be rude," she said, "but really, if your spirit guardian can't protect you on her own, she should call for help, don't you think? I mean, I'm your mother, but I still ask her to help me watch you." My mother huffed as if disgusted and insulted by her spirit guardian's overbearing pride and lack of common sense. "Finally, I had to get rough with her.

" 'Induk,' I said, using her personal name to show how upset I was, 'this Red Death is too much for an old lady spirit like you!'

"When the Birth Grandmother did not answer, I knew I had been too blunt, but I could not waste time massaging the ego of a fickle spirit. 'Call on the Seven Stars, or I will find a new Birth Grandmother and you will be just another lost ghost,' I told her. 'My daughter is dying.' "

When I choked, my mother interrupted her story to scold me. "Pay attention." She scowled. "I told you this was serious."

The Birth Grandmother, responding to either her threats or her plea, must have listened to my mother, because a path of white light cracked the red cloud. My mother walked through— "Floated," she said. "I didn't even have to move my feet"— and found herself transported to my side in the bathtub.

She peeled the blankets from my body, stripping me naked. When I shivered, she placed each of the seven strips of bedsheet—one for each of the Star Sisters—on my body. Starting from my head, she smoothed the linen against my contours, asking for blessings from the protective spirits. She ran her hands down my face, throat, arms, torso, legs, and when she touched my feet, her hands vibrated.

"The Sisters were telling me where the *honyaek* entered your body. This," my mother said as she tapped at my feet, which I could barely feel under their wrap, "is your weak point. Didn't I always say you got them from your father?

"They were balloons—so swollen, red, and tender," she said, "they melted into pus when I touched them. I took a razor from the medicine cabinet and —zhaa! zhaa! just like gutting fish—opened your feet to let the sickness out." My mother brandished imaginary knives, slicing the air with sure, quick strokes, reliving her battle. "Red Death shot from your feet, fouling the air with its stench of rotting meat and rat feces. I cut deeper, catching and killing the poison with the bandages blessed by the spirits. At first, as soon as I placed the cloth by your feet, the whole thing turned red, becoming slick and saturated with Red Death. I was like a demon myself, possessed, pushing clean cloths against your feet with one hand, pulling away the ones drenched in Red Death with the other hand. And all the while, I could see the battle between the Sisters and the *honyaek* on the strips of cloth, as the good spirits fought to turn the bandages back to pure white.

"Finally, toward the morning, when all the Red Death had been sucked from the room through the balls of your feet, when all the bandages were white again—even the one against your feet, which by then wept only clear water—the arrowhead, the *sal* triggered by the *honyaek,* popped out. Wait, I'll show you." My mother scuttled off the bed and rushed into the kitchen. I could hear her rummaging through the glass cupboard, and when she returned, she held above her head like a small trophy a Smucker's jelly jar.

She shook the jar in my face, and what looked like bits of bone jumped and rattled around the bottom. "*Sal,*" she announced. "This is the shattered arrowhead working its way out, making all kinds of trouble. We've got to watch for more of these."

I took the jar from her, interested in something I could touch from the spirit world, something tangible from the place where my mother lived half her life. I looked into the jar, then shook the contents onto my palm.

"Don't make that face," my mother said as I stared at the *sal.* "Wrinkles will freeze in your forehead." When I didn't say anything, she knelt beside me and wailed, "It's not my fault! In Korea, everything is safe for the mother and baby— you're not even supposed to leave the bed for two weeks after you give birth! Here, anybody, any man, can come right into the delivery room and cut you, so how could I protect you when you first came into this world? At first I thought since you were half-American you would be immune. But now I see that in your second life transition, the arrows are coming home."

I cupped my mother's chin in my hand, forcing her to look at me, worried that she was losing the present and drifting away from me. "Mom? What are you talking about? Where are you?"

She slapped my hand down. "Sometimes you ask stupid questions," she said. "I am explaining to you how the *sal* got in your body and what we can do about it. This is the critical year, the year you become a woman and vulnerable—just like when a snake first sheds his skin—so we got to purge the clouds of Red Disaster from the home—done—and then this building and then the school. Then we got to purify your mind. You got to—"

"Stop, Mommy, stop!" I held my palm toward her, displaying the white flecks. "This isn't *sal* or an arrow or whatever; it's coral."

"Coral?" My mother picked up a small piece and rolled it in her fingers.

"Yeah," I said, carefully dropping the rest of the rocks back into the jar so I wouldn't have to look at her. "You know, like stones from the sea."

"Yes," my mother said, her words measured, as if she were talking to someone mentally slow. "*Sal* is like stones from the sea."

"No, I mean coral is stones from the sea." I took a deep breath and exhaled in a rush. "I rode a bus and went swimming on a field trip. I lied to you before. I'm sorry. No need to watch me anymore."

My mother lifted the jar from my hands and swirled it until the coral skimmed across the bottom in an even hum. "I know you went swimming," she said. "The office called to tell me your bus would be getting back to school late."

"So you lied!" I yelled. "You know it's not *sal.*"

My mother slammed the glass down on the night table. Bits of coral flew across the bed and onto the floor at her feet. "It is *sal,*" she screamed back at me. "That's what made you lie in the first place. It's what made your feet swell up and stink. And I can see you still have more *sal* in your mouth, making it mean and stupid. Now—" Here my mother suddenly quieted and dropped down to kiss me on the forehead. "You are not well. Just rest. I'm going to keep you safe. I will watch for *sal* and pluck them out when you show the signs."

Juk
Wing Tek Lum

was what I used to eat
a lot of—like everyday
I'd cross the street to Hong Wah's
for a take-out. On seeing me
the owner by the register
would try to outguess me.
"Wat Gai Juk," she'd bellow
in a knowing way,
as if it were my name.

It was a game we played.
Depending on my whim
I'd simply nod my head, assenting,
or correct her, smiling:
"For Op"—to which she'd call
the order out again,
so that the waiter down the aisle
could write it for the kitchen.

Later, if she got a chance,
she'd go back personally.
You could see her through the open door:
first, with a ladle scooping
the soup, a light sprinkle
of scallions, and then the quick plop
of a handful of duck, chopped
in chunks, covered
I knew with lots of skin.

She would fill out a few orders
like this: soup
in the red containers, the dishes

of rice and noodles
into white boxes. In turn,
they would all be dropped
into bags, which she'd carry
—maybe three to an arm—
as she rushed, waddling,
up to the front.
                Sometimes,
I wondered if the hectic pace
would kill her in a year.
At other times I felt:
she's probably now a millionaire.
No one has made as good
a juk since then. I hope it tasted
as good to her
                as it did to me.

Oyako-Donburi
Sera Nakachi

Some people need bourbon
at 10 a.m., a Vegas weekend,
a new John now and then.
I need oyako donburi.

Maybe it's the duet of chicken
and poached egg set bland against
the counterpointing green
onion and shrill soy sauce.

Perhaps it's the earth-hum
of black mushroom, the rising
silence of steaming rice,
the hide and seek
of white wine
through
bamboo shoots.

Oyako donburi has everything
to do with heavy earthenware,
handpainted, and placed
"so"
by a woman who uses both
hands   then bows.

Girls, Are They Worth It?
Jonathan Kim

"Eh, look over there. There's a new guy."

"Moki, try call the dude over here. Tell him I like talk to him."

"Okay, I call him for you, Leroy."

"You want to talk to me?"

"Yeah, I want to talk to you. What's your name?"

"Troy, Troy Arakaki."

"What Bra, you one Pake?"

"No, I'm a Jap."

"You don't look like one Kamikazi. What you in here for?"

"Nothing."

"Eh Bra, nobody comes to Koolau for nothing."

"Well it all started at the beginning of the school year."

"What grade you stay in?"

"Eleventh."

When I started getting interested in girls, I used to go bananas over the chicks in my school but could never seem to score any of them. I'd watch movies every night and study how the guys on TV would always pick up chicks. They made it look so easy. I tried some of the lines The Fonz uses, but whenever I looked at a girl I liked and said, "EEEEEHHHeeeeee," they used to look at me queer like and walk away. Sometimes I used to use real macho lines like, "Eh Baby, what you doing tonight?" You know, the kind Charles Bronson says. But it never worked. They'd just walk away.

I noticed that the chicks in my class always went for the real local guys. You know, the guys with the dark skin and long hair. In my class there were four guys like that, and they always had girlfriends. Their names were Russel,

Sammy, Ray, and Guy. They used to be so rowdy and yell so much in class that the girls used to laugh and smile at them all the time.

I figured if I wanted the chicks to like me, that I had to be like Ray and Guy and their friends. They were called The Foursome, and I wanted to be part of The Foursome so I could have girlfriends like they had. At first I started sitting by them in class and during lunch period so they would recognize me and I would get to know them. They'd always be talking about surfing and girls, and sometimes they'd ask me what girls I liked and who I thought was cute. It made me feel good when they talked to me, and I always tried to say things that would make them laugh and enjoy my company. Sometimes they'd make fun of me, but I didn't care, as long as I got to hang around them. Not just anyone could hang around The Foursome. They were the roughest guys in the school and didn't let any "Turks," as Russel would call the panties of the school, hang around them.

I got to know them real good, and they'd always talk to me during lunch time. "Eh Troy. Go take back my tray and treat me to one ice cream, okay bra?" It made me feel wanted when they talked to me like that. Ray, he was the nicest guy and always talked to me a lot. He even suggested that if I wanted to attract girls that I should dress like them. I never realized it, but they did dress differently from everyone else. They used to wear tee shirts or sweat jackets that had something rough-looking printed on it, like, WAIANAE CANOE CLUB, or something in Hawaiian that you couldn't understand but looked pretty local. They would always wear swim shorts, I guess to show off their dark tanned legs and all the scars they got from surfing the shallow reefs after school.

I bought myself a tee shirt at Crazy Shirts in Ala Moana that said "Shaka Brudah" on the back. It looked pretty local to me, and with a pair of Hang Ten swim shorts with these little feet printed on the pocket I figured I looked almost as rough as they did, except for their long hair and dark tan. l decided that l wouldn't cut my hair and let it grow long like theirs was. I wanted to be like them so much that I even tried talking like them, but whenever I said something like "Eh bra, you going beef the guy or what?" I just didn't sound like one of them. I went to the beach every day after school, and I got pretty dark, just as dark as The Foursome. My hair was down to the middle of my back, and I felt as if I were one of them. I looked like them, and they more or less accepted me. Even the girls that hung around Ray and Sammy started talking to me a lot. These girls were different than the other girls that l used to try my movie star lines on. These chicks never wore bras and were super foxy. God. Did I like that! That's what I liked about being like The Four-some: they hung around classy chicks, not the hard-to-get, stuck-up type.

I started cutting out of classes and doing real rowdy stuff to make the chicks like me the way they liked The Foursome. Sammy and Guy really helped me a lot in becoming rowdy. One time Sammy gave me a whole package of fireworks to set off in the boys' bathroom. We cut out of English class one day and I set them off. It made such a gigantic BOOM that the whole school heard it. During lunch time that day, Guy told all the chicks that I had set the fireworks off, and they all came and sat around me. It made me feel so big to have all these girls eating lunch with me. That was the biggest day of my life.

Just before Easter Vacation, we had an Easter dance at the school. The Foursome said they'd pick me up and we could all go to the dance together. I was glad they were going to pick me up. It made me feel as if they wanted me around. They picked me up in Russel's car at about 8:45. Russel was 18 years old and had bought a cold pack of beer before picking me up. They had already finished off half of the cold pack of Oly by the time they picked me up. They were acting so silly and laughing so much you could tell they were drunk. Sammy offered me a can of beer, but I turned it down. I had never gotten drunk before and I was kind of scared of what might happen. They started calling me "Panty" and "Sissy" because I wouldn't take it and I could tell they were getting kind of mad at me because I was copping out. Ray told me that it was cool to drink and get drunk, because then the chicks like you even more. That's why I wanted to be like them, so the girls would like me, so I took the can of beer and gulped it down. They all laughed and yelled and started laughing after I drank it, but I just felt kind of nauseated. I asked Ray if I was sick or if I was drunk, and he said I just had to drink another beer and all this nausea I was feeling would disappear. I gulped another one down and boy did it taste terrible. Ray was right. All that nausea disappeared and I was feeling great.

Before I realized it we were parked in the school parking lot. I don't know how long we were there, but before that I thought we were driving on the freeway, until I saw Jerry, one of the guys from school, dancing on the hood of the car. I guess he was drunk or something. I really don't remember. I started to get really scared. I don't know why, but I was scared. I asked Sammy what it was like when you're drunk, and he just looked at me and laughed. I got even more scared when he laughed at me, and I think I started to cry. I really don't remember. Ray jumped in the back seat where I was and sat between me and Sammy. He put his arm around me and tried to comfort me. That made me feel good. He said I was drunk and that I shouldn't be afraid because all the guys were around and nothing could happen to me. He said that I should be having fun and laughing like Russel and Sammy were, and that what I needed was another drink to get my spirits up. It sounded good and I drank another Oly. After that I felt really good. When we walked from the car to the auditorium, it seemed as if my legs weren't even moving, but I could see the pavement moving beneath my feet. It was really neat. I started laughing and laughing, and everyone started laughing. Whenever I looked around, it seemed as if everyone was staring at me, but I knew they weren't. I was just drunk. We walked into the auditorium where the dance was, and everything was so unreal. Ray paid for me to get in, because I couldn't seem to understand what the girl at the entrance was trying to say to me. She was really cute. All the chicks that night were cute. At least that's what I thought. When we got in, the music was so loud, I couldn't hear anyone talking. I could see their lips moving, but I just couldn't hear what they were saying. We walked over to the back of the auditorium and leaned against the wall. The vibrations from the music ran through my body, and I seemed to be paralyzed until the song was over. I stopped leaning against the wall because I was afraid I might not be able to move when the next song started.

The music was really good. At least I thought it was. I wanted to dance in the worst way, but I was afraid I might fall down or dance into the wall or something. This one song was really good, and this super cute Haole chick asked me to dance. I wanted to dance, but I was afraid. Ray and Guy kept on pushing me and telling me to dance, but I told the girl I wasn't feeling well and that I didn't want to dance. After she left I felt really bad that I had turned her down, so the next song I asked her to dance. It was a good song and I had been doing alright until I tripped and fell on the girl next to me. When I fell I grabbed her to keep me from falling. I'd torn her blouse, and she wasn't wearing a bra or anything underneath. She ran out screaming and I didn't know what to do. I started to run after her to apologize, but some guy grabbed me and hit me in the face. I tried to get up and explain to this guy who I assumed was her boyfriend that it was an accident, but he just kept on hitting me and hitting me. That's when I got really mad. I had never gotten into a fight or even hit anyone before, but at that time I wanted to kill the bastard. I don't know what came over me. I guess it was the beer or something, but I ran over to Russel and asked him for his knife. He always carried a knife when he went out at night, and I knew he'd lend it to me if I was in a fight. With the knife in my hand I ran up to the guy and stabbed him with it. I just kept stabbing him and stabbing him. I just couldn't stop.

The next morning I woke up and found myself in a hospital. I don't know how I got there, and the nurses wouldn't even talk to me. They treated me like a criminal or something. My parents were there, and they seemed really upset. I told them I couldn't help what happened and that that other guy kept on hitting me, but they just looked at me queer like and my mother ran out of the room crying. My dad said I was crazy so I told him, "The hell with you you old bastard. I don't need you." He spit on my face and walked out.

I had some kind of juvenile trial to decide what they should do with me. They said I killed that guy at the dance, and that I would be sent to a home where everyone was like me. I never understood what that meant, but here I am.

"Eh Bra. You telling me that you stay in here just because you wanted one chick for like you?"

"What? I said I killed a guy at a dance, that's why I'm in here."

"Yeah. But if you never like be like those four guys, then you wouldn't have gotten drunk, and you wouldn't have stabbed that guy at the dance. Right?"

"Yeah. I guess so."

"Girls. Are they worth it?"

(Jonathan Kim was an 11th-grader at University Laboratory School when he wrote "Girls, Are They Worth It?")

A Small Rebuttal

Barbara B. Robinson

Some people say
Honolulu is just a
rotten cement city.
Too many beehive buildings
full of rotten piggy people.
Just noise and pollution
and crime.
And you can't see the ocean
from Kalakaua Avenue.
But just today—
I saw a mynah bird ring
at Makiki Park.
And I saw two blocks of cars
stop
and wait
for a puppy to cross
Beretania Street
and no horns beeped.

And I saw
A small girl chase a dime
an old Filipino man
had dropped
and carry it back to him.
And his fierce pock-marked face
lit up in Aloha,
and he gave her
the hibiscus from his hat band—
and—
she carried it away
like a crimson beacon
to show her friend.

Lost Sister
Cathy Song

1

In China,
even the peasants
named their first daughters
Jade—
the stone that in the far fields
could moisten the dry season,
could make men move mountains
for the healing green of the inner hills
glistening like slices of winter melon.

And the daughters were grateful:
they never left home.
To move freely was a luxury
stolen from them at birth.
Instead, they gathered patience,
learning to walk in shoes
the size of teacups,
without breaking—
the arc of their movements
as dormant as the rooted willow,
as redundant as the farmyard hens.
But they travelled far
in surviving,
learning to stretch the family rice,
to quiet the demons,
the noisy stomachs.

2

There is a sister
across the ocean,
who relinquished her name,
diluting jade green
with the blue of the Pacific.
Rising with a tide of locusts,
she swarmed with others
to inundate another shore.
In America,
there are many roads
and women can stride along with men.

But in another wilderness,
the possibilities,
the loneliness,
can strangulate like jungle vines.
The meager provisions and sentiments
of once belonging—
fermented roots, Mah-Jongg tiles and firecrackers—
set but a flimsy household
in a forest of nightless cities.
A giant snake rattles above,
spewing black clouds into your kitchen.
Dough-faced landlords
slip in and out of your keyholes,
making claims you don't understand,
tapping into your communication systems
of laundry lines and restaurant chains.

You find you need China:
your one fragile identification,
a jade link
handcuffed to your wrist.

You remember your mother
who walked for centuries,
footless—
and like her,
you have left no footprints,
but only because
there is an ocean in between,
the unremitting space of your rebellion.

Oranges Are Lucky
Darrell H.Y. Lum

CAST

DEBBIE, *a young woman in her early twenties.*
JON, *a young man in his early twenties, Debbie's boyfriend.*
AUNTY ESTHER, *a middle-aged woman, bilingual, Ah Po's daughter.*
UNCLE PETE, *Aunty Esther's husband.*
AH PO, *elderly grandmother of Debbie, Ricky, etc.; confined to a wheelchair.*
RICKY, *a young man in his late twenties, grandson of Ah Po.*
DANE, *a young man in his middle twenties, grandson of Ah Po, Ricky's brother.*
DENNIS, *a young man in his early thirties.*

THE SETTING: *A small, simple Chinese restaurant. The walls are plain and bare except for a folding oriental screen painted and inlaid with garish scenes of Chinese village life. There is an electric fan in the corner with a couple of red ribbons fluttering from the wire shield. There is a round table center stage set for a nine-course dinner. Two other tables, similarly set, flank the main table.*

(DEBBIE *and her boyfriend* JON *are the first to arrive at the restaurant. Jon carries a birthday cake in a card-board box and a lei in a plastic bag.)*

DEBBIE (*enters, looks around, makes a face at the restaurant's plainness, hesitantly speaks*): Well, Bahk

Hoo said this place serves good food. Da main ting is dat dey give lots for our family.

JON: Yeah, your uncle always like dis kine no class kine place. Remembah las' time he went pick da restaurant? He went pick someplace in Chinatown dat everybody come in and eat in their undershirt. Ass too much dat!

DEBBIE: Maybe we can put crepe paper or something, get one drugstore down da street.

JON (*sarcastically*): And maybe we can get some of those toot horns and party hats and dose tings dat shoot out and uncurl when you blow 'em . . .

(JON *and* DEBBIE *sit at the table and look unhappy: DEBBIE takes off the flower in her hair and arranges it in the middle of the table as a centerpiece.*)

JON: Look kinda had it yeah?

DEBBIE: Shut up . . . you got da lei?

JON (*irritably*): I got the lei, I got 'em.

(AUNTY ESTHER, UNCLE PETE *and* AH PO *enter. AH PO is in a wheelchair and PETE is pushing her. AH PO looks about distractedly and has a shawl and a lap blanket. She pulls the shawl closer to her shoulders and clutches her handbag as she looks around.*)

ESTHER (*reading the plates*): Here Ah Po. Hou Hou Chop Suey . . . Very Good Chop Suey . . . one ting fo' sure, da pakes not shame when dey name restaurants. (*Looks around quickly.*) It nice, Ah Po . . . nice. Look Debbie and Jon stay already.

(PETE *wheels* AH PO *into the middle seat of the center table.* JON *moves a chair out of the way.* DEBBIE *comes up and kisses* AH PO *on the cheek and presses an envelope into the woman's hand.* AH PO *does not recognize* DEBBIE *and looks around confused.* PETE *and* ESTHER *sit on either side of AH PO.*)

DEBBIE: Happy birthday Ah Po. This is Jon, my friend.

ESTHER (*whispering, interpreting for* AH PO): Ah Debbie

. . . Debbie boyfriend . . . lo. (ESTHER *takes the enve-lope from* AH PO's *hand, rips it open and records the amount of the gift in a notebook.*) Debbie, ten dollars.

DEBBIE (*corrects* ESTHER): Das from me and Jon, Aunty.

ESTHER: Yeah, yeah, Debbie and Jon. *(Scribbles.)*

AH PO: (*Still confused, she suddenly recognizes the voice and breaks into a smile. She reaches out and takes* DEBBIE's *hand.*) Ah Yin, eh? tank you eh . . . dough jay . . . tank you . . . yahk chiahng . . . eat orangee? (*AH PO rummages about at her feet as if there were a bag of oranges there. She offers* DEBBIE *an imaginary or-ange.*) Nicee girl . . . nicee girl.

DEBBIE: No, Ah Po, I no like oranges. Bumbye come fat . . .

ESTHER (*laughing, repeats loudly to* AH PO): She say bumbye she come fat . . .

AH PO (*leans toward* ESTHER *to catch her words*): Ah . . . bumbye come fat like Ah Po . . . Ah Po fat, but she get good children, good grandchildren even if dey all too skinny. (JON approaches AH PO with the lei. He bends over and presents it to her quickly, pecking her on the cheek. He steps back next to DEBBIE.)

JON: Happy birthday . . . um . . . Ah Po?

ESTHER: Debbie boyfriend, Jon (*Louder.*) Debbie . . . Ah Yin . . . boyfriend, Jon. (*Scribbles in notebook.*) Lei from Jon.

AH PO: (*She sticks out her hand formally for a handshake.* JON *comes forward and shakes it softly.*) Tank you, tank you. (AH PO *looks* JON *over then whispers to* ESTHER.) What kine boy?

ESTHER: Japanee boy, nice boy. Work shipyard with Pete. Nice boy, hard worker.

AH PO (*looks disapproving*): Japanee boy? Get plenty Chinee boy, why she like Japanee boy? You sure he nice boy?

ESTHER: Yes, yes. He nice boy, hard worker. Pete say.

(She reaches over and fills a small teacup with tea and motions to JON *to serve it to* AH PO.)

JON: Here Ah Po. You like tea? I bring you tea ...

AH PO: Ahh ... yum cha ... drink tea ... I like tea ... nice boy.

(AH PO starts to rummage through her purse for lee-see, money wrapped in red paper to give as a gift. She cannot find any so she pulls out a sheaf of red papers. She looks through her wallet but brings no money out and folds an empty lee-see for JON. JON *is uncomfortable as* AH PO *hands him the red paper.)*

AH PO: Here you nicee boy ... tank you ... tank you.

JON *(starts to refuse the gift)*: No, no need nothing, it's your birthday ...

DEBBIE: Take 'em Jon. Bumbye Ah Po tink you too good for her.

AH PO: Nice boy ... nice Japanee boy ... Ah Goong, you fahdah Esther, before time he say, Japanee no good ... no good marry Japanee. Must keep da family strong ... alla same blood, keep 'em pure. I everytime tell him dat da Japanee buy at his store all da time and he still talk bad about dem. He say dat business dat ... business okay but marry is different ... marry Japanee no good ... business okay. He say Japanee like spend dey money anyway, so mo' bettah da Chinee man take from dem den da haole man. Chinee man mo' fair den haole man store. Ah Goong he say dat but I watch him sometime when da Japanee man come buy meat, he leave da bone and plenny fat on top da meat ... or when he weigh da chicken he leave da liver and gizzard and da chicken head on da scale. Chinee man come inside da store, never mind Ah Goong don't know da man, as long as Chinee man, he cut off da fat and he no weigh da liver and gizzard and he let anybody Chinee come pick chicken feet from da scrap bin fo' free. Even he save da

pig blood fo' da Filipino man fo' free everytime he kill
pig. But da Japanee mans dat come inside da store he no
give dem nutting. He say Japanee man no treat wahine
good but da Japanee ice man always nice to me when he
come. He treat me good. Ah Goong he go wild if he tink
I talk to da ice man. He say we gotta teach our daughter
right so no talk to Japanee. So I have to listen to him . . .
he my husband so I have to listen. But I tink Japanee not
so bad. Japanee smart for grow garden. One time I ask
da ice man how to grow vegetable good . . . he tell me
put egg shell inside da dirt and put milk water inside da
dirt. When Chew Mung, you folks Ah Goong, eat da
cabbage he ask me where I learn how grow so good
cabbage, I like tell him from da Japanee ice man but I no
can say dat. I jes' smile and say it da secret of my
garden. (*To* JON.) You nicee Japanee boy . . . you take
care of my grandchild. You be nice husban to her . . .
you my secret in the garden.

JON: Tanks, Ah Po, tank you, but we not going get married
yet . . .

ESTHER: Shhh . . . Jon, enough . . .

DEBBIE: 'Nuff already Jon . . . she likes you, pau.
    (*Lights lowered, single spot on AH PO.*)

AH PO: Shh, Ah Po . . . should not speak to the Japanese.
Chew Mung will punish you and not permit you to play
mah jong on Sundays . . . he will not let you buy sweet
oranges or go into Chinatown to talk and shop. He will
make you go to the temple every day and chant and pray
with the bald-headed monks . . . all the monks are fat . . .
there are no thin monks. It must be their poverty . . . ha . . .
do the monks cheat like how Chew Mung cheats the
Japanese? Do they pray less for those who cannot make
a big offering? Does the Buddha know? Sometimes
when I kneel and chant and pray with my eyes closed
tightly I can see the great Buddha's arm move. It is a

blessing to see the Buddha's arm move, just a fraction of
an inch. A sign. I wonder if the monks see that or
perhaps it is they who make it move. Debbie has a
Japanese boyfriend . . . she asks her Ah Goong for his
blessing, Chew Mung. Will your eyes soften and move
so slightly in your way of saying yes? I shall go to the
temple to see if the Buddha's hand moves. I think it will.
I cannot defy you Chew Mung, I talked to the ice man . . .
he taught me how to grow the vegetables . . . but you
liked the vegetables . . . his Japanese soul is in those
eggshells and milk water that fed the cabbages . . . and
you ate them Chew Mung . . . you ate the Japanese
man's love for the plants. Does that make you part of the
man's soul? Does that make your blood impure?
(*Lights start to come up again.*)
 You folks grandfahdah, your Ah Goong, going know
that I never listen to him when we meet again in heaven . . .
He not going to let me come until I pray some more.
You going bring me food and burn money for me until I
reach da end of da journey, Esther? You going do dat fo'
me? And after one month you going back to da temple
for da end of da journey, Esther? You going do dat fo'
me? And after one month you going back to da temple
for ask da monk if I went go heaven okay. No let da fat
monks cheat you. Maybe you going have to bring some
more offerings and fold and burn some more dead
people's money . . . maybe more den for anybody else
because I never listen to my husband and I never follow
his word and I mock da fat monks and talk to da Japanee
ice man . . . his vegetables dey grow so good . . .
ESTHER: Ah Po, Ah Po . . . mama, enough already . . .
stop. No talk dat kine.
(JON *is still standing at her feet, frozen, his hands
clutching the red paper lee-see.* RICKY *and* DANE, *two
brothers, enter.* DANE *is long-haired and comfortably*

dressed, RICKY *is nattily dressed and chic.* DANE
approaches AH PO *and gives her a red envelope. She
looks around confused until* ESTHER *introduces* DANE.)

ESTHER: Dis Ah Kong's youngest boy, Dane . . . what's
you Chinese name? You know, Ah Goong name all you
folks. Your grandfahdah give da Chinese name to all the
grandchildren.

DANE: Hoong Gnip . . . Ah Gnip . . .

AH PO: (*She recognizes the name and reaches up to touch*
DANE *and fingers his hair. She mutters something
about hair.*): . . . jes' like your brothers when dey little,
Esther . . .

ESTHER: Ah Po say you should braid your hair into a
queue like the old Chinese plantation workers. She say
she used to put fish hooks inside da braid so when da
Hawaiian kids tease and pull your fahdah's hair they get
poked in da hand.

DANE: Aw . . . Ah Po . . . maybe I cut for you . . . (*Makes a
cutting motion.*)

AH PO (*laughs*): No cut . . . no cut. Nice hair, keep good
hair . . . you fahdah no more hair bumbye, so one son
must have hair for fahdah and son. Goodoo boy. Tank
you, dough jay . . . yahk orangee . . . eat orange, lucky . . .
(*Starts to rummage around again in her purse. Gives*
ESTHER *the envelope.* ESTHER *opens and records the
gift.*)

DANE: No Ah Po . . . umm yahk . . . no like.

AH PO (*offers an imaginary orange*): Here yahk orange,
goodoo boy . . . eat . . . lucky.

DANE (*accepts* AH PO's *gift from her empty hands*):
Dough jay Ah Po . . . dough jay . . . tank you.

AH PO (*smiling to* ESTHER): Dis boy always like eat
orangee . . . only when he eat orangee he talk Chinee, he
say "dough jay" . . . he say "dough jay Ah Po," no?

ESTHER (*patiently*): Yes, Ah Po.

DANE: Aunty Esther when you going ask Ah Po for tell me about long time ago? You went tell her what I tol you? It important for get em all down before she die. Da family tree, la dat. So dat everybody can tell how was in da olden days.

ESTHER: Yeah, yeah . . . no talk like she going die already. You only get her upset. She only talk about dat kine stuff when she feel like it anyway. Sometimes I tink she make up all her stories, so waste time. She cannot jes' sit and talk to you anyway . . . you lo-lo in Chinese.

DANE: I know Aunty, ass why I need you for help. All you gotta do is call me whenever she feel like talking or else I lend you my tape recorder or you can jes' write 'em down afterwards . . .

ESTHER: Waste time dat kine. If we was royalty or something maybe worth it. But you Ah Po only from one court official's family, small potatoes dat.

DANE: Yeah but Ah Po feet dey was bound eh? So dat must mean dey was kinda important eh?

ESTHER: No mean nutting dat. Probably mean your great grandfahdah had big ideas . . . jes like your Uncle Pete, all bullshit ideas. Besides, if you so hot on dis kine family tree stuff why you never learn Chinese in da first place?

DANE: Chee Aunty dat was small kid time . . . everybody like be American, no good be China jack. You gotta fit when you small kid time. I know we stupid dat, cause now I no can understand nutting . . . yahk chiahng, yahk chiahng ... eat oranges, ass all I know . . .

DEBBIE: Yeah no? You know, before time, I thot Ah Po was one dumb dodo because all she ever ask me was "yahk something . . ." eat orange or eat rice la dat . . . and I always say no cause shame eh?

JON (*teasing*): No look like you always said "no."

DEBBIE: Shaddup Jon . . .

DANE: Aunty Esther, you try ask Ah Po for me . . . C'mon Aunty. No tell me she no talk anykine stuff with you.

ESTHER: Ass all old stuff, no good talk about long time ago. No use . . . ancient history . . . you was right when you was small kid, da Chinese ways waste time, might as well be American. Too much dat kine talk no good for Ah Po. Bumbye she tink too much about dying and den she like go back China fo' die. Nope, no good dat.

AH PO: Ah Gnip, Ah Gnip . . .

DANE: Yes, Ah Po.

AH PO: Ah Gnip, you can not get married until Ah Jiu find one wife, okay? You wait fo' him . . . dat show respect . . .

DANE: Yes, Ah Po. You no need worry.

AH PO: Ah Jiu, where Ah Jiu?

ESTHER: Ricky, come. Ah Po like talk to you.

PETE: Hey Ricky, come have one beer . . .

RICKY: Okay, what you got?

PETE: Only Primo. I know you folks is Michelob people but ass all I got.

RICKY: Nah, Primo is good.

ESTHER: Ricky, Ricky . . . Ah Po like ask you something. Ah Po, dis Ricky over hea, Ah Kong's number one son.

RICKY: Yeah, yeah. Howsit grandma . . . how's it goin' . . . oh, I get a little something here fo' you. (*Reaches into his wallet and withdraws a five, looks up to see* ESTHER *watching him, then withdraws another five dollar bill. He spreads them out and presses it into* AH PO's *hands.*)

AH PO (*looks around to* ESTHER): Where Ah Jiu? . . . Ah Jiu, Ah Kong's boy . . .

ESTHER: Right here Ah Po . . .

RICKY: Yeah, I right here grandma . . . I right here . . . Ricky. I give you present. (*Points to* AH PO's *hands.*) Aunty, tell her ass me dat talking.

AH PO: Where Ah Jiu? First, Ah Jiu find nice Chinee girl. Ah Jiu, you get married so Ah Gnip can marry. You numbah one boy, marry first, den take care you fahdah . . .

ESTHER: Ricky, Ah Po ask if you married yet. She like you find one nice Chinee girl. I tink she like set you up with one rich widow at da temple . . . not too nice body but plenny money! (ESTHER *laughs and tells her joke to* AH PO.)

AH PO: Hai-lo . . . yes . . . get nice lady at da temple for Ah Jiu. (*Turns serious.*) What about da Yim's daughter? She schoolteacher no? Ah Jiu, you like Yim's daughter? Nice girl fo' you. She make plenty children fo' you. She come from good family, too. Ah Jiu you like orangee? Yahk chiahng. (*Begins to rummage about again. Her hands open and drop the money to the floor. She offers* RICKY *an imaginary orange.*)

RICKY: Ah Po, your money on da floor. I no like orange. I no like get married. I no like Yim's daughter. I no like Chinee girls . . . (*Increasingly loud, turns to* ESTHER.) Eh, she senile already. I dunno why I bother, waste time. Pete, where my beer?

AH PO (*frightened at the ruckus*): Ah Jiu, Ah Jiu.

RICKY: Ah Jiu . . . I dunno who Ah Jiu is . . . Ah Jiu no stay grandma . . . (*Laughs cruelly.*)

ESTHER (*to* AH PO): Ricky . . . Ah Jiu . . . he work hard today. Ah Jiu give you lee-see Ah Po. (*Bends over to pick up the money, puts it back into* AH PO's *hand.*)

AH PO: He no like Chinee girl? He no marry? Wassamalla him? Chinee girl good for Ah Jiu. She cook fo' him, she make plenny children for him . . . why he no like? Ah Goong name Hoong Jiu. Dat mean ''successful business-man'' . . . and all da grandchildren have da Chinese name "successful" . . . Ah Jiu everytime he quiet boy . . . no talk, him . . . aie, I no bring coconut candy for Ah Jiu. Maybe next time he tell me he get married. You tell him

no need be Chinee girl. Now modern days, okay marry
Japanese, maybe haole . . . anykine girl okay. Ah Jiu get
married be happy, den Ah Gnip get married. I go temple
and pray fo' Ah Jiu . . . maybe da Buddha help me find
one nice girl for Ah Jiu. Bumbye no marry, no have
children for da family name . . .

(*Lights begin to lower.*)

Mama, who is that man who came to talk to daddy? Am
I to marry him, he is old! That is Chew Mung's father?
Am I to marry Chew Mung? What is he like? Why
cannot I see Chew Mung? Oh great Buddha, please
make my husband happy and make me be a good wife.
They say he is a wise man. I hear so many things about
Chew Mung . . . he comes from a scholar's family, he is
a professor of philosophy, he can do calligraphy, he can
write poems . . . he is the most important man in the
world. But mama, we are not rich . . . we have a good
family name but I am not educated. What if Chew Mung
does not want to marry me? What if he disobeys his
father and does not want to marry me? I cannot do
calligraphy, we do not have many servants . . . my feet
are bound . . . I do not know the wise sayings . . . I
cannot be a good wife mama, say that I need not marry
Chew Mung . . . tell daddy that I cannot marry, that I am
barren and cannot have children . . . I will go to the
temple to live . . . I will learn to cook for the monks . . . I
cannot become an important lady in this family of good
name . . . I cannot even become a simple farmer . . . my
feet are useless . . . say that to him . . . I cannot marry
Chew Mung . . .

(*Lights come up.*)

When I see you Ah Goong he look mean. He say da
wisdom of our fahdahs is greatest and we gotta listen to
them. He brought me candy and sweet oranges. Ah Jiu,
he was a good man, he has a good name.

ESTHER: Ah Po, time fo' eat. I tell da manager to start
     bringing da food eh? Yahk fahn Ah Po . . . time fo' eat
     rice, Ah Po . . . everybody sit down, the food coming . . .
RICKY: Da old lady stop running off at da mout? Jeesus,
     might as well shoot me if I evah come la dat. Crazy, man
     . . . old age, senile already.
DEBBIE (*trying to smooth things over*): Ricky come sit
     over hea by us. You still working post office?
RICKY: Oh yeah, thru rain and snow and sleet and hail . . .
DANE: And thru goofing off and pay raises and slow mail . . .
PETE: Chee all you gov'ment workers da same ... you tink you
     ripping off Uncle Sam? Das me you ripping off, ass my tax
     money . . .
DANE: I thot you was Uncle Pete . . .
PETE: I put da stamps on top da envelope and still take
     three days fo' my letter get across da Pali . . . I used to
     have one carrier pigeon dat could fly across da Pali and
     back in ten hours. Dey oughta replace all you guys with
     a bunch of birds. (*Everybody laughs.*)
DANE: Dey already close uncle, all da carriers get bird brain
     anyway.
RICKY: You guys jes' jealous.
     (*Waitress brings the first course.*)
ESTHER: Bird nest soup everybody. Put your bowls close
     . . . Jon you scoop out da soup . . . you da only one here
     not related so you can scoop da most even . . . bumbye
     everybody say when I serve, get favortism . . . dis bunch
     fo' complain.
JON: Here Ah Po . . . da first bowl.
ESTHER: Ah Po Jon-boy give you soup . . . he nice boy . . .
AH PO: Goodoo boy . . . you scoop fo' you Ah Goong too . . .
     he like fresh parsley and with one jigger whiskey inside.
PETE: Right Ah Po . . . likker . . . who like likker? For put
     inside da soup . . . bring you jigger, everybody bring you
     jigger. Ricky, you drunkard, where you jigger, you pilute?

RICKY: Right here.

ESTHER: Jon, no forget make bowls for Gary and his wife . . .
and Cousin Dennis never come yet, make one bowl for
him too.

PETE: Who no mo' likker? Debbie put some tea inside your
jigger so make 'em look like whiskey, so you can toast
Ah Po. Okay, everybody ready . . . okay Ah Po . . .
(*Everybody raises their jigger and stands.*) To our Ah
Po, who is eighty-one years old today. Happy birthday
Ah Po. (*Some start to sit. PETE stops them.*) Wait you
guys, one mo' round . . . gotta toast da soup. You gotta
do dis right, bumbye bad luck . . .

DEBBIE (*to* JON): My Uncle Pete famous for making da
toasts. Dis way he get loaded by da fifth course and den,
you watch, he going play Chinese jun-ken-a-po by da ninth
course . . . ass one game where da loser gotta drink one
jigger, so my Uncle everytime lose on purpose. Funny man,
when you get two guys trying fo' to lose on purpose . . .

PETE (*completes refilling the jiggers*): Okay, everybody
bottoms up to da soup.

RICKY, DANE, JON (*together*): To da soup.

AH PO (*observing the toasting*): Pete, you forget pour fo'
Chew Mung. You not supposed to drink until da
children's goong goong went drink.
(*Lights dim.*)
I have forgotten my place Chew Mung. I will do as you
say and pray for forgiveness. I do not think forgiveness
will come until morning. I am sorry I disgraced you in
front of your scholarly friends. You are of such a high
position and I am so lowly. My feet are bound but it is
not an indication of court life, it is a mistake. I am too
lowly for you. There is a way for everything you say.
And it is through these ways that we learn respect and
the order of things. The children must have respect. I
have to earn my respect by respecting you, Chew Mung.

You are so solemn. You only speak to me when I do
wrong . . . and you speak in level and even tones . . . as
you would to a simple person or child. You wish the
children to stay at home and to study as you study. You
wish them to be doctors and poets and historians. They
fear you, your children do. They mock and mimic your
stern and solemn ways . . . they do not like school and
the town talks of the professor's children who have no
respect for their elders . . . noisy, boisterous children
who do not listen, they only ask why, why, why . . .
drink Chew Mung . . . drink your whiskey and study
your poems and while you sleep I shall comfort the
children and play with them and put them finally to bed,
then I shall hold your head in my lap and look into your
face to catch some of the wisdom that you give off in
your sleep . . . I shall clip the hairs in your nose and your
ears and stroke the one long hair from your mole, you
treasure it so . . . Chew Mung, I am not wise enough for
you. You cannot discuss philosophy with me and I
cannot discuss the children with you.

(*Lights brighten.*)

PETE (*loudly*): Everybody put one shot whiskey inside da
soup. Make 'em ono boy. C'mon Debbie jes' little bit, I
no tell your muddah . . . dis going make your complexion come smooth . . . give you rosy cheeks.

DEBBIE: Sure, uncle, sure . . . make me real drunk too eh?

ESTHER: Where dose cousins of yours Debbie, their soup
getting cold . . .

RICKY: Yeah, might as well I eat 'em . . . no good let 'em get
cold . . . (*Silence.*) Jeesus, you guys leave one bowl out for
grandpa . . . he's dead . . . you leave bowl out for people
who probably no goin' come . . . maybe dey never going
come . . . why? 'Cause das da custom. Custom gotta have
meaning, you guys gotta tink about what da meaning of
tings. If tings don't have meaning what's da use!

ESTHER: Ricky, serve you Ah Po tea . . . use two hands now.

DEBBIE: Here comes da late kung-fu master. Eh, Dennis where you was . . . out at some bar fighting evil?
(*Dennis enters, dressed in black with white patent leather belt and shoes. A jade medallion hangs from his chest.*)

DENNIS: Eh, howsit everybody. I sorry I late Ah Po. Where da tea, I supposed to serve Ah Po tea, eh?

PETE: Aw, you just bucking for get one lee-see you buggah.

DENNIS: (*pours some tea and serves it to* Ah Po. *He leaves an envelope in front of her on the table.*) Here Ah Po, happy birthday. I sorry I late.

ESTHER: Ah Po, dis Ah Yong . . . Ah Yong.

DENNIS: Aunty Esther, tell Ah Po I sorry I late. Tell her I bring some grapefruit, some boo-look? Nice kine. Tell her as from da tree Ah Goong plant for my daddy when he get married and den my daddy plant for me when I got married. Still come out sweet dese buggahs. (*Takes a few fruit out of a paper bag and passes it around the table. Each person in turn holds it for awhile then passes it on to* AH PO.)

AH PO (*confused as to where all the large fruit are coming from.*): Ai-ya? Boo-look . . . who get boo-look? Look like da boo-look you Ah Goong bring me when we get married . . .
(*Lights dim.*)
We must stack the fruit in the window Chew Mung . . . so that they can ripen and sweeten. I will stack them in pyramids of grapefruit and oranges and tangerines. The Chinese celebrate around citrus fruits. They are lucky fruit. To fruit is to have children and to be abundant. To be fruitful is to be prosperous. You wanted to be fruitful Chew Mung. You are such an important person but you

saw a land of fruit. Hawai'i, where there are trees that bear oranges the year long they told you. You left your friends in China, all the ones who came to you for advice because of your wisdom and your station and your education. Your friends with whom you discussed your calligraphy and your poetry. I told you to be a pioneer then, if it is your fate to go to Hawai'i. You would give up your name and your station to go to America? In America there are no classes They do not listen to their elders. Respect is earned there, it is not automatic. They do not respect mere family names . . . they respect the person. Respect in America is better, it is earned and it is more reliable in the end. Sometimes I forget that when I expect the children and the grandchildren to listen to me. They are all good children Chew Mung, you have not failed. I have failed because my feet are useless to you in the new land. I am a burden to you on this ship. It is a long journey and I insist that you carry me up and down the boat stairs because I am too slow to hobble after you up and down the decks . . . and I left my home of oranges and fruits and sweet air to ride a boat to come with you to Hawai'i, an adventure I thought. I always thought I would be going to another land of oranges and to become like them. I am bored with the life of a court official's daughter. I was tired of your fruit, the fruit you brought me because it was how you were instructed to behave. I am tired of your fruit Chew Mung! (*Picks up grapefruit and throws it weakly.*) I want adventures. I do not wish to watch your fruit ripen in my window.

(*Lights brighten. Everyone is eating heartily.*)

ESTHER: Ah Po, eat chicken, hau yau chicken, oyster sauce chicken.

PETE: Drink everybody . . . drink to the chicken. C'mon Ricky, Dane no scared 'em. Drink up. Dennis I no need ask him twice, da pilute. Better hide da bottle from him.

DENNIS: Chee you guys only tease eh? My hands stay
deadly weapons. You bettah watch out . . . they might
jes' flick out dere and injure and maim you . . .

PETE: Ha, da only deadly ting about you is you mout . . .

RICKY: Or his futs . . . dey silent and sneaky. . .

ESTHER: Shhh, you boys enough.

DANE: Whoa, the next one here already. You guys better
eat faster. Uncle, your toasts, dey slowing down . . . you
not keeping up wit da courses.

ESTHER: You not forgetting to leave some on Gary and his
wife plate, eh?

RICKY: Sure, and for Ah Goong, and for his Ah Goong and
for the grandfather of his grandfather . . .

PETE: Ass Ricky getting smart? Cut off his likker supply,
let him die of thirst.

RICKY (*gasping in mock horror*): No, no anything but dat .
. . Ah Po, Ah Po . . . I making plate for Ah Goong. He
going enjoy his plate . . . (*Begins to pick at the plate set
aside for* Ah Goong.) Lemme test one piece here . . . oh
goong goong, dis buggah is ono. You oughta try one
piece. What, you let me try for you? Okay . . . eh, Ah
Goong, you should be here whacking 'em in . . . Man
you get good life when you dead . . . jes' like when we
lug the roast pig up to Manoa cemetery every year, rain
or shine. We always wait until the candles all burn down
before we put da food away. Dose candles signify da
repast of da dead. We burn dead people's money for you
to spend in heaven, Ah Goong. We leave one bowl of
food by da side of da gravestone for da caretaker of you
grave and da guardian of your soul. You sucker, you
sucking Ah Goong . . . you suck us dry with your
Chinese ways . . . waste time Ah Goong, waste time.
(*Louder and louder, the table is deadly quiet.*) Ah Po
you good for nuttin . . . nobody can understand you and

you no can understand us. So what's the use . . . you're
just as good as dead.

ESTHER: Ricky, keep quiet. Ah Po can understand you when
you mad.

AH PO: Ah Jiu yahk orangee, yahk fruit . . . you eat, have
good luck . . . . you eat . . .

ESTHER: Pete, start getting the cake ready so we can sing
Happy Birthday.

JON: I help you put da candles.

PETE: You went bring eighty candles? Mo' bettah just put
one propane torch on top dis cake. We go just put some
so dat Ah Po get something fo' blow out.

AH PO: When your Ah Goong say we come to Hawai'i, I
say good, good. I keep telling him I no like live like my
muddah and fahdah, I want something new and exciting.
So you Ah Goong quit being professor and he save his
money and sell his house. He say he start one school in
Hawaii . . . one Chinee language school.

(*Lights dim.*)

I hate this boat Chew Mung . . . I hate the ocean . . . the
motion of the boat makes me ill and my feet make it
hard for me to go on the deck to get fresh air. I curse
you, Chew Mung. I want to go back home. There are
only poor people on this boat. There are no servants.
Only common people. I will not cook rice, that is
servant's work. Ah Goong, he did his best to please me.
He would buy salted fish and oranges and cook the rice.
He would make me eat and not speak of home anymore.
He did not write any more poetry and he did not seek out
people to talk philosophy . . . these are useless occupa-
tions he said. He worked in the ship kitchen and became
a meat cutter . . . he learned bookkeeping from a man
who could make the abacus beads fly. He never talked of
starting the school again. I kept asking him . . . I asked
him over and over . . . Chew Mung our house in

Hawai'i, how many rooms will it have? How many servants will we have? How many orange trees can we have? . . . He always said we will have enough. Not more or less. We will have enough. Chew Mung said when we come to Hawai'i we must be like Americans and do things in the right way. We must learn English and the new ways. I had no big house, no servants, no orange trees. I stayed in the house and refused to learn English. We lived above the store where he worked. I want to move out of here Chew Mung. You say that poetry and philosophy is worthless, waste time you say. It is good that you learned meat cutting and bookkeeping. I will only talk Chinese to you. I will only go to the Chinese stores. I will only eat Chinese food. Things American are no good. I do not want my children to become American. Why don't they listen to me? Chew Mung, why don't they listen to me . . .
(*Lights brighten.*)

ESTHER: Blow out da candles Ah Po. It good luck, you blow out da candles. Good luck Ah Po . . . jes' like orange.

DEBBIE: Make one wish first Ah Po . . . hurry up before da candles burn down. (AH PO *looks confused, she doesn't understand what's going on.*)

ESTHER: Ah Po, you make one wish . . . something that you want to make you happy, den you blow out da candles. If you blow out all da candles one time, you lucky and you wish come true.

AH PO: I make a wish . . . I want . . .

DEBBIE: Ah Po, you not supposed to say da wish aloud . . .

AH PO (*looks around quizzically*): . . . I make wish . . . I wish to be American . . . da first president is George Washington.

(AH PO *takes a deep breath, gets ready to blow. Lights go out.*)

Ancestry
Eric Chock

You ask me who I am? I say
I come from a long line of skinny old men.
Someday my hair will thin like a baby's
and I'll have a beard longer than a goat's.
When it's time for me to walk with a stick
I'll walk slowly,
and as I squeeze the gnarled handle
I'll think of all the bad men
I wanted to hit just once; I will
think of all the good men I wanted
to put my arms around; I will
smile at the young ladies that pass like butterflies
and I'll stumble at the street corner, frantically
hitting the earth with my cane . . .
The earth is always there, waiting.
Now I think I know why it spins.
If you listen closely at night
you can hear the music of its spinning.
I come from a long line of skinny old men
who want to be notes for a song.

Here I Am
Gary Tachiyama

Looking back
not to Dwight D.
Benny Harrison
or some foreign notion
of independence
               but to an empty
                     purple kimono
          ripping and tearing
       thread by thread
            in the wind
               over a Big Island
         plantation town

My heritage

But here I am
wearing jeans and T- shirts
with a crystal Seiko
analog on my wrist
eating rice on a plate
with a fork
sometimes in a bowl
with chili
rapping with my Sansei brothers
all in their twenties
sitting in class
beginning to learn the language
and about World War II
the plantation
and Issei ancestors

cause there ain't much
of the cloth left—
couple of threads
and no way to see
the plum blossoms
and I thought we came
just to cut cane
and I thought we'd go home
                    dancing
and I thought we'd go
the same as we came
like Japan
          just like Japan

Old Kimono
Marie Hara

From the moment she saw it folded neatly on the top of the pile of old clothing, she was sure it would look good on her.

"One of a kind, a perfect find."

The color was right, a sophisticated black crepe. The design was just what she hoped for, "Japanese-y" and clearly ethnic, plus the incredible price. It was second hand, of course, but the jagged scrap of masking tape stuck on to it read three dollars. Three dollars. For something antique and classy. You couldn't go wrong.

People she knew or had heard about, women her age, were using old kimonos in intriguing ways, pleating them for sophisticated skirts and cutting them up for fashionable blouses and vests. If they couldn't sew, they found dressmakers. And why not? Old material turns worthless forgotten in camphor chests or left in closets as termite food. And the patterns . . . you couldn't find that kind of design on bolts anymore . . . they had become priceless. Her own creative idea was simple: this one would be the perfect robe over a silky, black nightgown. No matter whose it had once been, it was destined to be part of her own wardrobe now, finally appreciated for its true worth, its one-of-a-kind lining, its fashion statement, subtle, but bold.

She held it up to the two elderly Japanese women who were tending their booth. The crowd at the Shinshu Mission Bazaar milled through the displays of housewares and knickknacks. Most people stepped right past the rack of dark "Baba-san" dresses and assorted heaps of cast-off garments.

The annual fair attracted a varied clump of people to the temple on a winding street off the heart of downtown Honolulu. Shoppers moved through tents and stalls. Some waited for the next batch of homemade sushi while a wave of smoke from the huli-huli chicken barbecue next door forced the bystanders to move aside or cover their watering eyes. The temple, a vestige of the 1920s, was bright pink, concrete East Indian style architecture. Easy to spot but hard to figure how it could have been built by Japanese Americans in Hawai'i, the temple now rarely attracted the young, except at Bon Dance time or the fair. So her first reaction whenever she visited was to open her eyes to take it all in once again. Here lay evidence of good luck, the very blessing she remembered a priest telling her grandmother she would receive for faithfully visiting the memorials to the dead.

The two old ladies saw her growing interest. As the women examined the garment, they noted her enthusiasm by exchanging questioning looks. She ran her hands over the elaborate design one more time. Her action was closely watched by the hunchbacked old lady whose neck was frozen in a perpetual bow.

"Young girlu-san." She got her attention.

"Saah . . . befo' time . . . you know Watanabe-san? Yuriko? The family wen' donate all her clothes after the one-year service." This from the elderly woman with mottled age spots all over her face and arms.

With annoyance at the unasked-for information, the young woman shook her head. "Maybe my grandma might have, but I nevah come to temple nowadays."

"You know how fo' wear this kind?"

"Sure, but I might change it and maybe cut it all up, too. I don't wanna wear dis kine old-fashion stuff. In Hawai'i, too hot."

As the other one stared, the young woman pressed three bills into the hand of the silent old lady and quickly packed the neat kimono—now a precisely folded rectangle—into her designer-label satchel. Without a word the hunched one handed her a stained, cotton obi, more a child's sash than a proper waist piece. She noted also that neither of the two women thanked her, even as they carefully watched her walk away.

Hypocrites. They think they know how to do things right . . . but it's always their way or no way. Typical! In her mind's eye she saw a long line of Japanese mothers, aunties and other older women lecturing young girls relentlessly about how to do things correctly, what they meant was *perfectly.* Even creasing a line in paper had to be done just so, with the edge of a fingernail. Crazy women. She would never do it their way. Leaving them far behind in her thoughts, she freed the kimono from any further association with such negative types.

No matter what anyone might say—and it would be some old lady for sure—she wouldn't tell where she bought it. This black silk kimono held so many possibilities. Even the glossy satin collar lining was quite elegant in a crisp way; there wasn't a single stain or moth hole. Not a whiff of camphor clung to the garment. Under her stroking touch, as she felt it in her handbag on the bus ride home, the kimono took on the form of a dozen different outfits, all hers.

The frame house on Pua Lane was surrounded by helter-skelter plantings. The varicolored ornamental growth winding along a flourishing garden of rows of green onion and lettuce ruffled out all around the neatly painted building. Vaguely similar to the other homes which formed a short row along the street, the brown cottage could have been a variant of the standard, now vanished plantation house. Littered with assorted slippers and shoes, the front porch where she dashed off her sandals stopped her motion for only the briefest moment.

She stood fixed in front of a full-length mirror. She sighed in satisfaction at the blackness of the top half of the kimono held next to her skin. The mirror gave proof that her choice, the sophisticated black and exquisite design work were exactly right for her. She would look bold and new:

Asian, not oriental. Sexy, not cute. The silky fabric confirmed her choice.

Once she turned the garment inside out to satisfy herself, she saw how painstakingly it had been made. Every seam was hidden by a double fold; every visible stitch, each identical to the eye, had been put in with stunning regularity since they were not machine made. Delighted, she said aloud, "My precision kimono!" held it to her chest, then frowned when she rechecked the sewing. She began to turn the kimono rapidly, then frantically. Where would the knots go? They had to be there or the whole thing would have fallen apart. All the finely matched rectangular pieces would break away. She chewed the logic of no anchor knots. Certainly they must be subtly hidden under the precise seams, of course.

At this comforting thought, she caught a glimpse of her mom's arrangement of what she called boy flawahs, anthuriums, in a blue vase placed on a bureau behind her. The red and pink flowers with their knobby pistils and sturdy stems, seemed—the only word she could call up to fit—crude. Not only were they ordinary and not placed in any particular order, they were also in no way fragile or aesthetic. They were so . . . local. Only hours away from the yard with its motley vegetation, the anthuriums shone out in their robust colors. They had been inserted into the vase for no particular reason, one more thing that her mother did by habit, not design.

By contrast the pattern of cranes and tortoises in a bamboo forest with a garden lantern, wisteria vines and chrysanthemums worked into a delicate but elaborate balance at the bottom of the kimono, spoke of art. Here lay the world where every fine line of distinguishing detail existed to make a difference. And then the crest needed some accounting for as well. On either breast, at the center back line and at two places below the shoulders, a tiny *mon* had been meticulously embroidered in white-gold thread. Whoever sewed it must have been a red hot seamstress, maybe a professional who had studied hard and aimed for perfection. She couldn't make out what the symbol meant but recognized a flower and the shape of a bird in the quarter of an inch allotted. The beak was sharply delineated.

Considering the imagery as she ran her hand wistfully over the garment now carefully spread out over the bed, she decided wearing it would make her not only look fashionably Japanese but also like someone who was used to wearing one. The only problem was that she'd have to learn all the finer points: what kind of under kimono and undergarments to wear, how to fix her hair just so, how to get her feet to walk together right and maybe even more. The kimono looked like the first step on a tiresome road of tasks to learn.

So she would use it as a simple robe. It looked like something from a fashion magazine. She was flexible. Easy elegance, that was just what she wanted from the moment she saw it. How would it look with a wide open neck and a flowing, loose sash?

When she saw herself in it for the first time, she felt a curious prickle run down her neck. It fit perfectly. That word again. She used the lightweight sash to tie herself in tightly. She wouldn't have to worry about a new hem, since it had been sewn precisely into an expert roll of one-fourth inch at the bottom edge. As she gazed at herself in the long mirror, she saw a young woman who, when she swept her full head of hair upward to form a ponytail, then a tight bun, was transformed into someone very much like a traditional Japanese woman, suddenly more demurely feminine than she had ever looked. Her form was elegantly contained in the decorated kimono column.

Oddly, she had a hard time meeting her own eyes in the mirror. She had to first look up and break out of the posture of her head bowed toward the kimono's border and the floor. She suppressed an impulse to move toward the kitchen to prepare a kettle of green tea.

Mother would bust laughing.

She chuckled, too, to think of the necessity to trot absurdly in this tight garment. Hilarious. She positioned her feet slightly inward so that the right pigeon-toed stance greeted her eyes when she admired herself again.

The blackness of the silk crepe glistened under the overhead light. To be so encased began to feel seductive. She could imagine being totally in control of an audience of observers who followed every movement she made . . . as if she were about to demonstrate an important cultural activity, explaining the reasons why people should choose this way, the proper one. Not that way, and why it looked so much more graceful, much better in the way that she had presented the action. What was the action? Just the way, actually the exquisite style with which she lifted her forearm and readied her own now elegant, elongated hand in a formal gesture of pointing to her slender form in the mirror. Her hand looked much longer, the nails subtly and perfectly shaped.

"Simple—absolutely simple—but correct, in fact, perfect." The last word came out in a pronouncement of satisfaction, although whispered.

She gazed at her image in the mirror. The Japanese-looking woman in disarray who returned the glance from the glass was vaguely familiar. With a realignment of her body posture, she saw what she would look like were she more attentive to details. The line of her back now had some starch to it, and her face grew masklike as if dreaming deeply. Erasing her individual expression, she had traded it for something more adequately female. Her eyes looked down.

One hand at her side, she fingered the cranes and tortoises and felt at home, no longer lost somewhere where the symbols meant nothing.

The figure in the sophisticated black kimono stared back at her without curiosity. With every tiny motion, her own breathing became part of a larger rhythm, something as ancient as the pattern on the cloth. She began to think about the Japan she had never seen, *tatami* mats and courtyards, wet garden stones and bustling street fronts, a Japan which she would never see, since it was all gone anyway. The romance of that charming past, replete with beckoning lanterns grew into colorful sweetmeats for her imagination. Lost in long, pleasant moments of a dream world layered with images from the Japanese movies she had gone to see with her grandma, her body began to fit the old kimono.

Her loyalty would never waver; she would serve her lord courageously. Her training would not let her do anything else. Her face would betray no emotion. Her feelings would be replaced by her purpose. She would learn what the great Lord Buddha taught about equanimity. Only her eyes would express how she regarded the universe: matter-of-factly, steadfastly seeing beauty in nature, in all the simple things, in respectfully acknowledging even bothersome people. She would lead by actions, not words.

The hour went by, the minutes unnoticed as she receded into deep thoughts about her role as a woman who appreciated the aesthetic above all. Beauty and pride, discipline and high endeavor ruled her very being.

When she let down her long hair in a straight mass against the back of the kimono, the black tresses looked like a silky waterfall with the light of the day outside picking up shiny glints in the flowing strands which moved together as one.

She pivoted slowly on one foot just to see if she could move correctly. Her hand daintily tucked back into her sleeve, she minced in tiny steps as if in time to a persistent koto melody. Back and forth, back and forth, she moved. Her face was determined as she disallowed herself a smile at the pleasing image of herself as a dancer, while she hid her hands within the kimono's delicate openings so that she looked more childlike and helpless. She cocked her head just so. No teeth, no fingernails, nothing sharp or jarring, broke her peaceful demeanor or the smooth lines of her softness dancing.

In the mirror someone diminutive and guileless reflected light. Music in her head, ringing with the rollicking cadences of koto and shamisen, rushed her into electric motion, back and forth, back and forth, until she collapsed on the bed, giggling at the spectacle.

She caught her breath when she looked backwards at the mirror. The woman in the black kimono was still dancing as if the music had increased its frantic rhythm. Back and forth, back and forth: her motions were hypnotic.

Lifting her face, the dancer, caught in the instant of clapping her hands, froze at the sight of the woman staring at her from the bed.

Both gasped, the young woman and the reflection in the mirror, when the bedroom door opened.

Her mother peered in from the darkened hallway.

"Oh. You. I thought I heard music. W'at did you put on? Hmmm . . . nice. But you have it on backwards. You wen' fo' get! Always wrap da kimono left over right or else you gonna look like one dead man. Fo' real! Anybody who know anyt'ing—all da people who see dat—dey gonna laugh at you."

She was ready to explain more and give examples from her experience.

Her daughter's face must have discouraged her, because she departed without waiting for a response.

The used kimono was left in a heap on the bed.

The Surfer
Asa Baber

During Rabbit's last weeks, when he knew and I knew that he was going to die, I sat with him at night.

I charted the times he was supposed to take Demerol and I gave him Thorazine when he needed it. The Thorazine was for the hiccups which came when he talked too much.

At night, Rabbit kept hearing a voice on the ridgeline at the top of the valley. I do not think the voice scared him so much as it interested him. He thought it was the spirit of his father calling to him.

Things like that happen in Hawai'i.

Then one night I heard the voice, too, although I tried to pretend that I did not. "You're stoned," I said to Rabbit when he asked me about it. "You've got too many pills in you." But I jumped again when I heard the voice clearly. It sounded like the call of a wolf.

"That's him, brah," Rabbit smiled. He called me 'brah'—Hawaiian lingo for 'brother'—not cheaply, like the mod crowd in Waikiki, but with love.

"It's just a dog or something," I said.

"That's Seki. He knows. He's waiting for me, Bobby. He's waiting."

Seki, Rabbit's father, had shot himself through the heart with a .22 pistol ten years ago. That was right after Lowell, Rabbit's brother, had been killed in a chopper crash in Laos. Right after the burial ceremony in Punchbowl with flags and rifles and a full bird Colonel and the smell of smog and ash in the slow Kona wind.

"Seki doesn't want you to die," I said.

"Yeah, I know," Rabbit nodded. "But if I have to die, Seki's saying he'll take care of me."

I did not know what to say, so I went back to talking surfing because that helped both of us.

For a short time we were not in a shack in Palolo Valley with a tin roof that rattled in the wind and a ball of opium in the saucer on the table. We moved out of there in our minds, leaving the pain, and we got back to the water where we belonged, where we had grown up together.

I told Rabbit what he already knew: that the summer waves were good on the South Shore and that there was sewage and sharks off of Sand Island and that Kaisers was as crowded as Publics and that Secrets had some long, heavy lefts with real power.

"You been to Cunahs?" Rabbit asked.

"Not this summer," I said. "It needs five feet to show. I'm working Cliffs mostly."

"You hotdog," Rabbit said. His eyes were closed but he was smiling.

"Hey!" I said. It was one of our old jokes. I surfed Diamond Head but Rabbit had never liked it there. The tour buses stopped at the top of Kuilei Cliffs on the wide part of Kahala Avenue and all day long the tourists watched us through binoculars as if we were toys on exhibit.

"You haole hotdog."

"Howl-lee, howl-lee," I exaggerated the word. "How come you always call me a haole, huh? I was raised here, too."

Rabbit was having trouble swallowing, so I kept talking to cover for him. "You call me a haole? OK, gook. Rabbit the gook. Here he is, folks. Rabbit the shy gook who surfs Secrets so nobody can see him. Awww." I pinched his thin cheeks. He tried to smile. His face was cold and there was something going on in his throat and chest that I did not understand. I waited to see if he was going to be sick but he got things under control. He was sweating.

"You think I could have another hit?" Rabbit asked later. "I don't know; maybe I shouldn't go out so stoned, huh? What do you think, Bobby?"

"It's been four hours," I lied. I propped him up so he could swallow another Demerol. As I helped him lie back on his pillows, I thought for a moment that he was one of my sons and that I was a full-time father again, nursing my children through the flu. It was a good feeling.

Sometimes I took a pill with Rabbit to try and float out of my own kind of pain. It was not Rabbit's pain of a diseased pancreas and a toxic bloodstream. But I missed my kids and I was losing my best friend and I had wasted my life. I was thirty-five years old and I should have been dead nine times over and I was burned out, wasted, like a spent shell casing. I knew there were as many kinds of pain as there were plants in the world, or trees or rocks or fish, and I knew that I was not coping with my pain as well as Rabbit was with his.

During those last days, as I watched Rabbit die slowly, I learned all over again that I am a racist and that I think there are genetic patterns, not in weaknesses but in strengths. Most Orientals handle pain better than most Caucasians.

Rabbit may have been a Sansei, the grandson of Tatshusho Harada and the son of Seki Harada, but there was a reservoir of Japan in him. Maybe he was part samurai or part priest. Maybe sometime back in the 16th Century one of his forebears had left Kyoto and gone into the mountains to practice calligraphy while he waited to die.

I do not know the exact history of the Harada family, but I do know that Rabbit was able to rise above his pain.

Towards the end, he decided to go without pills.

One of the best surfers I had ever seen, Rabbit had shrunk to a skeleton's weight, two operations in five months, the victim of various exotic therapies, but he sat up in the middle of what was to be his final night and he handed me the Darvon and Demerol and Thorazine and Vitamin B complex and Maalox and he said, "Wipe these out, brah."

"OK," I said. I moved the tray across the room.

"No. I mean out. Get rid of them." Rabbit waved his thin hands. He looked both old and child-like, the quilt around his shoulders, the gray sweatsuit covering his changed body, black felt slippers on his feet. He could have been a Montagnard or a tribal chief; say a chief who had signed a bad treaty and knew it.

"You sure?" I asked him. He did not answer. I took the tray into the kitchen and pretended to throw the bottles away. But when I walked into his room again, he was smiling at me.

"Bobby," he said, "I want them out of here. So do it."

I felt apart from him, and I knew that he had a special intuition now, something granted only to the dying, perhaps, and I did not argue with him. I walked through the garden and towards the road where I dumped the drugs in the trash pile.

It was past midnight and I stared up the valley towards the headwaters of the Waiomao Stream and I thought that I was on the moon, an astronaut in a deep crater close to the dark side of the moon, and I was almost dizzy as I tried to track the clouds crossing the ridge.

The thought that I was praying did not occur to me then, although I suppose I was, at least in my way; prayers to all the dead, of course, and to Buddha, to Jesus, to anything that might help, mixed with quick memories of the life that was passing in review.

Me, I am so twisted and scarred that I could not stand out there in the dark like that without also checking for trip wires, watching for ambushes, monitoring the ridgeline for the flash of tracers, and yes, I know it was peacetime in Honolulu, 1977, but for some of us it is always other times and other places, too. Always.

"Roberto," I said to myself, "you were present just before the destruction of a whole people."

That line came to me without my asking. It was delivered to me, and it was an awesome thought. So was the fact that Rabbit was passing into certain shadows as I stood in his vegetable garden. He had planted these flowering, budding things but he would not be around to harvest them.

"The destruction of a whole people," I said to myself again, remembering Kroong as he listened to the sounds of the prowling tiger near Sar Lang and Baap Can weeping at the funeral of his son and Maang-the-Deputy slicing the tendons on the hocks of the buffaloes before he cut their throats.

"Moi," the South Vietnamese called the Montagnards, "savages."

They are all gone now.

I was thinking about that when I heard the voice on the ridgeline again and I knew that Seki was telling me that Rabbit needed company. I walked back to the house.

"Bobby?" Rabbit whispered as I came into the room. He reached out for me. His eyes were closed.

"I'm here," I said. I held his hands. It was as if we were children in Manoa again, skipping school and planning where to surf for the day.

"Thanks, brah," Rabbit said.

"It's OK, brah."

"No pain," Rabbit said quietly.

I squeezed his hands. "All right."

I did not know what else to do, so I talked surfing again. Rabbit nodded sometimes.

I told him how next winter we would rent a house in Haleiwa and surf Sunset and the Bay and how he could ride the winter juice in The Pipeline and how Kapono, his sister, could come with us and surf Vals Reef and break the skeg on her board again at Kammieland. I took him all around O'ahu one last time, even after I could see he was not breathing any more.

"Goodbye, brah," I said. "You did good. Number One." I hugged the stick figure that had been my best friend. I felt sad and tired, but I was also relieved that it was over.

After a while I walked back to the gate and hiked down to the dealer's house to use his phone. I called Kapono at the hospital. She said she would come right up but I told her to finish her shift. "I'll stay with him until you get here, lady," I said. "He wouldn't want any fuss." I went on to tell her we would take Rabbit's ashes out in the Hobie Cat the way he wanted, and we would sink the urn somewhere past the reef.

When I got off the phone, the dealer offered me a joint and we smoked in silence.

"You want me to go with you?" he asked me as I got up to leave.

"No," I said, "that's OK. I'm not afraid of dead people. Some of them are my best friends."

The dealer had a poster of Jimi Hendrix on his front door and he had a vegetable garden in his yard with huge cabbage heads that looked like seaflowers in the early morning light.

I walked back up the path, past the grove of papaya trees and the palms and the high grasses. I was thinking that I was very old and that I probably did not deserve to be alive.

I decided that I did not want to be around when the valley was bought up and turned into a resort and the path was paved for tour buses and there were building cranes standing like metal birds on the tops of new condominiums.

Sitting on my Lightning Bolt tanker in the front yard, peeling old wax off the board, I heard sounds on the ridgeline.

There were two voices this time.

Ramble Round Hawai'i
from *The Echo of Our Song*
**Translated and edited by Mary K. Pukui & Alfons
L. Korn**

The Chant was sometimes recited for its own sake, but it
could also be performed as a string game. The various
figures were manipulated so as to suggest a panarama of
changing landscape as seen while traveling counter-clock-
wise from one to another of the six ancient districts of the
island of Hawai'i.

He Huaka'i Ka'apuni ma Hawai'i

Kū e ho'opi'o ka lā
Ka lā i ke kula o Ahu-'ena
Komo i ka la'i o Kai-lua e—

'O Kona:
'O Kona ia i ke kai malino
Ke hele la i waho o Kapu-lau
Kani ka 'a'o i Wai-'ula'ula
A he alani e waiho nei
A ke kanaka e hele ai la

'O Ka'ū:
'O Ka'ū ia, o Ka'ū kua makani
He ipu kai Pōhina nā ke A'e-loa
Lele koa'e i Kau-maea la e—

'O Puna:
'O Puna paia 'ala i ka hala
Kea'au 'ili'ili nehe 'ōlelo i ke kai
'O Puna ia la e—

'O Hilo:
'O Hilo ia o ka ua kinakinai
Ka ua mao 'ole o Hilo
He ua lū lehua ia nō Pana-'ewa e—
'O Hāmākua:
'O Hāmākua ia o ka pali Ko'olau
Ke ku'uku'u la i ke kaula
Ke 'aki la ka niho i ka ipu
I ka pali 'o Koholā-lele
'O Waipi'o, 'o Wai-manu e—

'O Kohala:
'O Kohala-iki, 'o Kohala-nui
'O Kohala-loko, 'o Kohala-waho
'O Pili, 'o Ka-lā-hiki-ola
Nā pu'u haele lua o Kohala

English Translation

The rising sun travels in an arc
reaches the flatlands of Ahu-'ena
enters Kai-lua's gentle landscape

This is Kona:
coastal Kona along the unruffled sea
where the sun rides ahead to Kapu-lau
where cry of the puffin-bird at Wai-'ula'ula
breaks the silence of the traveler's trail

And here's Ka'ū:
Ka'ū of the wind-swept back
where Pōhina's a pungent dish in the salty wind
while shining leapers at Kau-maea
soar like *koa'e*-birds through the air

And Puna:
where *hala*'s fragrance blows from Puna's branching bowers
and pebbles at Kea'au whisper to the sea
Puna's forever there

With Hilo:
Hilo of perpetual rains
rains in a never-clearing gusty sky
scattering the fringed *lehua* of Pana-'ewa

And Hāmākua:
Hāmākua of the windward Ko'olau hills
where the traveler lowering himself by rope
grips the net of his carrying calabash between his teeth
descends the cliff at Koholā-lele
and those sheer-sided valleys Wai-pi'o and Wai-manu

Kohala last:
lesser Kohala, greater Kohala
inner Kohala, outer Kohala
and then Pili and Ka-lā-hiki-ola
companion hills traveling as a twain

Son of the Shark-God
(A Mythological Legend of Hawai'i)

**Suggested by Emma M. Nakuina's
"The Legend of the Shark-Man, Nanaue" (1896),
retold by Alfons L. Korn (1968)**

Note

The legend index at the main branch of the Library of
Hawai'i contains a hoard of titles listing stories about
Hawaiian sharks, shark-gods, king-sharks, shark-warriors,
boy-sharks, blond sharks, and their various habitats, customs, favorite foods, adventures, love-affairs, triumphs, and
defeats. Some of these tales have been collected (and occasionally retold) by well-known figures in the history of
Hawaiian folk-lore, including Thomas G. Thrum,
W. D. Westervelt, Eric Knudsen, and Mary Kawena Pukui
and Caroline Curtis. Padraic Colum included a skillful
rendering of one of the shark-boy stories in his *Bright
Islands,* "When the Little Blond Shark Went Visiting."

My source for the following re-telling of the Tale of
Nanaue, shark-boy of Waipi'o Valley, Island of Hawai'i, is a
version originally collected by Mrs. Emma Metcalf Nakuina
(1847–1929) during the 1890s and first published in the
Fourth Annual Report of the Hawaiian Historical Society,
Honolulu, 1896, pp. 10–19. Mrs. Nakuina had a scholarly
interest in the traditions of her Hawaiian ancestors. At the
end of her version of "The Legend of the Shark-Man,
Nanaue," she provided an informative note as to the source
of the story in the form she published it. One of her infor-
mants was a ninety-year old woman of Waipi'o Valley and
the other was a *kama'āina* of Moloka'i, David Napela.

> This story was obtained from Kamakau. She
> was born at the time of the building of Kīholo.
> Details of the latter part of the story on Molokaʻi
> were obtained from D. Napela, who was born and
> lived all his lifetime in the vicinity of the scene of
> the story. He was quite an intelligent old man, and
> had been the government school teacher at
> Waialua, Molokaʻi.

The D. Napela mentioned by Mrs. Nakuina was probably David Napela, a relative (possibly son) of Jonathan
Napela, who was one of the first Hawaiians to become a
Mormon convert and one of several Hawaiians who helped
to translate the Book of Mormon into Hawaiian. Jonathan
Napela was assistant supervisor of the Kalaupapa settlement
in 1873 at the time of Father Damien's arrival. He was of
chiefly ancestry, as was his wife Kiti Richardson Napela,
and both husband and wife must have had an extensive
knowledge of old Hawaiʻi. Little is known about David
Napela, but the family tradition and the Molokaʻi setting,
steeped in folklore, are enough to account for David
Napela's interest in the story of how Nanaue finally met his
death on Molokaʻi.

In my re-telling of Mrs. Nakuina's version of the story of
Nanaue, I have freely expanded the bare outline of the 1896
text, in an attempt to make the setting (Hawaiʻi, Maui,
Molokaʻi) more vivid, the action more exciting and sensa-
tional, the character of Nanaue more memorable, and the
mixture of horror and humor in the tale somewhat more
highly seasoned. The only important episode I have invented
out of whole cloth is my account of Nanaue's unfortunate
domestic adventures on Maui and his ordeal of having to live
with his brother-in-law, Puʻupuʻu, the *kōnane* (checkers)
champion of Maui. Even this episode, however, has traditional roots, one of them being a famous scene in the life of

the hero Lono-i-ka-makahiki, when he "broke the *kōnane* board after an argument with Ka-iki-lani, a woman." (See "The Story of Lono-i-ka-makahiki," in Samuel M. Kamakau, *Ruling Chiefs of Hawai'i,* Honolulu, 1961.)

My re-telling of the story is intended not for small children but for teen-agers and grown-ups. My use of a rather more extensive and sometimes "literary" vocabulary than is usually encountered in this type of Hawaiian folk-tale is deliberate. Hence I have not necessarily deleted the first word that occurred to me to suggest an important idea or distinction or to convey a certain tone that, for me at least, seemed natural and effective in the context: "marina," "stipulation," "configuration," "superficial," "mandible," "par excellence," "dietary," "proclivity," etc.

Alfons Korn
May 1968
Honolulu, Hawai'i

In the reign of King Umi, there lived in Waipi'o Valley on the Island of Hawai'i a handsome girl called Kalei, who was very fond of eating shellfish. She regularly went to find them at a spot called Kuiopihi, at the mouth of the Waipi'o River, where the freshwater stream flows out of the valley by several descending marina-like terraces down into the sea. Kalei usually joined a party of other women for these fishing excursions, but if the sea was a little too rough, or if the weather was unfavorable and her companions too afraid to venture out on the wild dangerous beach, Kalei would often go by herself, rather than do without her favorite sea-food.

In those days the Waipi'o River emptied over a low fall into a basin, partly open to the sea, which is now completely filled up with rocks from some later volcanic event, or perhaps as a result of an earthquake. The ancient basin, a deep mirror to the sky above and the surrounding cliffs, was an ideal place for all the bathers of the valley to congregate and swim, dive, indulge in water sports, or simply enjoy themselves.

The King-Shark-God, none other than Kamohoali'i himself, used to visit this pool very often to disport himself in the fresh waters of the Waipi'o. Of course he had his other favorite habitats stretching all along the bottom of the palisades that extend from Waipi'o towards Kohala, on the Island of Hawai'i. A favorite haunt was an islet called Maiaukiu in the sea just opposite and abreast of serene Waipi'o Valley. It is not surprising that from this vantage point, Kamohoali'i was sometimes tempted to investigate more closely, for the purpose of sheer amusement, the beach on the mainland itself, just at the point where the river's mouth opens out upon the surf. It should be remembered that Kamohoali'i had a deep appreciation not only of scenic charm, but also of the human variety, particularly as found in young women.

Kalei, as was to be expected, since she had been born and brought up in Waipi'o Valley, was an expert swimmer, a champion diver, in fact a girl who was noted especially for the neatness and grace with which she could *lelekawa* — jump from the rocks into deep water without producing the slightest sign of a splash. This is a most difficult feat for unskilled and clumsy swimmers and divers, but it was not for Kalei. It seems that Kamohoali'i, the King-Shark, had made due note of Kalei's expert jump-diving, which he admired as an example of the girl's technique as an athlete, but also because this display of physical prowess was accompanied by the loveliness of her bodily presence, her unaffected air of calm, unhurried delight. Assuming the shape of a very good-looking man, Kamohoali'i walked on the beach one rather rough morning in mid-May, waiting for Kalei to put in her appearance.

Now the very enchantment of the scene—the wildness of the surrounding elements, surf and shore, terraced ledge, gleaming basin and pool, and perhaps above all the noble background of the towering cliffs surrounding the valley on three sides—provided a matchless setting for one of Kamohoali'i's most picturesque love-adventures.

On one morning in particular, when the surf was unusually rough, Kalei arrived on the beach alone. She was unaccompanied by any of her usual friends, because these had all been discouraged by the stiff winds and the rising waves. Even Kalei, one of the most agile and quick of rock-fishers, man or woman, who had ever lived in the valley during all its centuries, made several well-executed but unsuccessful springs to escape a high threatening wave raised by the Shark-God himself. This monster wave almost engulfed her. If it had not been for the prompt and effective assistance of the thoughtful stranger, Kalei would certainly have been swept out to sea and probably would never have been heard from again.

Thus an acquaintanceship was established. The casual meeting at a moment of crisis led naturally enough to a warm comradeship, and this phase ripened into deeper love.

There was soon no lack (for a time at least) of perfect
tenderness on each side. In any event, Kalei continued to
meet the stranger from time to time. After a period of some
months, she consented very willingly to become his bride.

Some little while before she expected to become a
mother, her husband, who all this time would only come
home at night, told her of his true nature. He told her
gravely, with a note of sadness in his revelations, that he
would have to leave her soon. With a most gentle admoni-
tion he gave Kalei orders about the regimen he recom-
mended for bringing up his future child. He especially
cautioned the mother never to let her baby, whether boy or
girl, be fed on animal flesh of any kind. This rather harsh
rule was the result of the dual nature of the anticipated
infant. There was no doubt about it. The child would be a
sort of demi-god. Or if not a regular demi-god, at least he
would participate in the nature of both his father and mother.
He would undergo the kind of life and the experiences
appropriate to both sharks and human beings—though not
usually, as in this case, fused together. One of his most
marvelous and disturbing powers, perhaps to himself as well
as to others, would be the ability of his dual nature to change
his bodily form at will. In the twinkling of an eye he would
be able to assume the shape and appearance and behavior of
a human being. And vice versa, of course, if he so desired
and if the occasion seemed to call for such a metamorphosis.

In time Kalei gave birth to a fine-looking healthy boy,
apparently the same as any other child. He had, however,
besides the normal mouth of a human being, a shark's mouth
on his back, a little to one side of his right shoulder-blade.
Kalei, not utterly surprised or disappointed by this singular
feature of her baby, had fortunately told her family earlier
about what kind of a man her husband was. They all agreed
to keep the matter of the shark-mouth a dark family secret,
for there was no knowing what fears and superstitions might

be aroused in the minds of the King and high chiefs by such an abnormal creature. Indeed, the child would run some danger of being killed for his innocent oddity. He was named Nanaue.

The old grandfather, far from heeding the warning given by Kamohoali'i as to diet and nutrition, did exactly what he was supposed not to do. He let himself spoil the child irreparably, as soon as the boy was old enough to come under the *kapu* regulating the segregated eating customs of the two sexes. The boy thus had to take his meals at the *mua* house with the men-folks of the family. It was by his grandfather's wicked or wickedly foolish disregard of Kamohoali'i's prohibition against his son's eating meat that the small boy was started on the long tortuous journey that was to end in his destruction. The grandfather went to special pains to stuff the little fellow with both dog meat and pork. Possibly the grandfather meant well. He had visions of his grandson growing up to be a famous warrior. There was no knowing what opportunities lay before a skillful warrior in the promising days of King Umi. So the grandfather fed the boy on meat, whenever it was obtainable. The boy thrived, grew sturdy, big-shouldered, a handsome fellow like his father (in his human form), and with something of his mother's poised grace. People often remarked that even as a six-year-old Nanaue was as glorious to look at as the *lama* tree, sacred tree-of-life, celebrated by lovers of the old Hawaiian hula and of its mistress, the demi-goddess Laka, who presides over song, dance, and the chanting of poetry.

Beside the pool at the mouth of the Waipi'o, there was another pool nearer Kalei's house, at the bottom of the last cascade in upper Waipi'o. There the boy went regularly to swim, where his mother could easily keep an eye on him as she sat watching from the bank. Just before the youngster shot—presto!—into the stream, he would change automatically in mid-air, as it seemed, into a shark. After racing back and forth a moment or two, plunging, rising, rolling his merry eyes about to make his mother laugh, he would often turn over on his belly, as if searching for something on the stream-bed. For a little while he would seem to be resting. Then, suddenly, he would dart about chasing the small fish that abound in the fresh-water pool, eating as many as he liked, until he had had his fill of them. When he became old enough to understand such matters, his mother impressed upon Nanaue the importance of concealing his shark identity from other people, especially from those his own age and their families and friends. He was very good about accepting the fact of his difference from other children. Nor did he seem to be in the least disturbed about some of his mother's important detailed instructions, such as always keeping his back covered with his *kapa kīhei,* his shoulder mantle.

Although the pool at the falls was a favorite bathing place for the entire village, Nanaue never accompanied other village children when they went there to bathe. Always he went his own way alone. On those early occasions while his mother watched over him, she would sit on the bank holding tight in her arms the boy's folded *kapa* scarf. She always chose the same place to sit, a certain rock well-shaded from the sun's glare, but a spot where she could easily spy out the approach of anyone else and yet keep Nanaue well in view. By no fault of Kalei would her son's secret ever become known.

As the days passed, she learned to read the rippling shadows and glints in the water as signals of a shark's movements. She proudly realized that she was mother of a champion boy-swimmer. She was always happy, as well as much relieved, when at last her gleaming ten- or eleven-year-old son was covered and clothed again in his human form, especially from left hip to right shoulder-blade.

When Nanaue was about fifteen, his appetite for fish and flesh, indulged regularly since childhood, had grown so strong that a human being's ordinary allowance was no

longer sufficient to satisfy Nanaue's capacity. By that time his old grandfather had died, and the family had to depend on what food was supplied by Nanaue's step-father and by his two slow-witted uncles. First, of course, all the relatives teased him, but finally they began scolding him for what they called his greedy habits. In the end, by unanimous agreement reached after a full family conclave, he was dubbed with the nickname of *manōhae*—meaning "ravenous shark," or a man who is extremely gluttonous and voracious, especially in his desire for raw meat.

During these years of his very young manhood, Nanaue roamed a good deal about his own neighborhood alone. He liked especially to spend hour after hour at one or the other of his two favorite pools, the one inland along the upper stretch of the river, or the other down at the lower channel, where the Waipi'o pours into the awaiting sea.

In the course of time, as was to be expected, there was increasing gossip in the valley about Nanaue and his singular ways. Great was the speculation about why he always kept his *kapa* mantle fastidiously draped over his right shoulder. For such a well-shaped, athletic youth, his invariable attire naturally aroused curiosity, for it was not at all exceptional for even a very modest young man in those days to appear naked from the waist upward. But not only did Nanaue avoid the two pools, which other persons and especially those his age habitually used for bathing and swimming, he also held himself aloof from all games and pastimes of the young people, for fear that a gust of wind or some sudden unexpected or perhaps awkward movement of someone else or of his own might dislodge the *kapa* shoulder-scarf and reveal his secret.

Yet Nanaue's apparent unsociability, as he reached his eighteenth year, was balanced by several redeeming features. When not fishing by himself or bathing in invisible solitude and bliss, he was almost always to be found working away in his mother's two potato patches. When many of the neighbors would pass Nanaue, while he was busy pulling taro or digging up potatoes, he liked to hail them with a jaunty greeting and inquiry about where they were going. If they answered "To bathe in the pool," or "Fishing," Nanaue would answer, "Watch out, or you may disappear head and tail!"

More and more people began to notice that whenever Nanaue addressed them in this neighborly manner, sooner or later some member of the fishing-party would be bitten savagely by a shark. Indeed, for several years certain children of the valley began to disappear mysteriously, leaving behind them not the slightest trace. In fact, even grownups began disappearing. None of these vanished persons provided any clue about what might have happened to them, not so much as an anklet or earring or any other article of use or adornment.

Nanaue was a full-grown man, just turned twenty-one, when Umi, King of Hawai'i, issued a royal command that every man dwelling in Waipi'o should go to work on the royal plantation, the *kōele,* tilling the soil of the King. Certain days during a ten-day period, an *anahulu,* were to be set aside for such feudal obligation. On the allotted days every man, woman, and child had to render service, except the very old, the decrepit, the sick, and infants in arms.

On the first day under the new work-schedule, every-body went to the fields except Nanaue. To the astonishment of all persons who had occasion to greet him, he simply continued as usual planting, weeding, irrigating, pulling and digging in his mother's patches. Nanaue's behavior was speedily reported to King Umi, and several of the King's stalwart lesser chieftains were dispatched to fetch Nanaue and bring him at once before the King. Nanaue of course approached the King in the correct manner, crawling along on his knees, still wearing his *kapa kīhei,* his invariable shoulder mantle.

"They tell me, Nanaue," said King Umi, "that you do not labor on the *Ko'ele* along with everybody else. Why don't you?"

"Sire," said Nanaue, "I was not aware that such labor had been demanded of me."

King Umi could not help admiring the bold, forthright, free bearing of the young man, scarcely more than a sturdy adolescent boy. The King carefully took stock of Nanaue's broad shoulders and glistening biceps. He decided then and there that this was a young man who ought to make excellent material for a superb warrior. King Umi's reign, as it happened, was a time when notable careers at court could sometimes be carved out of a very humble calabash, and when young men of promise of all classes, but especially first-rate athletes and potential warriors, could quite easily find a speedy avenue of advancement. Nevertheless King Umi, having made his mental observation, merely dismissed his handsome young subject, ordering him to report forthwith in the fields and patches, exactly like everyone else, at least among his loyal commoners.

Nanaue obeyed. He appeared without delay, but still wearing his *kapa kīhei*. He immediately identified a particular headman, a *luna* who looked intelligent, and fell into place beside him in the field. Nanaue did not, however, lay aside his *kapa* mantle from his shoulders, though it would have been far more practical to remove so useless and uncomfortable an encumbrance before settling down to such punishing labor in the field. The sight of the independent and aloof Nanaue, lifting heavy stones and, as he sweated at every pore, dragging great gnarled *'ohi'a* tree-roots to a spot where other men were chopping them to pieces with their stone adzes, made a most satisfying picture in the eyes of the other workmen who had known Nanaue since his boyhood. They found it pleasant to hear him grunt and heave. They grinned when they saw the sweat trickle down his forehead, fall in heavy drops from his dirty ear-lobes. One man in particular, a close friend of Nanaue's lazy uncles, envied the easy way Nanaue without even lunging could toss a huge root backward over his shoulder. To a sullen-faced comrade the man whispered a certain insulting expression. The second man allowed a smile to creep over his own sullen face. Then looking round at his nearest neighbors he repeated the same rude expression. The joke caught on like wildfire. Soon all dusty faces were baring upper and lower molars, heads were nodding, elbows nudging, lips whispering the same insulting password: *"Manōhae"*— "Greedy shark."

But it was a mere nine-year-old youngster, one who in years almost could have been Nanaue's own son, who brushed past his uplifted arm in such a way as to tear off, as if by accident, the *kapa kīhei.* At that instant almost everyone in the field beheld for the first time a sight all had heard about since childhood, but which none had ever encountered before with his own eyes. It was quite obvious that Nanaue had two mouths.

One mouth, which he spoke with, was entirely normal and located in the usual part of his anatomy. The other, which had begun at birth simply as a slight swelling or healed-over scar, had developed and flowered finally into a second muscular mouth or slot, with a throat-like opening, situated on his back a little to one side under his right shoulder-blade. When closed, its powerful lips resembled something that was not quite a seam nor exactly a gash. Although none of the teeth at the moment were visible, slight indentations on the superficial skin revealed the underlying bony mandible-like structure. While human lips are normally darker than their surrounding area, Nanaue's shark-mouth lips were lighter than the rest of his skin, resembling the dead white of fish-belly, or the slightly yellow-white of fine old ivory jewelry. Because the protective shield of the *kīhei* covered a portion of Nanaue's back, now there appeared a

slash of almost ghostly pale skin where no sunburn had ever
before directly penetrated. The slash reached from Nanaue's
right shoulder down to his left hip. The strong mouth-slit lay
entirely in the concealed strip of snowy pigmentation.

All the crowd instantly comprehended Nanaue's secret.
Those who had started lifting stones let them drop to the
ground. Even the small children carrying their little lauhala
play-baskets of waste and rubble gazed in the direction
where uniformly all their parents' eyes were riveted as if
hypnotized.

Nanaue's response to his new situation was no less
spontaneous. In his sudden predicament he now for the first
time in his life, certainly in public, lost all his capacity (thus
far well-controlled and trained) for rigorous will-power and
self-discipline. His shark's nature had almost automatically
become predominant even though he remained in his human
form.

As when a flung switch-blade whisks through the air, or
when some razor-sharp bird-beak or spur falls suddenly upon
its helpless prey, Nanaue swiftly pivoted and turned round.
Then in a flash of blinding motion he bit several of the
nearest bystanders. His dorsal shark-mouth snapped open
and shut, shut and open, making at the same time an odd
clicking sound such as sharks notoriously are known to make
when balked of a victim.

The news of Shark-Mouth Nanaue and his carnivorous
predatory behavior was quickly carried by special runner to
King Umi, who was deeply concerned. Now all of a sudden
everyone was full of old tales about bathers who had disappeared in the surf, but more especially about the decidedly
mysterious disappearance of bathers who had gone for a swim
in the pools frequented by young Nanaue. Some professed to
remember that Nanaue, as they passed by his mother's potato
patches, had given them pretended warnings, and that only
their own skill as swimmers had later enabled them to escape

with merely a flesh-wound or a slight but painful graze. Many knew of a certain cousin or brother-in-law, or somebody's foster-mother's sister, who had disappeared from the community and had never been heard of again. Surely these lost individuals must have been devoured by the shark-man.

King Umi had not the slightest doubt that these surmises and charges were true. He accordingly ordered all field-work to cease instantly. When basket and sledge and adze had been laid aside, all hands were instructed to prepare at once a great bonfire. As soon as proper arrangements could be completed, Nanaue was to be thrown upon the punitive funeral pyre and burned to death alive.

Now as everyone knows, a shark's muscles and brain can on occasion function almost with the speed of angelic light. When wretched Nanaue realized what he had done, and at the same time clearly took in what fate lay before him, he called out by name to the Shark-God, his father: "Kamohoali'i! Kamohoali'i!" Bursting the ropes he had been bound with for his cremation, he dashed with almost invisible speed into the ranks of the assembled warriors. Though the entire throng of strapping men attempted to detain him, he easily slipped through the *malo*-clad human barrier and raced with incredible swiftness in the direction of the ocean. No man in Waipi'o had ever been known to cover the distance with such superhuman speed.

Nanaue did not slacken his pace until he had reached the very brink of the lower pool, the paradisiacal palm-fringed basin that drained into the last stretch of the river before descending into the sea. Pausing for a moment on a ledge of rocks bordering the pool, favorite taking-off place for divers, Nanaue waited nonchalantly until the foremost of his pursuers were almost within an arm's reach. Then, at that precise instant, he leaped upward and next shot downward into the pool, having changed in mid-air into a giant silver shark. He was as fierce in appearance as he was beautiful.

Sometimes he swam on the surface of the water and sometimes several feet beneath, but always in full view of the Waipi'o multitude. These people could only stand cemented in their places by fright, their gaze transfixed by the antics of the son of the Shark-God. The number of watchers was being constantly increased by new arrivals, ranging from the very old to mere toddlers, and including one or two persons who were actually blind but did not want to miss this historic occasion.

From their stations on each side of the river the crowd could frequently catch lightning glimpses of Nanaue in his new shark form. He would sometimes lie brazenly on his back on the surface of the water, then flip himself over on his belly, exposing to his audience the dark silver shaft of his unblemished back. Next he would raise his head partly above the water, snort once or twice, spurt and spray jets of fresh water in five directions, and finally snap his teeth at the stupefied spectators. They gazed at him with eyes agog like an audience in an obscene circus.

By this time the swarming valley-folk had completely lined both banks of the Waipi'o River for many yards, like an overflow crowd at an open-air boxing match. Finally, as if in derision of his onlookers, Nanaue swung himself swiftly about, making a kind of gleaming arc as he pivoted, flirted his tail at the rapt gazers, and swam away to the lower end of the pool, where in a single splendid dive he entered the last stretch of the river and headed out toward the open sea.

After this last gesture of defiance, most of the excited watchers could hardly do more than catch their breath. However, not a few hotheads, with several women among them, and even including a number of hysterical children, wanted to kill Nanaue's mother and all her bad-blooded relatives at once. What else could such a monstrous woman deserve for having given birth to such a monstrous son? The leaders of the mob even went so far as to seize Kalei and her brothers, bind them with strong *olonā* fiber, and drag the

whole lot of them off to where King Umi was holding court
in special session. The outcry and clamor of the community
was loud and virtually unanimous—death to all. Among the
more practical suggestions was a proposal that Kalei and the
uncles should be thrown into the bonfire being kindled for
the escaped Nanaue.

But Umi was a wise king and could not consent to any
such summary proceedings. King Umi ordered that Kalei be
permitted to crawl on her knees, still bound hand and foot,
and approach him so that he might ask a few questions about
her terrible offspring. The aggrieved mother told King Umi
everything, the whole story in many ways so wonderful
concerning the boy's uncommon paternity and his careful
upbringing. And she also told Umi about the warning given
him by Nanaue's sea-father.

After meticulous weighing of the evidence, King Umi
came to the conclusion that the great King-Shark
Kamohoali'i was on the whole a beneficent as well as a
powerful deity. Indeed, if the relatives, especially the
mother, of his princely son should be killed, there would
then be no possible means of checking the ravages of
Nanaue, now apparently committed without reservation to
satisfying his predatory appetites. For in all probability
Nanaue would take to lurking about the coasts, creeks, caves,
inlets, and deltas of Hawai'i, assuming a human shape at
will. Through his mysterious power of self-generated
metamorphosis, he was quite capable of traveling inland on
foot, in fact to any place he might fancy, even to the most
remote homesteads and out-of-the-way *ahupua'a* and
kuleana of an island where he would then reassume his fish
form and lie in wait in hundreds of deep pools, in the most
secluded forests inland or in the more popular marine waters
and beaches, with their alluring coral-gardens. Certainly he
would have no reason to lack victims.

With all these considerations in mind, King Umi wisely ordered Kalei and her relations to be set at liberty. This decision was put into the form of a royal proclamation announced by runners in all localities where the information was likely to prove useful. The King further commanded that various priests and shark-*kahuna* should make appropriate invocations, prayers, and sacrificial offerings to Kamohoali'i. Through their prayers and devotions the priests were to make the Shark-God's wishes known.

How this intercommunication with the god might be conducted was well understood during the reign of King Umi. In those times every coastal village of any pretensions was always provided with at least three or four disciples of the Shark-God, experts who were adept as spirit-mediums. If only Kamohoali'i would allow his spirit to take possession of one of the *haka*—a trance-medium—in that way the god could express to humanity his desires regarding the fate of his problem-son. Everyone agreed that Nanaue's cannibalism, his shark's taste for human flesh, was a practice completely at variance with Kamohoali'i's own benign tastes and designs.

Kamohoali'i made his policy known through the mediumship of a certain *haka,* a rather masculine-looking elderly widow named Paniku Hua, who was a descendant of a once-famous chieftain who was himself a remote relation of the Shark-God. Kamohoali'i thus spoke eloquently of his grief over the actions of his wayward son. Those who heard Kamohoali'i's elegiac address, much of it in poetry, said that it was as if the Shark-God's voice sometimes seemed to be speaking—or emanating—through the *haka*'s rumbling belly. At other moments, however, the impression given was that Kamohoali'i's voice was uttering his thoughts just above the left shoulder of Paniku Hua, as if the god had perched himself there in the atmosphere, at about the level of the medium's head. The voice, for it did not sound quite human, resembled that of some talking-bird, heard speaking sharply but very wisely from the branches of an invisible tree.

Kamohoali'i told his listeners that the old grandfather was the one rightly to be blamed for the troubles of Nanaue by catering to little Nanaue's lust for animal flesh, thus going flatly contrary to the clear and firm orders of his divine shark-father. Indeed, if it had not been for this extenuating circumstance—namely, that Nanaue could hardly be held accountable for the gross dietary neglect of his elders—Kamohoali'i announced that he would happily have ordered his son to be executed at once.

In view of Nanaue's original innocence, Kamohoali'i concluded, he had decided to send the young man into banishment. From this day forth his son should live as an exile on some other island, less populated preferably, and less well supplied with seductive bathing facilities, than windward Hawai'i. But if Nanaue should be so foolhardy or depraved as to ignore his father's ban upon his movements, and certainly if the son were ever discovered by any of his father's shark-soldiers on the Island of Hawai'i, Nanaue would then be destroyed.

The last words heard to issue from somewhere in the region of the slightly moving lips of the *haka* sounded as if they had been actually uttered from a spot about two feet above the old woman's wild grey head.

"I bid you lastly," said Kamohoali'i, who seems to have preserved a certain affection for his human wife, "to promise me faithfully that Kalei, her relations, and all their descendants, are to be forever free from all persecution either by the malice of individuals or by the exercise of historical but now obsolete rules and taboos. Only in this way," continued the Shark-God kindly, "can the evil deeply rooted in my own son's nature be purged—that is, by banning and expelling him from these your lovely shores and valleys, basins, rivers, and pools."

At this point in Kamohoali'i's heavenly discourse he launched off on a flight of poetry, selected very appropriately for the unusual occasion.

> On all sides of Waipiʻo the cliffs face each other,
> Enfold Waipiʻo with their whole beauty
> Even on that one side of Waipiʻo where
> Green tumbling water in cliff upon cliff
> Rolls in from a foam-crested sea!

"But if you should disobey me in this my wish," added Kamohoaliʻi, "and violate my command and persecute the kin of Nanaue, then you must forfeit because of your cruelty to others who are innocent your own wretched freedom—you will not be worthy of it, nor of my own just prerequisites and taboos. In that event I shall free my son from his present taboo and he will thereupon again assuredly return to your beautiful island and its precious but dangerous waters. Thereafter he will bring upon you unending pangs and sorrows!"

When the *haka* gradually came out of her trance, the large audience of listeners looked at one another with expressions in which consternation was mixed with relieved willingness and resolve. They needed no further persuasion to carry out Kamohoaliʻi's command and stipulation to the very letter.

II

Within less than an hour while Kamohoaliʻi was addressing the valley-folk through the *haka,* Nanaue in solitude bade farewell to the Island of Hawaiʻi and to the scenes of his happy childhood. It was thus a direct consequence of his father the Shark-God's wishes that the son and demi-shark crossed over the channel between Hawaiʻi and Maui. On landing at Kipahulu on the latter island, Nanaue immediately adopted his human shape. Clad once more in a *kapa kīhei,* brand new, and displaying this time an intricate saw-tooth pattern, he at once set forth on a sight-seeing tour of his new domain. Many *kama'āina* old-timers noticed the arrival of a strikingly good-looking malahini stranger with the clear bronze-copper complexion and gracefully athletic bearing, his dancer's movements and his animated actor's eyes. As he was a most approachable fellow, many of the Maui folk soon found themselves engaged in social chit-chat with the newcomer. He told them, truthfully, that he was a traveler from Hawai'i. He also remarked that he had landed at Hāna planning to spend an extended holiday, if he cared for the place. Could anyone recommend to him some of the items of chief scenic interest on the island, especially in the form of places for swimming and bathing? Nanaue was so good-looking and engaging that he had no trouble attracting a circle of new friends.

One of the petty chiefs, Kipu'upu'u, known as Pu'upu'u for short, took to Nanaue so completely that soon this person was announcing to everyone that Nanaue was Kipu'upu'u's *aikāne,* his special guest, comrade, dining-partner, and *kōnane* companion par excellence. Kipu'upu'u, it so happened, was the *kōnane* champion of Maui. The chief not only invited Nanaue to become a permanent non-paying member of his household. He even went so far as to offer Nanaue his younger sister, Lanihuli, as a bride. Pu'upu'u did not merely offer the girl—he implored, he insisted.

This domestic arrangement pleased Nanaue quite well. He did, however, demur a little at first on the grounds that, after all, he was still much of a stranger and hardly deserved such a prompt demonstration of Maui hospitality. Without further discussions, Nanaue agreed to take Lanihuli as his wife, although he would be obliged to set up one important stipulation. His sleeping quarters, he said, should be entirely separate from Lanihuli's.

"I am a rather restless sleeper, you see," explained Nanaue, "and unfortunately I am also a very loud snorer—have been since childhood. Naturally I dislike torturing other

persons," he went on in his winning way, "with my unfortunate unsocial nasal proclivity. Also, I have made a vow to
Lono that I must henceforth sleep in perfect solitude. Besides, I have to admit I can't bear it when other persons are
snoring around me."

Since the petty chieftain knew that Lanihuli had also
been a chronic snorer from childhood, he readily agreed to
the terms of the match, knowing that Lanihuli would fully
understand. This she did, and for a while her sweet accom-
modating disposition and gentle childlike ways quite capti-
vated Nanaue's heart, curbing and channeling the darker
subterranean currents of his shark-personality. He seemed in
many ways an altered, in fact a reformed, character, who
kept close to home and, like the rest of the family, preferred
to keep to a very sedate routine for meals, in-between
refreshments, and sonorous sleeping. He largely confined his
outdoor activities to strolling in the forest uplands with his
girl-bride in search of wild herbs and berries, confiding to
her romantic memories of his boyhood on Hawai'i—his
family, he said, enjoyed the protection of the High Chief—
and in playing games, outdoor sports in particular. But on
Maui the only game Nanaue played was indoor *kōnane*— a
form of checkers—endless games of *kōnane*.

The setting for these contests was the spacious lanai of
Pu'upu'u's long-house. There gradually came a time,
unfortunately, when the novelty of his new way of life wore
off for Nanaue. During his strolls with his wife, his own
silences grew long and then longer as he listened—or rather
ceased to listen—to her idle prattle. And in truth Lanihuli
was not distinguished for intelligence or humor, however
much she was admirable for the evenness of her tempera-
ment and her adorable unassuming ways. Beauty and charm,
of course, were not what Nanaue hungered for. Never before
had he found his life so burdensome, disturbing, and empty.

Sometimes while playing *kōnane* with Puʻupuʻu, especially when the game became unendurably sluggish, Nanaue himself would almost fall asleep. If an observant onlooker from outside had been present he would certainly have concluded that Nanaue had fallen into some sort of trance or trance-like stupor. This, of course, was a most unnatural state of mind for someone of Nanaue's disposition and back-ground—his complex, energetic, occasionally wild sportive nature, in which his shark's attributes were so precariously balanced with his mother's heredity.

But what might have appeared as stupor to others was actually a state of dreaming. Nanaue never confided the content of any of these dreams to Lanihuli. Certainly not to Puʻupuʻu. Yet if the stupor were really a reverie, a state of suspended but inspired animation, it is not difficult to surmise the direction whither Nanaue's day-dreaming was tending. It is easy in the mind's eye to imagine those pan-oramic visions in which there flashed and glowed in front of Nanaue's sightless eyes all the streams, pools, brooks, basins, grottoes, sea-caverns and sunken coral-gardens he had known at first hand at least since adolescence, if not much earlier. It all began perhaps when his pretty mother had supervised his first swimming exercises.

There came a time, inevitably, when the mirror of Nanaue's imagination could no longer contain itself, and he would willingly—more than half-willingly, at least—have smashed the submarine looking-glass and its reeling and writhing phantasms into a thousand flying fragments. Nanaue could not bear his condition any longer. Without excusing himself, in the midst of an unusually drawn-out game of *kōnane,* he rose from the floor to his feet, pushed away the draft-board and the *kōnane* pebbles, so that they rolled in nineteen directions around the floor. Then, stum-bling across the lauhala mats he at last reached the side door and hurled himself out into the bright moonlight in the direction of the sea.

Though it was a night of unusual beauty, with the assembled stars congregated across the black heavens, Nanaue began running at maximum speed, comparable to that of the wild north wind in a tornado-storm. Never had he run so fast before, not since that day when the valley-people had pursued him into the pounding surf at Waipi'o. Where it exactly was that Nanaue ran this time, after the upsetting of the *kōnane* board, is not known; but it is reasonable to assume that he was seeking, and found, some pool or stretch of rippling surf where he could slake his need: the need that tingled in his limbs, spoke mysterious signals in the lobes of his brain, stirred at the roots of his spine and in his loins, and made the very jaws of his two mouths—especially the covered-up dorsal mouth—ache with what seemed to him to be an entirely normal and natural longing.

Nanaue was gone from his home on Maui shared with Lanihuli and Pu'upu'u exactly one month and five days. Where he spent that month is not known, although certain mysterious disappearances of fisherwomen from O'ahu, and also the successive vanishing of six children from Lāna'i, bear out the theory that Nanaue may have paid several, or more than several, calls at those islands. How many other unreported missing persons he made away with will never be known.

That Nanaue did return to Maui, to the arms of Lanihuli, and to the company of Pu'upu'u and the ever-ready *kōnane*-board, is certain. However, his relations with wife and brother-in-law became progressively less and less cozy. Nanaue no longer took the slightest interest in the affairs of the petty chief's uneventful household. He hardly spared a word to his wife, but confined his use of the place almost entirely to his own private sleeping-quarters. He totally ignored the kindly invitation of Pu'upu'u to join him in an evening game.

So it is not at all surprising that rumors began to be heard on Maui, many of them encouraged by his host's servants, that Nanaue had taken to spending his nights on the beaches, roaming the inlets of streams, lurking about irrigation canals and places in general where there was flowing water and where young lovers could be counted on to meet for their flirtations or more serious romantic endeavors. In fact, though Nanaue grew quite careless about keeping up appearances, he was eventually detected in the very act—not after dusk but in glaring daylight—of shoving a young girl from a ledge into the sea. His leap in after her was virtually simultaneous with the girl's tumbling fall. In midair, like some aerial-trapeze artist shedding one disguise after another, Nanaue metamorphosed himself into a shark.

The hypnotized crowd stood on the broad ledge with mouths agape as Nanaue began to their horror to rip open the girl's belly, slash at her thighs, mangle her bloody ribs and buttocks, and finally impale her throat between his open jaws.

When the crowd of sickened fisherfolk raised an alarm, Nanaue instantly abandoned the remains of his prey in the contaminated water and prudently turned round, heading at great speed for Moloka'i. And again, as he pivoted about, making several intricate circles like a revolving sea-dervish whirling in the ecstasy of his dream, the shark-man flirted his tail two or three times in the faces of his audience. Then he disappeared from view beneath the surface of his waters, leaving no trace of his presence except a few gobbets of the girl's hair and shreds of her *kapa*-skirt, bobbing about in what looked like the red sediment that forms a kind of bloody dye in many Hawaiian streams in flood-time.

III

On Moloka'i, Nanaue made his next home in a comfortable grass house at Oniohua, adjoining the ancient *ahupua'a* of Kainalu. This pleasant pastoral spot was part of a prosperous homestead, owned and maintained by a high-born widow, extending from the beach into the valley, and then reaching upward and beyond into the remoter bird-forests and stream-fed uplands. After his sophisticated stay on Maui, Nanaue had decided to settle on an island where he could live the life of a simple farmer and fisherman, in a manner similar to that of his own earliest Waipi'o ancestors. But Nanaue was certainly no farmer. Neither was he, except in a rather special sense, a fisherman, not honestly. It was not long before he had reverted to his practice of observing with a peculiar glint in the corner of his eyes the old inhabitants of the place, especially their sons and daughters. Sometimes Nanaue would accost passing travelers, giving them one of his genial warnings. Then, after following them to the seashore in his human shape, he would seize the prey of his choice, whether boy or girl, and in his shark manifestation carry the victim out to the ocean, to devour his trophy there on its briny floor.

In the excitement of these lurid occurrences, potential victims were likely to become confused. They would be thrown off the track by Nanaue's sudden disappearances from the scene, then by his equally abrupt reappearance at some other spot distant from the throng of fisher folk. It was hard to figure out how he ever got there. Usually, when glimpsed from afar, he was simply taken for somebody else engaging in the useful, entertaining arts of shrimping or crabbing.

This disturbing pattern of events continued for many months. It went on and on until the harassed and by now terrified people of the district became determined to consult a shark-*kahuna* to look into the whole dreadful affair.

Indeed, by now morale in this region on Moloka'i had
deteriorated so much that the local chief felt impelled to
declare a taboo on all kinds of fishing. People began to say
that it was no longer safe to venture anywhere near the sea,
even in the shallowest water. After questioning his clients,
the *kahuna* told everyone to take courage and lie in wait for
Nanaue. "When Nanaue predicts that such-and-such a person
will be eaten, head and tail," said the kahuna, "have your
strongest men instantly seize him. Then, remove his *kapa
kīhei*—don't hesitate a second. Simply strip it off. You will
certainly find a shark's mouth," concluded the *kahuna*
sagely, "or at least the next thing to it."

With their hopes greatly raised by the *kahuna*'s optimis-
tic instructions, the worried volunteers and Nanaue's fanatic
enemies did exactly as they were told. Without need of
rehearsal, they seized Nanaue, stripped away the modest
kapa kīhei, beheld the now opening and closing shark lips
with a shudder—all to the disquieting accompaniment of the
famous clicking sound. Nevertheless the shark-man was so
strong that whenever they did their best to bind him with
olona-cord, he easily broke loose from their grip each time.

He was at last overpowered, but only after harrowing
efforts, on the slopes of the hillside just where the lowest
incline approaches the vacant beach. He was seized at almost
the very moment he was about to race his last 100 yards
before plunging into the sea. By this time his body bore
numerous bruises and even several very deep wounds in the
breast and groin.

This time his captors were able to bind Nanaue tightly,
his knees propped under his chin, his hands tied behind his
back, his bound ankles fettered. It was a most uncomfortable
position for Nanaue, but obviously a very effective solution
to the problem of keeping him a captive. By common
consent the inhabitants of the district then turned their
earnest attention to finding a permanent remedy. All present

joined hands in gathering dry weeds, brush, and firewood to burn Nanaue, for it was well known that only by being totally consumed by fire can a man-shark be thoroughly destroyed. Otherwise, if he is merely partly eliminated, the monster may take possession of the body of some fish-shark who might then be incited to perform all the agile, purposeful, and vicious acts of a human shark.

As Nanaue, bound but not gagged, lay on his back on the sandy beach with the sun beating down into his staring eyes, he tried to wriggle his neck. After several jerking efforts he was able to turn his head just enough to determine the fact (which he had been anxiously anticipating) that at last the tide was beginning to turn—now it was moving into shore. With his two dry gullets Nanaue swallowed once or twice, clenched his double shark-power mandible teeth, and by thrusting with every muscle of his shoulders, thighs, and buttocks, he somehow managed to roll himself over. He was able to perform this act of tremendous exertion unnoticed because the Moloka'i folk were all busy with their task of gathering firewood.

Nanaue's wrestler's body-thrust was completely successful, as he could tell by the feeling of the cool water on his flanks and cheeks. For all practical purposes he had already cleared the way for returning to his ocean-home, his briny currents, the palisaded depths where green waters were traversed by shafts of shadow and dim light and spoke a language he could understand. Here the pull and flow of the tide could rock him in its familiar embrace, a state resembling sleep, or trance, or unbroken dream. As there were no witnesses around at the moment, it is uncertain when Nanaue changed himself for the last time into a shark. But it was in the form of a giant shark, trussed and bound in a mass of fishnet, that he now lay breathing heavily in the still listless incoming tide.

Two women standing about fifty feet up the bank, firewood-gatherers, decided to take a rest. They straightened up, the bundles of firewood at their feet. One of them happened to glance down to the beach. No sooner had she noticed what Nanaue had been able to achieve than she began signalling and shouting to all her relations and friends. Certainly none of the Moloka'i people were willing to let the shark-man elude them so easily. In answer to the shrieking, two younger men came running down and quickly installed several rows of strong fish-net *ma kai* and counterwise to the languid but strengthening thrust and release of the tide. For a fair distance out, the water was still shallow.

Of course Nanaue's flippers were still shackled by the ropes with which the man Nanaue had been bound. This circumstance, combined with the shallowness of the water, prevented Nanaue from exerting his full strength to advantage. He did, however, by agonizing lurches and other spasmodic movements of the appropriate muscles, manage to reach the area of the ever-stronger incoming breakers. It was unfortunate, as he lay amid the familiar spume and debris of the now eager surf, that momentarily he should be growing weaker from his steady loss of blood. As he continued to dash and fling himself with as much force as he could muster always in the direction of the open sea, he began finally to feel recurrent waves of rhythmic pain such as he had never known before. The prison of the net prevented any further true progress. As he lay prone and bound in the churned-up water, now discolored by the mixture of Nanaue's dark red blood and the boiling black sand, everyone within striking distance smote him with whatever weapon or instrument came to hand—clubs, stone adzes, bamboo knives with razor-fine edges, jagged rocks, fragments of leaden driftwood—in other words, with anything that could be employed to hurt, maim, or kill the shark-man. Only in this way could the people prevent the shark-man's escape. One

Amazonian wife of a leading chief was even seen to rip from her neck a splendid whale's tooth *palaoa* necklace, which she proceeded to wield as an aristocratic weapon of battle. Using the central tusk as a gouge, the chiefess succeeded in blinding Nanaue in one of his eyes.

Despite such ferocious measures, Nanaue would un-doubtedly have won his way clear, if only his opponents had not called to their aid their local demi-god, Unauna, who lived in the mountains of Upper Kainalu. The struggle by then was a contest of *Akua vs. Akua,* or demi-god vs. demi-god. Unauna was merely a young and relatively inexperienced demi-god, and therefore could not yet be expected to demonstrate his full supernatural authority. Nanaue's vigor was not to be scorned. Both as full-grown man and as shark, he was a creature of formidable self-discipline as well as of tormenting—and self-torment-ing—powers. If Nanaue had not been under so severe a physical handicap, because of the net and the binding cords and the loss of blood, he might still have got the better of the presiding local deity. But his bodily prison held him and there was no watery tunnel of escape. The contest was agonizing on both sides, and Nanaue's recurrent death throes were great, losing force little by little with each repetition. They continued for well over two hours, before the shark-man at last lay absolutely motionless, to all appear-ances dead.

During this interval the Moloka'i people made elaborate preparations for hauling Nanaue's great body up the slopes to Kainalu Hill, the place selected for his funeral pyre and final sacrifice. Travelers and tourists who have visited Moloka'i insist that the shallow ravine, caused in the hillside by the passage of Nanaue's immense body over the light black sand soil of Kainalu Hill, can be seen on the island to this day. Also to be seen is a ring or deep groove completely encircling the top of the tall mutilated rock very near the summit of Kainalu Hill. It was around this rock that Unauna drew the stout rope by means of which the giant shark was hauled up the hillside. The place has ever since been known as Puʻu-manō Hill, Shark Hill.

Because Nanaue was so huge in the final form he took as a gigantic shark, the attempt at first to incinerate him was not at all successful. Great jets of spurting blood and sprayclouds of oozing water or steam poured and simmered out of his burning body. These liquid explosions put out the fire several times. But Unauna the demi-god had no intention of letting himself be outwitted by the vital juices working and flowing in and through the shark-son of Kamohaliʻi. The young Unauna acted decisively. He ordered a throng of the local inhabitants to fetch a vast number of bamboo trunks from the sacred upland grove of Kainalu. Then the laborers were commanded to split the magic bamboo staves into sharp knives, suitable for use as two-handed bayonet swords, or, in the case of the smaller boys, wooden cutlasses. By this means the shark-flesh of Nanaue was cut into strips, sliced rather thin, partly dried, and finally burnt to light grey ashes, though it took the entire bamboo grove to provide enough weaponry for carving up and dissecting so monumental a demi-god fish.

Nanaue's father, Kamohaliʻi, though he conceded the justice of his son's annihilation, was so angered at the desecration of the fine bamboo grove, and more probably by the repulsive use to which it had been put, that he took away all edge and sharpness from the bamboo trees of this grove forever after. To this day the bamboo of Kainalu differs from that of any other forest on Molokaʻi or on any other island. In fact, it is of such poor quality that it even has less use than the most miserable species of common wood, which can at least serve as kindling to start a fire.

The life story of Nanaue, shark-boy and shark-man, ends with the ceremonial episode of his piecemeal extinction by fire. After Unauna's gruesome triumph and Kamohaliʻi's somewhat petulant revenge upon the bamboo stand of Kainalu, nothing further has been heard or seen of Nanaue in Hawai'i, either in his shape as shark or in his role of man. His name and his deeds pass, if not quite into oblivion, definitely into legend. Possibly future watchers of the island skies will occasionally notice certain meteors that appear to flash across the Hawaiian firmament like celestial skin-divers, silver-glinting flares in the night sky, torn away from some parent star-galaxy. It is easy to conceive of these sky divers as shark-sons, supernatural creatures fashioned of earth, air, water, and fire, but with the elements of water and fire predominant in their highly combustible natures. They may be thought of as lost fish-divers, perennially seeking to return to their true homes, the submarine caverns and grottoes and weird cathedral chapels in the depths of the Hawaiian seas.

When one of these starry acrobats is noticed performing his exploits in regions of mountain and cliff, like Diamond Head, it is appropriate to imagine him as still another embodiment of Kamohoali'i, the Shark-God of King Umi's time, father of Nanaue, the ill-fated boy and man who became a swimming demi-god of grievous fame. Likewise when Hawaiian boys disport themselves today, swimming, bathing, and surfing in safety along the beaches and streams of their ancient shores, it is pleasing and poetic to picture in these bronzed youngsters the boy Nanaue, son of mortal Kalei and of the Shark-God Kamohoali'i, freed at last from his tormenting self-division of part human being and part fish. No longer is the Nanaue of today doomed to endure more than the usual measure of loneliness found in human experience. No longer need he live an exile from his island home.

The Pool
John Dominis Holt

It was perhaps as large as a good-sized house. It tended to be round in shape. At the far southern end of Kawela Bay, it sat open to the wind, the sun. Scattered clumps of coconut grew around it, splashing shade with the look of Rorschach ink blots here and there at the edges of the water.

Fresh water fed into it from underground arteries, blended with warmer water pushed in by the tide from the sea through a volcanic umbilical cord. "The lagoon," as we called it, had a definitive link to the sea, being joined as it was by virtue of this unique tubular connection.

We were always afraid of "the lagoon." For one thing it was alleged to be so deep as to be way beyond anyone's imagination like the idea of endless space to the universe or the unending possibilities of time. Its dark blue-green waters were testament to the fact of the pool being deep according to our elders. We accepted their calculation, but not entirely. It was deep to be sure, but not depthless.

Within "the lagoon," huge ulua, a local variety of pompano or crevalle, would suddenly appear in ravenous groups of three or four, chasing mullet in from the sea. Once in the confines of this small body of water the mullet were no match for the larger carnivorous predators. Ulua could grow to the size of three or four feet and weigh nearly a hundred pounds. The mullet feasts by ulua in the lagoon were wild and unpleasant scenes. We would watch as children, both enthralled and frightened, as mullet leaped for their lives in glittering silvery schools of forty or fifty fish, some to fall with deadly precision into the jaws of the larger fish. The waters swirled then and sometimes became bloody. The old folks said this would attract sharks. They would wait at the opening of the tube in the ocean to prey on the ulua, whose bellies now were fat from feasting on mullet. These tumultuous invasions were not frequent, but they were reason enough to keep us from swimming in "the lagoon." Perhaps most fearful to us were the tales we heard offered by assorted adults that a goddess of ancient times inhabited these strange blue-green waters. Some knew her name and mentioned it. I have forgotten what it was. She was said to be a creature of unearthly beauty, a queen of the Polynesian spirit world, who revealed herself at times in the forms of great strands of limu, a special seaweed growing only in brackish water; her appearance depending on tides, the moon, winds, and certain cosmic manifestations we could not completely understand because they were mentioned in Hawaiian.

I wandered by the hour in the area of "the lagoon" and on the reefs nearby with an ancient, bearded sage who was our caretaker. His hut of clapboard and corrugated roofing sat near an old ku'ula, a fisherman's shrine, half-hidden under some hau bushes. His people had been fishermen from time immemorial. Some of his relatives lived a short distance down the coast toward Waimea Bay. Infrequent visits were made upon the old man by these ohana; usually three or four young men came to consult him about fishing. His knowledge of the north shore and its inhabitants in the sea was vast. Once or twice a year he paid a ritual visit to their little house standing in its tiny lawn surrounded by taro patches and sheltered at the front by clumps of coconut and lauhala trees. He spent hours explaining in Hawaiian, and in his own unique use of pidgin, the lore of the region, mentioning with distaste his wine-drinking nephews. I was only four or five years of age at the time. Much of his old-world ramblings is now lost to me.

But I do remember him mentioning that the sea entrance to "the lagoon" was too deep for him to take me to it. He was too old now to dive to those depths. He secretly led me to the kuʻula, a built-up rock shrine, round in shape, where we took small reef fish and crustacea we had speared. We would pray; the old man in Hawaiian, I in a mixture of the old native tongue and English. It was being impressed upon us now we must speak perfect English. The use of Hawaiian was discouraged. After prayers we would leave offerings on the kuʻula walls, walk to "the lagoon" where more prayers were said and the remaining bits of fish thrown into the pool as offerings to the beautiful goddess.

All of these activities fell within a definitive framework of time and circumstance. These were not helter-skelter rituals. I obeyed without question and I declared it untrue when confronted by my mother whose father, a half-white, had lived for years as a recluse in the native style in Iao Valley—that the old man of Kawela was teaching me pagan ways.

In horror one day I heard the old man say "hemo ia oe kou lolo—take off your clothes," which consisted of a pair of chopped-off dungarees.

"Hemo ia oe kou lole e holo oe a iʻa i ka lua wai—take off your clothes and swim like a fish across the pool." My body froze and goose bumps formed everywhere on my skin.

"Awiwi—hurry. "

I stood in sullen defiance, thinking: He is an old man, a servant. He cannot order me to do anything, anything.

"Au, keiki, Au! Swim, child, swim! Do not be afraid. They are with us."

I remained motionless.

"Auwe, heaha keia keiki kane? He kaika mahine puiwa paha? What is this child, a frightened girl?"

Thoughts came to me of past fishing expeditions when I clung to the old man's back and he dove with me into holes filled with lobsters and certain crabs. He would choose as time allowed, pluck them from the coral walls, hand me two. Then, I could cling to him with only the use of my legs. In time I learned to rise to the surface alone, clinging with all my might to the two lobsters the old man had handed me. What excitement the first of these expeditions created! I leaped and danced around the crawling catch. We went down for a second take. Again two were brought up. On the reef above they were crushed, one then left as an offering on the ku'ula walls, the other fed to the akua in the pool. I was four or five then and wild with joy.

There were other days when he took me to great caverns swarming with fish of such brilliant colors you were nearly blinded by the reds, yellows, greens, blues and stripes. Above on the reef he would name them for me. Patiently he named them, these reef fish, aglow in cavern waters: the lau'ipala, the manini, the uhu; the ala'ihi; the kihikihi with its black, yellow and white stripes; the humuhumu with its blue patch on throat and vibrant yellow and red fins.

On one very special day, a sacred day in his life and mine as well—for I was linked to the family gods, the aumakua—he took me, clinging to his back, to the great sandy places under the sharp lava edges of Oahu's North Shore, to the places where the great sharks lazed in the light of day. Breaks in the lava walls sent shafts of light to sandy ocean floors and then we could see the sometimes-dreaded monsters rolling from side to side in harmless, peaceful rest. Shooting up to the surface, the old man would breathlessly tell me the names of this or that shark—names given them by his contemporaries.

"Why names?" I would ask wonderingly.

"Are they not our parents, our guardians—our aumakua? Did you not see the old chief covered with limu and barnacles? He is the chief, the heir of Kamohoali'i. I used to feed him myself and clean the opala from his eyes. Now a younger member of my clan does that."

I could not absorb these calm, reassuring concerns of denizens I had been taught to dread from early years.

But had I not been down in their resting place, close enough to see yellow eyes, to almost feel the roughness of their skin scraping like sandpaper across my arms?

My dreams were wild for several nights and my parents, worried, held several conferences with the old man. He was chastened, but at my insistence we went several times more to the holes under coral ledges to see the aumakua lazing in the daytime hours.

And now, frozen at the edge of the green pool, I looked hatefully at this magnificent relic of a Hawai'i that was long vanished. I loved him. There was no question I loved him deeply. Ours was a special kind of love of a man for a child.

I was blond-haired. Exposed for weeks to the summer sun when we made long stays at Kawela, I became almost platinum blond.

The old man was bearded, tall and thin. Still muscular. He was pure Hawaiian. Blond though my hair might be and my skin fair, I was nonetheless three-eighths Hawaiian. I think this captured the old man's fancy—often he would say to me in pidgin, "You one haole boy, yet you one Hawaiian. I know you Hawaiian—you mama hapa-haole, you papa hapa-haole. How come you so white? Your hair ke'oke'o?" He would laugh, draw me close to him and rub his scruffy beard against my face as though in doing this he would rub some of his brownness off and ink forever the dark rich tones of a calabash into my pale skin.

It was love that finally led me to loosen the buttons of my shorts and kick them off and race plunging into the green pool. I swam with all the speed I could and reached in what seemed a very long time the opposite side. When I turned around, the old man was bent over with laughter. I had never seen him laugh with such gustatory abandon.

"Look you mea lii-lii. All dry up. Like one laho poka'o ka'o—like an old man's balls and penis. No can see now." He pointed and made fun of my privates, shriveled from a combination of cold water and fear. I turned away from him and raced home, naked.

Four days later I walked past the pool, across the sharp lava flats to the old man's hut. Flies buzzed in legion. The stench was unbearable. I opened the door. Lying face up and straight across his little bed, the old man lay in the first stages of putrefaction. Sometime during my absence the old man had died. At midday? In the cool of night? In the late afternoon, the time of lengthening shadows and the gathering of the brilliant array of gold-orange and red off the coast of Kaena to the south facing the sea of Kanaloa? When did the old man die? Why did he die? Tears began to stream down my cheeks.

I shut the door of the shack and went to sit in the shade of the hau branches near the kuʻula—my heart was pounding so I could hardly breathe. What should I do? Tears rolled in little salty rivulets down my cheeks. I enjoyed the taste when the moisture entered my mouth at the corners of my lips.

What should I do? Some instinct compelled me not to go home and tell my family of the death of the old man and the putrefaction that filled the cottage. Perhaps I was too stunned—perhaps it was perversity.

The family was gathering for a large weekend revel. Aunts, uncles, cousins—all the generations coming together. Usually I enjoyed these congregations of the family. There would be masses of food, music, games and the great lauhala mats spread on the lawn near the sandy beach. Someone would make a bonfire and the talk would begin. I would sit at the edges of the inner circle of elders as they ruminated on past events. Old chiefs, kings, queens, great house parties— scandals and gossip of one sort or another would billow up from the central core of adults and leap into the air like flames. I absorbed the heat of this talk and greedily absorbed my heritage for they spoke of family members and their circles of friends, mostly people from royalist families, the

Hawaiian and part-Hawaiian aristocracy during the last days
of the Monarchy. I heard of this carriage or that barouche or
landau, this house or that garden, this beautiful woman in
love with so-and-so, or that abiding "good and patient" soul
whose handsome husband dashed about town in a splendid
uniform, lavishing on his paramour a beautiful house, a
carriage and team, and flowing silk holokus fitted finely to
her ample figure. O, the tales that steamed up from those
gatherings on lauhala mats at Kawela's shores!

One of my great-aunts, an aberration of sorts, came once
in a while for the weekend. She brought a paid companion
and her Hawaiian maid. She looked like Ethel Barrymore
and talked with an English accent. Her gossip was spicy,
often vicious, and I loved it. She fascinated me as caged
baboons fascinate some people who go to zoos. She was also
forbidding. I thought she had strange powers.

Often the old man had joined us during these family
gatherings, and I would sit on his lap until I fell asleep.

There was something of great warmth and unforgettable
charm in these gatherings. Even as the talk raged over
romances, land dealings and money transactions long passed,
I revelled in hearing about them and loved everyone there,
particularly those who talked. There was an immense feeling
of comfort and safety, of lovingness for me on those long
nights of talk.

But now under the hau branches I scorned my family.
I hated them. I held them responsible, for some unknown
reason—a child's special reason I suppose; inexplicable and
slightly irrational.

I decided not to tell them of the old man's death but to
run down the path along the beach to the house where his
relatives lived. I would tell them. They must rescue him from
his rotting state; they must take him from the tomb of his
stench-filled shack. I ran down along the beach, sometimes
taking the path pressed into winding shape from human use
in the middle of grass and pohuehue vines.

The men were at home, mending fishing nets. This was a good sign. I ran to the rickety steps leading upward to the porch where they sat working at their nets.

"The old man is dead," I said forcefully.

One of the young men looked down at me.

"Ma'ke."

"Yes, he's ma'ke. His body is stink. He ma'ke long time." They put down their mending tools and came in a body to the top of the stairs.

"How you know?" one of them asked.

"We just came back from Punalu'u. I went to the old man's house. I saw plenny flies. I open the door and see him covered with flies. It was steenk." I spoke partly in pidgin to give greater credibility to my message.

They fussed around, called into the house, held a brief conference and faced me again.

"You wen' tell anybody?"

"No, nobody."

The four men took the path at a run. I was under the hau bushes, catching my breath, when they flew past me heading back to their house. I sat for what seemed like hours in the shade of hau. My sister appeared at the side of the pool. I ran to fend her off. She caught the stench from the shack.

"Something stinks."

"The old man has fish drying outside his shack."

"Where is he?"

"Down on the reef fishing."

"When are you coming home?"

"Pretty soon."

"Mamma is looking for you—Uncle Willson is here with those brats," she referred to his adopted grandchildren. Uncle Willson was a grand old relic. Something quite unreal. He was brimming always with stories of the past.

"Aunt Emily has arrived with Miss Rhodes and that other one," my sister added, referring to the maid whom she hated.

The cottages would be bulging and perhaps tents would be set up for the servants.

My sister swung around abruptly and took the path back to our cottage. She was always purposeful in her movements.

"Tell Mamma I'll be home soon and kiss Uncle Willson and Aunt Emily for me."

"Don't stay too long. You'll get sunburned."

I walked past the pool. It seemed purer in its color today. Deep blue, deep green. I was crying again. The stench filled the air with a stronger, punishing aroma as the sun rose high and began the afternoon descent beyond Kaena Point. I walked along the reef; the tide was rising. I peeked into holes the old man had shown me, watched idly the masses of fish swimming in joyous aimlessness it seemed.

What ruled their lives? There was life and death among them. They were continually in danger of being devoured by larger fish. Some grew old and died. I suppose, they die of old age.

Death. Such an angry, total thing. There was no escaping it.

I looked back at the shack and shook my fists. The old man's nephews had returned with gleaming cans. They poured the liquid which filled them all around the little house. I rushed back to the hau bushes as two of them threw lighted torches of newspaper at different places around the shack. Soon it was in flames which leaped to the sky; as the dry wood caught fire, it crackled angrily. The flies buzzed at a distance from the blaze as though waiting for it to die down. The heat was intense. The smell of burning rotting flesh unbearable.

I ran from the hau bushes toward the pool. One of the men saw me and yelled, "Go home, boy. Go home."

"Git da hell outa heah, you goddam haole," another one shouted. I was angry and stunned in not being accepted as a Hawaiian by the old man's nephews.

I ran around the pool at the side we seldom crossed. My family was massing nearby to watch the fiery spectacle.

"What's happening, son?" my father asked with more than usual kindness.

I ran to my mother and hugged her thighs.

"The old man is dead. I found him. He was stinking. I ran down to tell his family."

"And now the bastards are burning him up," my father said. "It's against the law."

Aunt Emily had arrived on the arms of her companion and maid. Her handsome face pointed its powerful features to the center of the burning mass.

"What is happening?" she asked in Hawaiian.

"Our caretaker died. Been dead for several days. The boy found him."

"What are they doing?"

"It's illegal. They're cremating him without going through the usual procedures."

Aunt Emily blasted forth with a number of her original and unrepeatable castigations. Everyone listened. They were gems of Hawaiian metaphor.

Uncle Willson and his man servant arrived.

"The poor old bastard finally died. He was the best fisherman of these parts in his younger days. No one could beat him. As a boy he was chosen to go down to the caverns and select the shark to be taken to use for the making of drums. His family were fishermen. One branch was famed as kahunas. He was a marvel in his day."

"But Willy," Aunt Emily was saying in a commanding tone. "Those brutes are burning his body. The boy here says it was rotten. He'd been dead for several days. The whole thing's a matter for the Board of Health authorities. The police should be called."

"No, no!" I screamed.

"Emily dear," Great Uncle Willson intervened. "He is one of us. His ohana, those young men, are part of us. Leave them alone. They are doing what they think best."

I had gone from my mother to my nurse Kulia, a round, happy sweet-smelling Hawaiian woman.

"No cry, baby. No cry. We all gotta die sometime. Da ole man was real old."

"Not that old," I whimpered.

Aunt Emily cast one of her iciest looks at me.

"Stop that sniveling. Stop it this instant. What utter foolishness to cry that way over a dirty, bearded old drunk."

She turned to my mother.

"This child was allowed to be too much with that old brute. I think his attachment was quite unnatural—quite unnatural."

"Another one of your theories, Aunt Emily," my mother snapped.

"Not a thing but good common sense. Look at him clinging to Kulia and whimpering like a girl."

Kulia took me away. We walked on the beach.

How I hated Aunt Emily's Ethel Barrymore profile and her English accent.

Late that day, in the early evening, the old man's nephews came back and carried off his charred remains in the empty cans of kerosene. No one ever found out what they did with them.

When did the old man die? Why did he die? This I will never know. We called him Bobada, but I remember from something Great Uncle Willson said on the night the shack was burned that Bobada's real name was Pali Kapihe.

Turtles
Lois-Ann Yamanaka

On the wall in Banjo's Taxidermy Shop
is two big, green turtles. They all shiny.
Banjo, he use varnish make um look wet.
Banjo say, before could catch turtles if you like
for the shell or for meat, but now,
he say not suppose to catch turtles
or else the police going arrest you.
He say, when you catch a turtle, the turtle he cry
a tear from his big, wet eye.
Banjo seen um when he went fish with his friend, Keone,
in a Boston whaler down South Point side.

He ask if I ever taste turtle meat.
He say, **Ono you know. I tell my wife cook
the frozen turtle meat one night and you come over
try some. Ask yo mama first.**
I thinking about the tear from the turtle eye.
I tell Banjo I no like.

Banjo say the turtle eggs look like ping pong balls.
He tell me, his friend Melvin, the lifeguard
down Punalu'u beach, seen turtle fin marks in the sand
couple weeks ago so him and Banjo wen' put all the eggs
in one hole and wen' put one cage over um
so nobody vandal it.

Late one Saturday afternoon, I was at Banjo's shop
helping him sweep up the loose feathers,
this white chemicals, and sheep wool off the floor,
the phone wen' ring and was Melvin.
Banjo stay all panic on the phone. **Okay, Okay.**

I going close the shop. C'mon, he tell me. **No need sweep.**
C'mon, c'mon. The turtles hatching. We never going see
this in our whole life again. Us get in the jeep and drive
fast down Punalu'u. **No speed, Banjo,** I tell him,
bumbye Officer Gomes give you one ticket.
But Banjo, he no listen.
When us get there, close to night time.

Get Melvin and his girlfriend, Coleen. Banjo's wife
stay too – she work the lei stand down the beach.
The little turtle babies, they pop their head
right out the black sand. They all black too.
And when one 'nother one about to come up,
the sand cave in a little bit around the turtle head.
Turtles, they know by instinct where is the ocean,
Banjo tell. **Watch.** And he turn a baby turtle
backwards to the mountain. Then the turtle he turn
his own self around and run to the water.

Get plenty. They all running to the water. They shine
when the wave hit them. And their heads stay bob up
and down in the ocean. Plenty little heads.
Banjo pick one up and give um to me.
Like take um home? Take um, take um, he tell me.
I think about the turtles on Banjo wall.
They look like they crying too.
Nah, I tell him. **I no like um.**
I take the baby turtle to the water edge,
his eye all glassy, his whole body shine,
and I put um down. **No cry now,** I tell um.
No cry.

"Great Grandfather of the Sandalwood Mountains"

Excerpted from *China Men*
Maxine Hong Kingston

Driving along Oʻahu's windward side, where sugarcane grew in my great-grandfathers' day, I like looking out at the ocean and seeing the pointed island offshore, not much bigger than a couple of houses, nothing else out in that ocean to catch the eye—Mokoliʻi Island, but nobody calls it that. I had a shock when I heard it's also named Chinaman's Hat. I had only encountered that slurred-together word in taunts when walking past racists. (They would be the ones loafing on a fence, and they said the chinaman was sitting on a fence " . . . trying to make a dollar out of fifty cents.") But Hawaiʻi people call us Pākē, which is their way of pronouncing Bak-ah, Uncle. They even call Chinese women Pākē.

When driving south, clockwise, there is an interesting optical illusion. At a certain point in the road, the sky is covered with Chinaman's Hat, which bulges huge, near. The closer you drive toward what seems like a mountain, the farther it shrinks away until there it is, quite far off, an island, a brim and crown on the water.

At first, I did not say Chinaman's Hat; I didn't call the island anything. "You see the island that looks like a Chinaman's hat?" locals ask, and visitors know right away which one they mean.

I swam out to Chinaman's Hat. We walked partway in low tide, then put on face masks. Once you open your eyes in the water, you become a flying creature. Schools of fish—zebra fish, rainbow fish, red fish—curve with the currents, swim alongside and away; balloon fish puff out their porcupine quills. How unlike a dead fish a live fish is. We swam through spangles of silver-white fish, their scales like sequins. Sometimes we entered cold spots, deserts, darkness under clouds, where the sand churned like gray fog, and sometimes we entered golden chambers. There are summer forests and winter forests down there. Sea cucumbers, holothurians, rocked side to side. A sea turtle glided by and that big shell is no encumbrance in the water. We saw no sharks, though they spawn in that area, and pilot fish swam ahead in front of our faces. The shores behind and ahead kept me unafraid.

Approaching Chinaman's Hat, we flew around and between a group of tall black stones like Stonehenge under-water, and through there, came up onto the land, where we rested with arms out holding on to the island. We walked among the palm trees and bushes that we had seen from the other shore. Large white birds were nesting on the ground under these bushes. We hurried to the unseen side of the island. Even such a tiny island has its windward and leeward. On the ocean side, we found a cave, a miniature pirate's cove with a finger of ocean for its river, a beach of fine yellow sand, a blowhole, brown and lavender cowry shells, not broken, black live crabs side-stepping and red dead crabs drying in the red sun, a lava rock shelf with tide pools as warm as baths and each one with its ecology. A brown fish with a face like a cartoon cow's mugged at me. A white globule quivered, swelled, flipped over or inside out, stretched and turned like a human being getting out of bed, opened and opened; two arms and two legs flexed, and feathery wings, webbing the arms and the legs to the body, unfolded and flared; its thighs tapered to a graceful tail, and its ankles had tiny wings on them—like Mercury; its back was muscled like a comic book superhero's—blue and silver metallic leotards outlined with black racing stripes. It's a spaceman, I thought. A tiny spaceman in a spacesuit. Scooping these critters into another tide pool, I got into theirs, and lying in it, saw nothing but sky and black rock, the ocean occasionally flicking cold spit.

At sunset we built a campfire and sat around it inside a cleft in the hillside. We cooked and ate the fish we caught. We were climbing along a ledge down to the shore, holding on to the face of the island in the twilight, when a howling like wolves, like singing, came rising out of the island. "Birds," somebody said. "The wind," said someone else. But the air was still, and the high, clear sound wound through the trees. It continued until we departed. It was, I know it, the island, the voice of the island singing, the sirens Odysseus heard.

The Navy continues to bomb Kahoʻolawe and the Army blasts the green skin off the red mountains of Oʻahu. But the land sings. We heard something.

It's a tribute to the pioneers to have a living island named after their work hat.

I have heard the land sing. I have seen the bright blue streaks of spirits whisking through the air. I again search for my American ancestors by listening in the cane.

The Hongo Store
29 Miles Volcano
Hilo, Hawai'i
Garrett Hongo

My parents felt those rumblings
Coming deep from the earth's belly.
Thudding like the bell of the Buddhist Church.
Echoes in the ground swayed the bassinet
Where I lay squalling in soapy water.

My mother carried me around the house,
Back through the orchids, ferns, and plumeria
Of that greenhouse world behind the store
And jumped between gas pumps into the car.

My father gave it the gun
And said "Be quiet" as he searched
The frequencies flipping for the right station,
The radio squealing more loudly than I could cry.

And then even the echoes stopped—
The only sound the Edsel's grinding
And the bark and the crackle of radio news
Saying stay home or go to church.

"Dees time she no blow!"
My father said driving back
Over the red ash covering the road.
"I worried she went go foa broke awreddy!"
So in this photograph the size of a matchbook,
The dark skinny man, shirtless and grinning,
A toothpick in the corner of his smile,
Lifts a naked baby above his head,
Behind him the plate glass of the store only cracked.

Excerpted from
Sachie, A Daughter of Hawai'i
Patsy Saiki

This excerpt is from Chapter Ten, in which Sachie, stringing leis for graduation, reviews her past educational experiences.

Sachie, A Daughter of Hawai'i is a novel about a young teenager emerging into awareness and therefore adulthood. Sachie comes from a home where only Japanese is spoken, except by her brothers, but Sachie hears and speaks only English at school. This part of the culture—language—is highly visible. More invisible are customs, religions, and the philosophy in the two mini-environments—the home and the school. Initially, Sachie spurns the Japanese culture in her haste and desire to become an "American," which her parents could never become. But because she must exist harmoniously with her parents and because it is already a part of her own "culture" to accept calmly and passively, she tolerates the Japanese culture. Eventually, aspects of the Japanese culture become a part of her, for although consciously she tries to become an "American," subconsciously she has learned to be and also is "Japanese," a fact symbolized by a triangular rice-ball. (From an introduction by Patsy Saiki.)

The day before graduation Sachie picked 900 white carnations and sat down to string them into a triple carnation lei. The lei would be for Ayako, for Haruo had planted the carnations for his mother, but it also had been for Ayako who someday might have lived in the Himeno home had Haruo lived.

After stringing the carnation lei, Sachie started on a pansy lei. The pansy lei was for Miss Case, the English teacher, who had been at Fraserville for three years and was now being transferred to Honolulu. Being assigned to a Honolulu school was every teacher's goal.

Sachie smiled, thinking of her many tussles with Miss Case in the one year she had had her for English.

Once Miss Case had wanted her to sit next to Chiyo, who had lice crawling over her black hair. Sachie refused to move.

"I'm going to have to send you to the principal," Miss Case warned. The threat did no good. Better to be sent to the principal than to have lice and have one's head doused with kerosene.

"Why don't you obey me?" Miss Case asked. Sachie couldn't say, "Chiyo has lice," even though everyone in the classroom, including Chiyo, knew it. By putting it into words, she would make Chiyo lose face. So Sachie was silent and sent to the principal's office with a note.

The principal, who knew Sachie as his daughter's friend but better as the girl who had spilled smelly cod liver oil on his suit one day, read the note.

"Now, what's the matter?" he asked. "Miss Case says you don't want to share a seat with another girl. Don't you know we don't have enough seats, and we have to share where we can?"

"Not just another girl. Chiyo!"

"What's wrong with Chiyo?"

"She has lice. Her mother should use this special kind of comb my mother used when I caught lice from her before. The teeth of the comb is so close together, it draws out the lice. Then her mother has to wash Chiyo's head with kerosene. But she has to wash more than once, because the nits hatch, and then there's lice all over again . . ."

Mr. Higgins turned pink. "Did you tell Miss Case why you didn't want to change seats?"

"In front of everybody? You think I want to make Chiyo feel shame?"

Mr. Higgins wrote a note and gave it to Sachie to give to Miss Case. Since it wasn't in an envelope and sealed, it couldn't be very private. Sachie sneaked a quick look. All it said was "Lice. Health Room."

Another confrontation Sachie had had with Miss Case was when she was sitting next to Rose. Rose had a habit of reading her words out loud when she concentrated. "Adjective, adverb, participle, gerund . . . ," she mumbled.

One day Miss Case, correcting papers, said, "I'm giving you free time today to review the chapter for tomorrow's test. You have lots to do, so I don't want to hear any whispering or talking. Is that clear?"

Concentration . . . Rose studied every sentence, every word, mouthing her words. Sachie read her chapter, then looked at Rose in amazement. How could Rose know what was in the chapter if she read words instead of the ideas in the combination of words and sentences?

Just then Miss Case raised her head. "Sachie, I thought I just said I didn't want any talking."

"I wasn't talking, Miss Case."

"Now you're lying, which is even worse."

"Ask Rose. Rose, was I talking to you?"

Rose turned red and lowered her head. To Miss Case, that was proof Sachie had been talking.

"Sachie, I told you I don't like people who lie. Will you please stand outside the door until you can learn courtesy for other members of the class."

The injustice, the unfairness of Miss Case not even checking with Rose, and Rose not supporting Sachie, was too much! Sachie grabbed her books, and instead of standing outside the door, walked to the cafeteria. There, the cafeteria manager, thinking her one of the student helpers, scolded, "Where's your cap? Put your cap on. Don't you know you're always to have a cap on when working in the cafeteria?"

Sachie found a cap in a corner, put it on, washed her hands, and then helped to spread butter on the bread. It wasn't real butter . . . it was peanut butter which had had milk added to it to make it thinner and to stretch it.

At first she buttered the bread angrily, but soon she began enjoying it. She had finished this job and was being assigned another, when a girl came dashing in.

"Sachie, Miss Case is looking all over for you. She even went to all the bathrooms!"

Sachie remembered. She was supposed to be standing outside the English classroom door.

"I didn't talk, and Miss Case said I did. She accused me of lying in front of everybody."

"We know. Miss Case found that out. She heard the talking even after you left so she watched us. She found it was Rose reading aloud. She said she would give Rose extra help in reading, and she apologized and began looking for you."

So after the fall came the pride. Miss Case was extra nice to her for weeks after that.

As Sachie sat stringing the pansies for Miss Case's lei, she thought of all the times Miss Case had shown interest in the Kakela children. She was different from the other teachers. Miss Roe, for instance, never got mad at anyone and never was really unfair, but she didn't care what happened to the students after school. Mr. Gobel was snobbish, and tried to associate with the white people in the big houses on the hill. Mr. Rhodes was nice, but he acted as if the Kakela children were beggar children, just because their Keds had holes or they had no shoes at all. But Miss Case, she was different.

"Go through high school, and then to college if you can," she encouraged. "With your intelligence, your alertness, it would be a shame to spend all your life working as laborers on the plantations. You can be doctors, lawyers, even representatives and senators in Congress if Hawai'i ever becomes a state. I have faith in you to be leaders of your community."

"We have the ambition, but we don't have the money."

"Don't be afraid to work. You can work in cafeterias while going through school. You can be maids and yardmen. That way, you get free room and board. You can work at the pineapple cannery during summers for spending money, for tuition. You can apply for scholarships."

To those who had a hard time in learning school work, she said, "But college isn't the only important place where you learn. You can learn while you work. The important thing is that you be happy, doing the work for which you're best suited. If you're going to be a chicken farmer, be a good one. If you want to be a mechanic, be reliable, for people's lives depend on you. That's such an important job."

As Sachie strung the lei, she thought, "Funny, about this time last year, I used to think most white people didn't respect the Japanese or looked down on them. But look at Miss Case. Look at Mr. Scott, how he takes care of us. Of course there are people like Bachman, but on the other hand, we have people like Mrs. Yamada, who won't share something good that she has."

A carnation lei and a pansy lei made with hundreds of flowers and hundreds of memories . . . that was June. June was the time friends and teachers parted, the end of a school year. But June was the time those who graduated began making something of themselves. June, and not January, was the time when a new life, a new year really began.

The Mystery Writer's Class Reunion
Lisa Horiuchi

The familiar cleft in the craggy cliff rose above John Parker like an ancient hand from the past. It sent an electric shiver up his arm, and the leather-covered steering wheel quivered slightly under his nervous touch. Tires clashed against rock for a split second; then he straightened his car and sped toward Kaiser High School.

He detested the thought, all his life, of coming to this class reunion. Laughed at by all—a fool, a failure. Walking into a gym full of successes, he'd be a weed in a patch of roses. At last, it has come to pass, John thought. This car is my soul and this road a symbol of my life.

In high school, John Joseph Parker had been a gangling runner, a poor mathematician, and the owner of a brilliant mind with a great ability for writing detective stories and untangling mysteries as if they were slipknots. He had a long, pensive face that looked like it could blossom into good looks at any second. English teachers had called him "outstanding" and "nothing short of genius" and his gift "a godsend," absolving him of his many imperfections. Even John himself dreamed that one day he would become a famous, billion-dollar-contract mystery writer and expected them to make TV movies of his greatest works. Maybe even cable TV movies. Everybody had expected it.

But John Parker had grown to be a failure. Just like his archrival, Hewitt Jensen had vowed. "You'll never amount to anything," he had hissed at their commencement exercises ten years ago. And he didn't, really.

Tears stung at John's weary blue eyes. Hewitt was a lawyer now, a graduate of Harvard Law School and had a practice in Boston. "What drives me down this cursed road?" John demanded aloud. "Courage," he said, answering himself. "That and foolishness. I could have been somebody. I could've been a great mystery writer—could have created another Sherlock Holmes! I could've this . . . I could've that . . . Who'm I kidding? I was clever enough to write a thousand mysteries, but not clever enough to BE a writer! I've failed at the only thing I knew how to do!

John Parker turned into the Hawaii Kai suburbs, his heart heavy with emotion, fear, embarrassment, apprehension—but most of all the gnawing, sinking feeling of failure. After all, what was a class reunion for but to show off accomplishments? And John Parker really didn't have any great accomplishments. Not even a two-book contract. Not even a short magazine piece. Not even a Harlequin romance. Nothing.

As the mud-splattered tires of John's car turned into the old parking lot, he began to formulate a plan in his head. He'd tell them he has been writing novels under an assumed name . . . yes! He'd tell them he feared publicity as a writer because he wanted a private life with his wife. They didn't have to know that he didn't have a wife. He'd tell them he'd written eight great novels and made two movies. Yes, that sounded about right.

But John Parker knew his plan would fail the minute he saw the crowd of people at the stairwell of Building II jump at the sight of his Jaguar pulling into a compact-car stall. "He's here!" he heard them screaming. "John Parker the movie star is here!" "It's John Parker, the ACTOR!"

"Can't I escape the madness, even here?" he asked himself. "Must they constantly remind me of my lack of integrity, my failure to become what I had been put on this earth to be?" He didn't call acting a profession; when he had first started acting, he had promised himself to do some mystery writing on the side. He had broken his own promise, and now ten years later, it was too late to turn back to the John Parker he had been — the *real* John Parker with *real* hopes and dreams of murders and exotic lands and jewel thieves. This man lived these dreams in the movies he acted in, but he didn't create them.

Slowly, with an aching back and stiff legs, he climbed out of his Jaguar, facing the crowd rushing toward him, hurling questions, hugs, and kisses at him.

At the reunion, he was unanimously voted "most successful" in a hoss election. Everybody knew him now. Everybody had been his "best" friend. They even read one of the short mystery pieces he had written in the ninth grade over the microphone while everyone had dessert. Nobody asked him what he had done with his writing talents. Nobody cared. John Parker was a success in their eyes.

John Joseph Parker, 6' 3", blonde, blue-eyed, the owner of a perfectly chiseled face that finally blossomed after graduation, owner of a once-brilliant mystery-writing mind, left the reunion early, after signing some autographs.

The familiar cleft in the craggy cliff watched after John Parker as he raced away from Kaiser High School in his brand-new Jaguar. He was beginning to feel sick. But he couldn't afford to. He was meeting his agent at 8:00 in the morning to discuss his next movie over breakfast.

He wished he had become a writer. He really did.

(Lisa Horiuchi was an 11th-grader at University Laboratory School when she wrote "The Mystery Writer's Class Reunion.")

'Awapuhi
Puanani Burgess

Mama loved the scent
of the wild yellow ginger,
growing thick on the slopes of Tantalus.

In its blooming season,
she would walk up that steep, curvy road
to pick two or three.

These she would weave into a brooch,
to be pinned to the inside
of her blouse—hidden,
but for that warm perfume.

On the day she was buried,
she wore a lei of wild yellow ginger,
freshly picked from the slopes of Tantalus.

And left for me,
in a blue shoe box,
a thousand, neatly-woven, dry,
       fragrant brooches.

A Fire
Ty Pak

Allen Shin found the sign, Bargains Galore, written on a termite-eaten board in Chinese ink. The windows were caked with dirt, and the grey paint was peeling everywhere on the store front. Allen pushed the hanging beads aside and stepped in. The inside was a jungle of used goods, chairs, bookshelves, clothes, lamps, all kinds of odds and ends piled on top of each other. Narrow passageways meandered through the chaos, overhung by precariously balanced chests of drawers, bed springs, plates, books.

"What are you looking for?" asked the old Chinese storekeeper, blinking his eyes over his spectacles that slid two-thirds down his nose.

"A bed," Allen said, discreetly turning from the old man's bad breath.

"Do you want a complete set, with the box spring and mattress, headboard, endtable, and dresser?"

"Yes, if you have something reasonable. Otherwise just a spring and mattress."

"I have a beauty for you in the back of the store. Has just come in. Not even unpacked yet. Come follow me."

The old man led the way briskly, then stopped.

"This is it," he said, turning around and making a proud sweeping gesture with his hand.

Allen was struck dumb. There was his entire household: dining set, TV, stereo, guitar, typewriter. Not a single item missing. So this was how Sunhee had disposed of it. The landlady had seemed mightily surprised when he'd turned up at the old apartment. Hadn't he met his wife at Los Angeles, where she said they were moving? No? As a special favor, the landlady had given back to Sunhee most of the security deposit, in cash, instead of waiting a month and sending a

check to their new address, as was the custom. The apartment had been taken. What a fool he must have appeared!

He could tell the storekeeper that these things were his,
that they were stolen goods, in a sense. He had paid for every
one of them with his own good money. He must have
cancelled checks somewhere to prove it. But prove what?
That his wife had run out on him after selling all his valuables?

"Did you buy the whole lot?"

"Yes, it was a moving sale."

"Can I offer you whatever you paid for it and $100
more?"

"Make it $200 more for moving and other incidentals."

"More than what?"

"$1,800."

Allen knew the man was lying but didn't make an issue
of it. He went nearer to the furniture. Here was the wreckage
of his life, in a heap. It was like looking at his own carcass.
Yet what he felt was more akin to amused curiosity than
bitterness or anger. The old man followed him around,
making encouraging comments. Allen's eyes fell on a
picture frame leaning against the leg of the writing desk, the
backside toward him. On the plywood backing he could still
read the date of the wedding picture.

"That's a rosewood frame," the old man said, lifting it
up. "Look at the exquisite carving. Nobody makes this kind
any more."

Allen knew well enough. He had special-ordered it from
Taiwan through China Imports in Waikiki. It had cost him over
two hundred dollars.

"All you have to do is take the picture out and put in your
own," the old man babbled on, running his palm across the dust
of the glass. It was still their picture all right, he in his tuxedo
and she in her innocent white gown. The old man apparently
didn't see the likeness between the groom in the picture and
Allen before him.

"Wedding picture," he said, blowing the dust off the glass and frame.

Allen stomped out of the store. The bitch hadn't even the decency to take out the photograph. He strode down River Street and crossed Nimitz Highway to the waterfront. Coming to Pier 15, he sat down on a bollard. A luxury liner with some foreign lettering, maybe Arabic, was docked at Pier 13. On the other side of the harbor a freshly painted Coast Guard frigate was moored at the Sand Island dock. A Matson ship was leaving harbor. A puff of steam left its chimney, and the whistle moaned deep yet shrill.

* * *

It was two summers ago. For the first time he had saved enough money to feel comfortable about taking a trip abroad. Rather than going to Europe or Mexico, he decided to go to Korea, the native land he had left at the age of four when he was adopted by Major Dunbar, the intelligence officer who had interrogated him. He'd been something of a wonder to the entire regiment. Barely able to walk, he had safely crossed the heavily mined no-man's land. "The lucky devil," the GI's said in amazement. "Not even a mouse could have made it alive."

The two-mile belt of land had separated several divisions of North Korean and Red Chinese troops on the north from a matching force of South Koreans and Americans on the south. The Armistice was about to be signed and battles raged to seize last-minute advantages of terrain. The area Allen had traversed toddling barefoot was in the Iron Triangle, over which both sides dumped tons upon tons of ammunition to saturation bomb and flush out the enemy from entrenchments.

Allen's house was on fire. The smoke blinded and choked him. The darting flames singed his hair, eyelashes,

and skin. The cotton in his quilt smoldered. He screamed for
his mother and father. But the crackling of the fire and the
thunder of shells and bombs hushed him. He ran to the door,
but it was on fire. A falling brand knocked him to the floor.
He crawled in the opposite direction. There was thick smoke
and leaping flame everywhere. The barn, hayrick, wood pile,
cowshed, everything burned. The houses next door were
ablaze, too. He limped and crawled and found his way to the
water-filled rice paddies. His burns smarted. He kept going
over dikes, roads, streams, away from the burning village,
the burning hell. He was now in the hills, but was scarcely
conscious of the sharp stones and underbrush that bruised
and cut him. The flash of gunfire and the thunder of explosions goaded him on all night, long after he had put hills and
valleys between him and his village.

Major Dunbar was a bachelor who had risen from the
ranks. He retired from the army soon after the Korean War
and settled in Honolulu. But Vietnam called him again and
he went, only to return soon after in an urn. Allen had not
known how much he loved this man until then. He had long
resented him for giving him the unsuitable name Dunbar. At
school he had been the butt of ceaseless teasing, an Oriental
with a Caucasian name. Now that the man was no longer
alive, he recalled Dunbar's every mannerism, his intonation,
his laughter. Dunbar had insisted on celebrating as Allen's
birthday, the day he had stumbled across the no-man's land
into the U.S. army unit. This had always infuriated Allen,
but now he was tearful thinking about it, hearing the old
man's croaking voice, "Happy birthday to you . . ." He
missed him terribly, his slouching posture, his shuffling gait,
his untidy habit of throwing clothes all over the floor and
furniture, his stink that no deodorant soap seemed to wash
off. If only he could get him back as he was . . . it was years
before he got over his loss. But never quite.

That's why he had decided to go to Korea. Perhaps his reintegration to his native land might help him forget everything, Dunbar, the U.S., the job, the acquaintances, all that clinging matter. He would find his original true being, uncluttered by spurious additions. He went to court and had his name changed to Shin, which he had picked at random from a list of a few dozen. He was sure Dunbar would understand. It had been like matrimony in a way and his loyalty should not extend beyond death. He was starting life all over again, with a new identity.

He went to Seoul, but the polluted, congested megalopolis with its nervous, fast-stepping population gave him no sense of homecoming. The real Korea, his native land, had to lie somewhere in the country. But what part of rural Korea? He had no idea where his village was. He remembered nothing distinctive about it. This was fine with him. The indubitable fact remained, his being Korean. Since he was not tied to any specific locality, he belonged to all of it, to any part of it. After inquiry at the Tourist Bureau he discovered that there were nearly twenty different Shin clans spread throughout the provinces. Again at random he chose a county in Kangwon Province near the Demilitarized Zone, just above the Iron Triangle of Korean War fame. The Shins live in several villages all over the county. The village of his choice was called Cholpori. It was a half-farming, half-fishing community of a hundred families. The letter of introduction he had brought from the Bureau was addressed to the alderman of the village. Allen was a Shin, returned from America in search of his roots. The entire county buzzed with the rumor and conjecture ran wild. Several families came from outlying areas with claims of kinship, to be turned away reluctantly with too many conflicting circumstances. His exact genealogy unsettled, he was nevertheless accepted as one of them. The alderman insisted on Allen's taking his own beach cottage, rent free, for as long as he liked. The villagers brought him food and supplies and he had a hard time making them accept money in return.

The cottage was some distance from the village and was occupied only during the fishing season in late fall. For the rest of the year it was left vacant and stored fishing gear. It sat in the middle of a sand dune, wind-swept and shifting, dotted by clumps of stunted conifers and hardy weeds. Allen read, swam, strolled, and occasionally strayed close to the village with its thatched, close-built houses, reeking with sewage. He could not, dared not, go too close to the people, these kindly, smiling brethren with faces similar to his own, who nevertheless shared with him little else. Their constant nodding, bowing, smirking, giggling, all good-natured and friendly, annoyed him unbearably. But he enjoyed the sea and the strips of sand and gravel punctuating the craggy shoreline. He loved to go to the edge of a promontory not far from the cottage and peer into the clear water that revealed the deep bottom where the sea plants swayed like sensuous dancing maidens and the fish gamboled. He loved the masculine austerity of the bleak sand dunes. It seemed he had truly found his element.

Then Sunhee came. She took over the supply of necessities and discouraged visitors, especially the gamesome village girls. She was the alderman's niece or something, and went to college in Seoul. It was some time before summer vacation. She must have cut school to devote herself to the task of ministering to him. Her English was halting and ungrammatical, but she made herself intelligible by vigorously signing and drawing. She had black eyes, rather thick eyebrows, a lumpy nose, full lips, and a square jaw—a far cry from a flaming beauty. But she made up for her deficiencies by her vivacity, her eagerness to communicate, her determined cheerfulness that would not be dampened by refusal.

"I want to teach you Korean," she said. "It's a shame you don't know your own language."

It sounded familiar. He had heard it from Korean tourists passing through Honolulu, gravely shaking their heads at the American Koreans who couldn't speak a word of Korean, hinting at ingratitude, even treachery. Ingratitude for what? Famine and war?

"But I am on vacation," Allen protested. "I don't want to labor with a foreign language when I am supposed to have fun."

"You call this fun, being cooped up here all by yourself?"

"But I like it. You have no idea how much."

"You'll soon lose your mind if you keep this up. I must help you, save you."

So Allen allowed her to do her best. The month was coming to an end, and it was time to leave. But Sunhee confronted him with the news that she was pregnant. When he offered to give her enough money for the abortion, she broke into tears. Did he think she was a machine he could turn on and off at will? She would kill herself first before she murdered her child. Did he have no humanity, no conscience, no fear of God? There was no other alternative but to marry her, duly witnessed by the Vice Consul at the American Embassy. He went to Honolulu first, at her strong urging. She would join him later, when her visa came through. There was a long waiting list, he was told. For eight months he sent $300 a month toward her support, not counting other gifts and allowances. Then, just before she left, she asked for $2,000 to settle her debts. He sent it, along with the air fare.

The person he met at the airport was not the big-bellied woman in her last month of pregnancy he had expected.

"I had a miscarriage," she said lightly.

"When?"

"Oh, a few months after you left."

"Why didn't you tell me?"

"I didn't want to worry you about it."

He glared at her.

"Were you ever pregnant?"

"Now, what is that supposed to mean?"

"Do you have the medical proof of your miscarriage?" he persisted. "Who was your doctor?"

"Do you doubt me, your own wife?" she shouted. "You have deceived me. You have never loved me. You have never trusted me. Is this love? Is this how husbands treat wives in America?"

Allen knew that he had been conned. All his plans had been shattered. There was not to be a new life. Knowing herself to be secure, now that she was on American soil, she openly scoffed at him. Did he think she would be tied down like a brood mare to start his dynasty, to make him the Adam of his race? She wanted to live, to savor in full the good life of America. She had to buy clothes at Carol and Mary, jewelry at the House of Adler, furniture at Jorgensen's. She had to eat out at the best restaurants. After two trips to the continental U.S. and a few trips to the outer islands, they had quite exhausted Allen's patrimony. When this fact was brought to her attention, and she was asked to cut down on her expenses, she went into hysterics. When he returned home from work, he found the dinner unprepared. She wasn't his slave. He had to cook, wash clothes, and clean the house. In the middle of the night he was jolted out of his sleep by a violent tug at his hair.

"What are all these deductions for?" she demanded, pointing at the pay statement.

Half asleep, rubbing his eyes, he studied the items. They were the medical insurance premium, union dues, social security payment, and installment payments to airline companies. She didn't believe it. She said it was a trick of his, borrowing money to stash away somewhere. No amount of reasoning helped. She was unalterable in her conviction. Night after night she woke him up to argue over the pay and the other women in his life, for whom he must be siphoning the money. Then she had a proposal. Since he was quite incapable of supporting her in her accustomed style, she was going to make her own money. She said she had met an old friend who worked at a bar, earning in one night as much as he made in a week. It so happened that there was an opening at the bar. He had to consent. Her hours were from evening till three or four in the morning. But she didn't come home after work. She said she slept at her friend's, since it was closer. She had to take care of shopping and other chores during the day. He was not home at the time anyway, so why should he care whether she was home or not?

His office sent him on a two-week training program to the head office in New York. He had a chance of being promoted to a managerial position, maybe even relocated to a better post. When he returned, there wasn't a penny left in their savings and checking accounts. He had to borrow from the credit union to pay the down payment on an unfurnished studio. After one night on the hard, uncarpeted floor, he sorely needed a bed.

Walking slowly back to Bargains Galore, he paid the amount the storekeeper asked for the picture frame and went with it to his studio.

* * *

Allen jumped in his sleep, screaming. He was having a nightmare. He had been caught in a burning house, and half his body had burned. The pain was so real that he ran his hand over himself for reassurance. He was drenched in sweat. He opened a window. The night lights of the city blinked drowsily. Muffled music ebbed and flowed from a nearby disco. A car screeched round the corner of the building. Late partying noise floated up from downstairs. He opened the refrigerator. There was no food. He took out a piece of ice from the freezer and put it in his mouth. Looking around the studio he noticed the picture frame, still wrapped in brown paper and resting against the wall. He picked it up and went to the oven. He opened the oven door and tried to slide the bundle in. It was too wide. But he didn't want to remove the wrapping. He took out the middle racks. Now he could squeeze it in sideways. Its length just fit the depth of the oven. The oven door clicked shut, and he turned the knob to broil. Then he went into the shower and fully opened both taps. As the water splashed his skin, he felt an exhilaration he had not known before. He sang at the top of his voice all the songs that came to his head. They kept coming one after another, astonishing even himself. He'd had no idea how extensive his repertoire was. He had come through fire and hell. He had beaten all odds. He was a lucky devil. Nothing could touch him.

* * *

The firemen had to axe the door down. The management had a good deal to explain and pay for. Several warnings of fire hazard had been issued against the building but had gone unheeded.

The Men Whose Tongues
Dana Naone

The men whose tongues have turned to iron
would say water tastes like rust
to them if they did not find it
so hard to speak. Words pile up,
they go through each day, their mouths full
of unsaid words. In dreams
they hang upside down and
ring like bells.

A Chant for a Wedding
Alfons L. Korn

Dusk covers day, clouds tilt, bud-shaped
cloudlets break and lean
against the sky

After lightning flashes, roar of thunder
echoes through darkness, echoing and re-echoing
again and again

For the lost has been found:
the one to cherish
the one to share
the one to keep against cold and
other skies: the one to keep
warm the house of welcome: the one
resting-place of love

Love asked you, who are two, to become one

Here then is your resting-place:
a place to poise
a place to perch
a place to reach out
a place to unite and together make
one earth and sky

Do you hear a trembling?
Do you hear a rumble and
rattle yonder, a rustle of
rolling pebbles below?

Remember: a house occupied
becomes a house of voices
Remember: when a house is empty
there are no voices,
there is not even a whisper, not
so much as a sigh

So you are two made one and
darkness, turning, begins to go while
daylight revives in the East and
bright day comes, comes at last
reawakening joy, staying until day becomes
dark, dark recovers day

United, the two of you are released, made free to each,
each to one, and to one another

The chant of your joining has taken flight

Flown into darkness, flown to the waters of night
let this chant go its way

The Grandmother
Susan Nunes

She was ninety-five years old, Frances said. For me, that was old, but she could have been one hundred and fifty for all the difference it would have made. I believed Frances. Mrs. Kawaradani was the oldest person I had ever seen in all my eight years, and in those years we lived on the hill, she never changed.

Frances teaches school in Honolulu now. I hear she is married and has two children. Her grandmother is long dead I am sure. And yet I cannot separate the old woman from the place, and I think I do not want to go back there now and see the house and the garden, because she will not be there.

I have never forgotten how she looked that first time, before I met her granddaughter who would be my best friend throughout childhood, before that frail, bent figure became a part of the place, a kind of fixture both fascinating and terrifying, like the hothouse with its sweaty flasks, or the cooking shed with its strange smells.

First I saw her feet—old, brown withered things in grass slippers, the toes thin and knotty, with the chalk-white nails long and curving toward the brown flesh. I remember that all quite clearly, sitting in the hedge close to the cooking shed with the smell of fish and old wood and charcoal burning.

Because we had only days before moved into the house on the hill, and because my parents were busy with cleaning, unpacking and putting away, I was left to wander about on my own, quite forgotten I am sure.

I had seen her feet so clearly, then her dress a moving white through the hedge. Moments after she passed my hiding place, I could hear noises coming from the shed. Curious, I crossed the narrow border path where she had walked only moments before, and edged along the right side of the low wooden shed. However, when I reached the open front and peered round to look inside, she was gone.

The room was small and square with a dirt floor and shelves running along three windowless walls. There were empty bottles and strange shaped flasks on the shelves, and in the rear boxes, stacked one on the other. Just inside the open front was a small cooking pit lined with stones with a wire grating on the top. Next to the pit was a low table and on it a wooden rice pot, a blackened water kettle, a plate of dried fish with a pair of long wooden cooking chopsticks laid across it. The room smelled of old things and charcoal burning.

Then I sensed a movement behind me, and as I turned, heard her low laugh.

That impression, in those moments before I ran, never left me completely, and because of the strength of that impression, caught there as I was, knowing that she knew I watched her only moments before, I was always in awe of that frail white-haired creature who was Frances' grandmother.

She comes to me sometimes, even now, just as she was that first day, a tiny, shriveled-up shell of a woman, standing sideways looking at me, her head sunk low into her narrow shoulders, her thin, brown arms with the knotted, veined hands all bent as if they clutched at something, and the way her dress fell from the hump on her back, fell all loose and hanging as if there were nothing underneath. And the low laughter.

"Furancesu," she would call. "Fu-ra-n-ce-su." I think Frances loved her, but I failed then to see any connection between old Mrs. Kawaradani and her granddaughter.

"She's calling you," I said to Frances one day as we sat in the old guava tree below the last terrace.

"I know," she said, with that solemn air she had about her. "You want to come?"

We went up toward the cooking shed, and standing there at the top of the rise was Mrs. Kawaradani, holding something in her apron, waiting. She didn't say a word as we approached, but turned and walked into the shed and knelt at the cooking pit. We stood behind her as she emptied the contents of her apron onto a newspaper. They were little brown wrinkled knobs like the tops of so many fingers. I looked at Frances.

"Sweet potatoes," she replied, answering my silent question. "She saves them for me. Watch."

The old woman poked at the ashes, her wooden chopsticks making a hole in the middle of the heap. Under the grey blanket of ashes, the coals glowed bright for a moment, then faded into fine pinpoints of orange. She put the potato ends into the hole and covered the little pile with the hot ashes.

"It doesn't take long," Frances said without looking at me. She was watching her grandmother.

We sat there, the three of us, old Mrs. Kawaradani on her low stool, Frances and I on the floor close to the fire. I could feel the heat against my legs and face. No one said anything, but occasionally the old woman would murmur "Francesu" and laugh quietly to herself. Frances watched the heap of coals.

When we could smell the potatoes, Mrs. Kawaradani reached for a newspaper, got up from her stool and squatted before the fire. Her chopsticks broke through the pile of ash and coals and she began picking out the little knobs, now grey and steaming, and put them one by one on the paper. Occasionally she blew gently to remove the ashes. When she was finished, she handed the newspaper to Frances.

"Come on," said Frances. "Let's go down to the tree."

We walked back down the path that cut through the rows and rows of orchid hybrids, down to the tree. I looked back, just once, and Mrs. Kawaradani was standing in front of the shed, old and bent in her faded dress with the white apron.

We ate the potatoes. They were sweet and earthy, but what I remember most is the lingering aftertaste of ashes.

Who can remember precisely when wonderment gives way to something else? Mrs. Kawaradani was old—I could see that—terribly old. She was also a grandmother. I knew that because Frances said it was so. But to me grandmothers were of another kind. When they smiled their gums didn't show. Mrs. Kawaradani was Frances' grandmother, and because everyone loved their grandmothers, Frances had to have loved her. I had not pondered upon this logic. It was just so.

But I saw that her face was more skull than flesh, and there was always about her the aura of old wood, and charcoal burning.

Frances' family raised orchid hybrids. Row after row of tree fern stump lined the terraced slope of their back yard, each stump topped with the pale green waxy plant. There were so many. It was a huge tangle of color with no visible attempt at order or design. A not untypical Hilo yard.

Frances and I often played in the greenhouse. It was built in a sheltered corner of the yard against an airy wall of tree fern. A red cinder path lined with azalea bushes led to an entrance framed with hanging wire baskets of maidenhair. Inside, the sunlight came through the slats in patterned stripes. All was transformed. The colors were more intense, the flasks glowed, and the air, laced with the damp smell of tree moss and the heady odor of the cattleya, was different.

The flasks contained hundreds of tiny orchid seedlings in their water medium. These were particularly vulnerable to disease so they grew quite apart in their sealed containers. I do not know how long it took them to mature and flower, but I believe it was a long, long time.

Frances and I came here often, but sometimes I came alone, just to be there in that otherness. And I would leave quietly, once more aware of the sharp stones under my bare feet.

It was at such a time that they found me there. Frances and her grandmother. I had not heard them approach, but the old woman's low laugh cut through the sunlight. She brushed gently past me, and I caught the smell of old wood and charcoal burning. She paused a few feet in front of me, reached among the red clay pots and singled out one plant, white rooted and moss covered, but with three deep purple blooms.

I felt the sharp bite of the cinder under my feet as she spoke in Japanese something I could not understand.

After a few moments of silence, Frances said, "That is the oldest. All the others come from this plant." She came from behind me and walked toward the old woman.

"My father says this one is older than he is."

She took the plant from her grandmother, placed it carefully back on the shelf and pulled at some bits of moss.

Again the old woman said something, most of which I did not understand. But I didn't miss the last word.

"Purebred."

And Frances said again, "It is very, very old." I hardly heard her though, because I was staring at that bony face, at the toothless mouth, at the shiny purple mottled flesh. Something in the meeting of the word and experience alienated me. I was alone. Not like them.

That is all I remember. I do not know what we did after that. It might have been any number of things, all lost. But I do know that it was in the weeks after that I decided to destroy the plant, to slowly crush each flower, to snap the thick stems and grind them into the sharp stones, to pull from the pot the hunk of tree fern which held the plant, and to rub from the red clay pot all traces of the white roots.

They never told my parents. Never complained. Frances and I played together until we reached intermediate school when different interests pulled us apart. Frances was my only and first Japanese friend. But she is as alien to me as that part of myself which is like her. As alien as her grandmother was. Old Mrs. Kawaradani.

Hybrid
For Susan
Juliet S. Kono

In Grandfather's cane fields
During planting, the old
Bent immigrant women
Worked the fields. They
Wore tabis, gloves, palaka
Shirts and men's old pants.
They'd do the "hoe-hana"
And sing songs of lament
That drifted saliently
With the down-winds.
After the plowing,
The women laid the "Pula-pula"
Into the long furrows.
One year, these young
Shoots were different.
"They are hybrids,"
Grandpa said, "Juicier,
Taller, creamier with less
Fiber, but strong."
He said that his harvest
Would be good in 2 years.

I see you now—
A woman of a night-dream—
Willowy as the cane,
Creamy and tall,
Moving comfortably
Among the "hoe-hana" women.
Your brown hair sparkling

And moving wispfully
Over your shoulders.
Your body gossamer,
Filtering in and out
Of our common ancestry.
You belong. You do not belong.
You have accepted that.

You float away
Across the fields.
Suddenly you're burning
At your feet. The flames
Grow fierce like cane fire.
There's no stopping it.
I run towards the field.
Before me, rising from
The smouldering dirt
Then blooming scent
And its blood,
A whole field of,
Purple hybrid orchids.

Bonsai
Frances Kakugawa

Knees knotted.
Veins frozen.
Legs rooted.
Arms perfected.
Years of toil
Plugged within.
His aged form
Sits serene.
Winds and rains
Beat on down
Only to quench
His thirsty tongue.
He sits unbent
In silent thoughts,
While all around
The sprouting young
Toss and stretch
Their adolescent arms.
He listens in silence
To all their dreams
Of conquerable feats,
Of emperors and kings.
He watches in silence
Their hairless limbs
Unaware still
Of their spiraled fences.
He watches them sway
In the bending wind,
His thoughts imprisoned
By adolescent walls.
Does he pity
Or does he envy?

Papio
Eric Chock

This one's for you, Uncle Bill.
I didn't want to club the life
from its blue and silver skin,
so I killed it by holding it
upside-down by the tail
and singing into the sunset.
It squeaked air three times
in a small dying chicken's voice,
and became a stiff curve
like a wave that had frozen
before the break into foam.

In the tidal pool
you used to stand in,
I held the fish and laughed
thinking how you called me
handsome at thirteen.
I slashed the scaled belly,
pulled gills and guts,
and a red flower bloomed
and disappeared with a wave like the last breath
your body heaved
on a smuggled Lucky Strike and Primo
in a hospital bed.
You wanted your ashes out at sea
but Aunty kept half on the hill.
She can't be swimming the waves at her age
and she wants you still.

The Million-Dollar Mango Tree
Ryan Monico

Our class was given a major end-of-the-year project. We had to come up with a business plan that would raise money for the class's Big Island field trip. Whoever raised the most money from their business plan would get an "A" for the course and the best room at the Big Island hotel.

I was at Perry Park with my friend Jeff. Jeff was my hapa-haole neighbor who was about a foot shorter than me, with light-brown hair and dark-brown eyes. We were trying to think of an idea for the project. I was hungry so I brought some pickled mango with me to snack on while we were thinking.

"Eh, Ryan, I like sample your pickled mango," my friend Jeff asked.

"Fifty cents one piece, five dollar one bag," I joked.

"No be uns, bu. I only like sample," Jeff pleaded.

"Okay, you can have one sample den, but you got to promise me that you going stop whining," I said so he would shut up.

"Yah, yah, yah, I going stop whining," Jeff answered quickly.

"Hea den!" I gave the mango to Jeff.

"Ho brah, the bugga is ono! Where you wen get 'em from?" asked Jeff.

"I when get 'em from my grandpa." I knew he was going to ask me where I wen get 'um from. I guess it was because he couldn't resist the crunchy, sweet, but vinegary taste. Just thinking about it makes my mouth water.

"Eh, Ryan, I can have just one moa sample?" Jeff asked. I gave him more and began to tell him the history of my grandpa's pickled mango.

About 25 years ago, my grandpa planted two cigar mango trees in the front and back yards of his home in Kalihi Valley. As the trees grew they became useful in many ways. They provided shade during family gatherings. They were used as jungle gyms with a tire swing by his grandchildren. And they were the main suppliers of mango for my grandpa's pickled mango.

Every mango season my grandpa would pick the biggest and best-tasting mangoes from the tree. He would skin the mangoes and cut them into long strips, then he would soak them in a semi-sweet pickle sauce for a week, giving them an onolicious taste.

"Eh, Ryan. Your grandpa still get pickled mango?" Jeff asked.

"Yah, why?"

"I get one idea for your school project."

"What is it?" I was eager to know because I didn't have an idea yet.

"We can sell your grandpa's pickled mango," Jeff answered.

"That's a great idea!" I said and set off for my grandpa's house with Jeff.

My grandpa has a typical Filipino house. It has a garden containing my grandma's favorite vegetables, like squash, paria, eggplant, and many others. My grandpa also grows a lot of trees. He has a plumeria tree, a *marunggay* tree, a mountain apple tree, a guava tree, and two mango trees. The inside of the house is decorated with souvenirs from the Philippines, family pictures, silk flowers and trophies. The living room furniture is draped with a bold-print covering, and the kitchen table is covered with plastic.

"Hi, Grandpa," I said as Jeff and I walked into the white two-story house.

"Grandpa, as part of our class project, I have to come up with a business plan to raise money for our Big Island field trip. Is it okay if I sell your pickled mango?" I asked.

"Okay. I have a big container full of pickled mango in deee ice box downstairs," my grandpa said with his Filipino accent. My grandpa was in his mid-sixties, had dark wrinkled skin, and mostly black hair.

"Thanks, Grandpa," I said.

Jeff and I went to the ice box and grabbed one of the big containers full of pickled mango. Then we filled Ziploc bags with pickled mango.

After filling 100 bags with pickled mango, we walked from house to house selling it for $3.00 a quarter pound, $6.00 a half pound, and $11 a full pound.

"Ryan, how much money you think we going make?" Jeff asked.

"I think we get enough to make a million dollars," I answered.

"Nah, for real? How much do you think we going make?" Jeff asked again, wanting a reasonable answer.

"One million dollars," I answered again.

"Well, I think that we'll make $3,000," Jeff said, confident that we would reach his mark.

We didn't make a million dollars or $3,000. Instead, we made $356, and that was enough to earn me an "A" for the course.

(Ryan Monico was an 8th-grader at University Laboratory School when he wrote "The Million-Dollar Mango Tree.")

More Precious than Pineapples
Vittorio Talerico

The wind is light
as we motor into the harbor,
the sails of no help.
While the others clean
and straighten below deck,
I volunteer to go up the hill
and get gas. The tank is below half.
A fisherman in his Jeep stops.
The road is winding
dry, mostly keawe trees.
"You been up Lanai City before?"
"Yeah about six years ago."
He smiles, "Nothing change."
"Where you guys from, Maui?"
"Yeah."
"Phooo Maui junk.
Everybody look stink eye.
Lanai mo' better. Plenty fish now,
everybody busy."
At Ohara's garage
I walk around back to pee.
Junk cars all over.
Old cars.
Studebakers, Packers, military jeeps,
dead school buses.
People here keep what they got.

Chinatown
Cathy Song

1

Chinatowns: they all look alike.
In the heart
of cities. Dead
center: fish eyes
blinking between
redlight & ghetto,
sleazy movie houses
& oily joints.

A network of yellow tumors,
throbbing insect wings.
Lanterns of moths
and other shady characters:
cricket bulbs & roach eggs
hatching in the night.

2

Grandmother is gambling.
Her teeth rattle: Mah-Jongg tiles.

She is the blood bank
we seek
for wobbly supports.

Building
on top of one another,
bamboo chopstick tenements
pile up like noodles.
Fungus mushrooming,
hoarding sunlight

from the neighbors
as if it were rice.
Lemon peels
off the walls so thin,
abalone skins.
Everyone can hear.

3

First question,
Can it be eaten?
If not, what good
is it, is anything?

Father's hair is gleaming
like black shoe polish.
Chopping pork & prawns,
his fingers emerge
unsliced, all ten intact.

Compact muscles taut,
the burning cigarette
dangling from his mouth,
is the fuse to the dynamite.

Combustible material.
Inflammable.
Igniting each other
when the old men talk
stories on street corners.
Words spark & flare out,
firecrackers popping on sidewalks.
Spitting insults, hurled garbage
exploding into rancid odors:
urine & water chestnuts.

4

Mother is swollen again.
Puffy & waterlogged.
Sour plums
fermenting in dank cellars.

She sends the children
up for air.
Sip it like tea.

5

The children are the dumplings
set afloat.
Little boats
bobbing up to surface
in the steamy cauldron.

The rice & the sunlight
have been saved for this:

Wrap the children
in wonton skins,
bright quilted bundles
sewn warm with five spices.

Jade, ginger root,
sesame seed, mother-of-pearl
& ivory.

Light incense to a strong wind.
Blow the children away,
one at a time.

A Haole Stops in Kaimuki
Jim Harstad

Mr. Perreira is the stocky, smiling Portuguese man who runs the Bank of Hawaii parking lot in Kaimuki Mondays, Tuesdays, and Wednesdays. He explains that he lets somebody else run the lot Thursdays and Fridays because he does not want to be a millionaire.

We have known each other since the early 1970s, when our sons played football for the Kapiolani Tigers in the Honolulu Pop Warner League. Whenever we see each other we shake hands and talk. I don't think he remembers my name. He calls me Handsome. He must know that, with my gray beard and bald head, I am flattered. I don't remember his first name. I call him Mr. Perreira.

Yesterday when I went to the bank to see how badly I was overdrawn and try to cover it, Mr. Perreira was wearing a lei of pikake and carnations. He shook my hand and said it was his birthday. He said he was 40. Mr. Perreira is a joker. I said he didn't look a day over 30. He laughed and said I looked more handsome every time he saw me. We both laughed. Mr. Perreira's face turns a jolly red when he laughs. He has a long, friendly face.

Then he said his wife gave him the lei. It was left over from yesterday, when it was her birthday. She was 62. Then Mr. Perreira said, again, that today was his birthday and that he was 40. And he laughed. The flowers on the lei were wilting and turning brown, but they still smelled good. Mr. Perreira said it was his birthday and I wanted it to be that way, though we both knew it would be ludicrous to believe either of us would ever see 40 again. He was older than me. Was he older than his wife? "Happy birthday, Mr. Perreira," I said. "I've got to go hold up the bank."

"OK, Handsome," he said. "Don't get caught."

We laughed again and stopped shaking hands. He handed me my parking ticket.

The line at the bank was long and slow moving. Only three windows were open, and at each was a businessperson with a whole week of life spread out on the counter in front of him. The tellers looked worried. They all seemed to be wondering whether something was missing.

I was leaning on the oak rail, wondering what to get Mr. Perreira for his birthday. I had never gotten him a birthday present before, but I felt I should, since I have known him for so long and like him so well. Thrifty Drugs is next door to the bank. I would check and see if they had sampler bottles of liquor. A sampler of Jack Daniel's black label seemed to me an appropriate gift for a 62-year-old man on his fortieth birthday.

Finally the businesspersons left the tellers' windows silently, almost at the same time, and the line began to move. The teller I got has been at Kaimuki Branch since I first started lending them my money, ten years or so ago. We don't know each other, but we are familiar faces. Hers is Japanese. She validated my parking ticket with a rubber stamp and seemed personally concerned that I had overdrawn my account by 36 dollars, even though the 100 dollars I deposited from the Credit Union more than covered the deficit. There would be penalty fees attached to my next bank statement. We both knew that and silently agreed to say nothing about it. It was unfortunate but could not be helped. We smiled and told each other to have a nice day.

Thrifty Drugs did not have sampler bottles of liquor, so I looked for something else. Maybe liquor would not have been appropriate after all? I found, instead, a small glass bottle of Martinelli's apple juice. The bottle was shaped like an apple, and the juice was golden through the clear glass. It was chilled perfectly. With tax, it came to 82 cents. I gave the Filipino lady at the counter a dollar bill and two pennies, which pleased her because the change came to a neat two dimes. She counted it out for me, "Eighty, ninety, and a hundred," just like they were crisp ten-dollar bills, not dimes. We smiled and wished each other a good morning.

When I got back to the parking lot, Mr. Perreira was busy stamping parking tickets on his time clock. He likes to be five or ten tickets ahead, so he can wander a little from his station and be friendly with his customers. He was whistling, and his back was turned, so he did not notice me. I said, "Mr. Perreira," and when he looked I handed him my validated parking ticket. "And this is for your fortieth birthday," I said, handing him the apple juice in a paper bag and walking toward my car.

"I can't take this," Mr. Perreira called after me.

"It's for your birthday."

"I was just kidding. Yesterday was my wife's birthday. Take it home for your kids."

"It's for your wife's birthday. It's good."

"All right, Handsome," he said, "and I just want you to know that my wife says you get better looking every time she sees you."

"That's right, Mr. Perreira," I said, "and mine tells me you don't look a day over 30."

And we both laughed as I got into the rusty 1968 VW bug I have owned since 1971. It was 10:33 a.m. on Wednesday, December 11, 1985. The sky was clear. The sun was warm. It was a beautiful morning.

Pele's Children
Alissa Fukushima

It lay basking in the warm rays of the tropical sunlight, its corrugated surface catching and refracting the light. The deep black coloring trapped and drew the heat into its very core. It was hard and solid, able to withstand all the weathering elements despite its small size. It was a marvel of creation, capable of defying even time itself as it lay dormant, patiently waiting.

Priscilla Harper carefully descended the metal stairs leading down from the airplane. A gusty wind whistled around the craft, creating a strong updraft. Her special Hawaii-bound hairdo, which had cost a small fortune, flattened out in all directions, clinging to her face and sticking in her lipstick. She pulled at her hair vainly, trying to prevent the strands from whipping into her eyes. Where were the dancing hula girls with arms overflowing with fragrant blossoms? She sure as heck didn't see any little grass huts, luscious green foliage, or fresh coconuts either. Coming to Hawaii for vacation was a mistake. She had been right all along. Why hadn't it been the French Riviera?

Close behind Priscilla followed her yawning and stretching husband, Jeff. He paused a moment at the top of the stairs. Fresh air filled his lungs as he inhaled deeply and took in the beauty of the cloudless blue sky. It felt great to be out of the airplane's cramped seats. He had two long weeks of nothing but leisurely sight-seeing ahead of him. Yes, this was going to be the vacation of a lifetime.

The hotel had a distinctly unique air about it, a special elegance, that neither of them had ever experienced. Tall, graceful palms lined the narrow straightaway leading up to the shining building.

At the entrance a brown-skinned local boy greeted them and took their bags. The lobby was spacious; creeping vines embraced the ivory pillars supporting the high open-beam ceiling. Sweet strains of island music floated throughout the room from some unseen source. Smoothly polished gourds and scowling wooden idols with mouths full of sharp teeth embellished the walls. The subtle primitive touches only enhanced the exotic flavor of the hotel.

As Priscilla and Jeff climbed the marble staircase, Jeff marveled at the dignified kings and queens of Old Hawaii that looked down at him from their exquisitely carved gold picture frames. He announced the long foreign-sounding name of each depicted royalty loudly in his best imitation Hawaiian accent. Even Priscilla had to suppress the smile that crept onto her lips.

Once inside their room Priscilla and Jeff quickly exchanged their travel clothing for comfortable, broken-in t-shirts and faded cutoff shorts. The bright sunshine and the out-of-doors beckoned to them. Unable to resist, they were soon back in their compact rent-a-car speeding off to the major tourist attraction in Hawaii, the volcanoes. The Hawaii Volcanoes Visitor Center was a colorful mecca of tourists milling about in fluorescent aloha apparel. Priscilla and her husband wandered amid the other people and display cases which held various types of lava rocks and native plants. Pictures and paintings of volcanoes erupting furiously hung from the walls. One picture in particular caught Priscilla's eye. In it was the silhouette of a volcano against a dark bluish night sky, red molten lava fountaining spectacularly into the air and spilling over its slopes. Clearly visible in the rising reddish smoke was the image of a woman's face, her long hair streaming behind her. The woman's expression was one of wild glee, as if she delighted in the flames and ongoing destruction around her. It was as if her impish,

piercing gaze was focused directly on Priscilla. Mesmerized completely, she did not realize someone had joined her.

"Beautiful isn't she?" a voice crackled. Priscilla jumped at the sound. Startled, she turned to stare at the voice's owner. Standing in back of her was a short, wrinkled man with hair of the purest white. Paying no attention to the embarrassed blush that colored Priscilla's face he said again, "Yes, she surely is." He gave a low whistle. "That," he informed her, nodding at the painting, "is Madame Pele herself, in all her fiery glory."

"Oh," was all she could get out at first. "Madame Pele, huh?"

"That's right, she is the goddess of these volcanoes, creator of this land."

"And you are Kimo. Correct?" she said, glancing at the tag attached to his shirt pocket. "You work around here?"

"Yes, I do. I'm a guide. I take visitors on tours of the crater in my van. Right now I have a group almost ready to depart. They're waiting for me outside. Would you like to come along?"

"Well, only if you have room for one more, my husband," she said, looking around for Jeff.

"No problem, there's always room for one more," replied Kimo smiling easily. "We'll be waiting outside in the van." With that he disappeared. Priscilla rushed off and found Jeff, who was reading an exhibit on volcano wildlife. She led him by the sleeve all the way into a yellow van, badly in need of a paint job, which stood idling in the parking lot.

The van was already crammed full and Priscilla had to squeeze into a seat with another couple while Jeff stood. The ride was short, but in the brief time period Kimo filled their heads with numerous tales of gay Hawaiian menehunes and legends about mischievous gods. He was an expert in his field, with an incredible knowledge of Hawaiian folklore. He laughed a lot, a funny wheezy sound in itself, well-worn smile creases appearing around his eyes.

As the van creaked to a stop, his expression changed. "Outside, there are many interesting things and unusual rocks, but you must not take the stones off these grounds. These are the lands sacred to Pele. The rocks are her children. According to Hawaiian legend, bad luck follows the one who is unfortunate and foolish enough to try and steal her children from her." He abruptly turned his back and swung open the squeaky door, allowing all the eager tourists to hop out.

Priscilla stepped out of the van and looked around. As far as the eye could see, there was nothing but layers of rock from a recent lava flow. No plants, no beetles or any living thing in the vast expanse of land, only the sound of the wind whistling through the cracks in the rock. The whole place seemed bleak, barren and desolate. This made her feel uneasy as, gazing downwards to her feet, she saw something gleaming in the sunlight. She stooped and picked it up. It was sunwarmed and a little sticky. There appeared to be little rainbows shining on its black, multifaceted surface. What an odd rock. She'd never seen anything like it before. Certainly neither had any of her friends back home. It would make a terrific souvenir. Just then Priscilla realized the intent of her thoughts. The rock thudded to the ground. Kimo had warned against taking these "children."

The rock, sitting placidly at her feet, glinted up at her. It was only one little rock. Surely Peelee or whatever her name was, if she really existed, wouldn't miss just one. That did it. Her eyes darted slyly from side to side. No one was looking. In one fluid movement she grabbed the rock up and slipped it into her pocket.

Just then Jeff walked over. "You about ready to go?" he asked. "I've had enough of this boring lava stuff. Whaddya say we hit the beach."

She smiled widely at him and said, "Yes, let's go already. I agree with you totally. I think I have had enough." She held out her hand to him.

"Hey, what happened to your hand?" he said, staring.

"Hmm?" Priscilla looked down at her hand, which now contained many small cuts that were beginning to bleed in tiny scarlet rivulets.

"Oh that, I must have scraped it on that dumb, old, rusty van door." She cradled her injured hand, trying hard to remember if that was what had really happened. That had to have been it. She was almost sure of it. Still, deep in the pit of her stomach, a small sick feeling started up.

That night Priscilla thought she would be exhausted after having such a busy day. Instead she tossed and turned. She tried to think of all the pleasant things she'd seen during the day, but her thoughts kept reverting back to Kimo's firm words of warning and then to the coal-black rock hidden away in the darkness of her closet. Finally, without realizing it, she fell into a shallow, restless sleep. She heard a whispery, thin voice calling her name, and through the shadowy mists of the dream world the face of Madame Pele materialized before her. Pele said not a word but stretched out her arms toward her.

"I don't have it," Priscilla heard herself say. A rhythmic drum beat reverberated in the background. It grew faster and faster. Suddenly she was falling face down, rushing towards a pit of fiery hot lava that was bubbling and boiling up to receive her. The intense heat started to sear the delicate skin of her face. It was too much and she jerked back into consciousness, just barely stifling the screams stuck within her throat. Her hair was plastered to her head in a cold sweat, and the heavy pounding in her chest sounded horribly irregular. The darkness all around her only amplified her fears and she groped for the light desperately. At last she found it and flicked it on. The remainder of the night she sat up rigidly, staring wide-eyed at the closet, her muscles tense.

When the dawn finally arrived, illuminating the paradise outside, Priscilla was still awake, barely holding open her red, glassy eyes. She threw off the covers, flung open the closet door, and grabbed the rock.

She ran outside and jumped into the car. Her hands were white and shaky, clutching the steering wheel unsteadily, causing the car to weave back and forth on the road, narrowly missing some pedestrians crossing the street. Undaunted, Priscilla sped on, flooring the accelerator relentlessly.

It was only early morning and as a result the visitors' center was deserted. Her footsteps echoed hollowly on the cold cement floor as she hurried around the exhibition area. She passed the picture that had virtually hypnotized her the previous day, not daring to look up. At last she spied a figure in the Information Booth. She ran up to the booth as fast as her shaking legs would carry her. Inside sat a comfortable-looking middle-aged woman with her hair done up in a no-nonsense bun. When she saw Priscilla, she stopped humming and said, "Aloha and good morning to you, miss. What may I do to help you?"

"Well, yesterday I took this rock from Madame Pele. No, I mean I took this rock from the crater, and ever since I have had nothing but bad luck and nightmares," Priscilla said breathlessly.

"Here, let me see this rock," the woman told her gently, removing the rock from Priscilla's clenched hands. She examined it carefully for a moment. The woman started to chuckle. "This is nothing but a piece of the new asphalt that the government laid because of the recent lava flow that destroyed the road. It is not a rock."

Priscilla's jaw dropped. She stared at the woman blankly.

"Could it be a bad conscience? You know you're not supposed to take stones out of the area. You were lucky it wasn't a real stone," the woman scolded. "We always tell all our visitors not to . . ."

"No, it was real. My hand, it bled and Pele, she came to me. I saw her, myself," Priscilla said, then she stopped. "I, well, I thought that," she faltered. Confusion rolled in her mind like thick clouds. She turned and ran back to the car.

The woman waved good-bye to the fast-disappearing car. She shook her head. They sure did get their share of the strange ones around here. Tourists could be so silly. Humming once again, she let loose her long black hair which streamed down her back. She picked up the rock and smiled. In a brilliant flash of fire and smoke, she too was gone.

(Alissa Fukushima was a student at Hawaii Preparatory Academy when she wrote "Pele's Children.")

Excerpt from
A Pilgrim's Kisses
James D. Houston

> On the way to Mecca, many dangers:
> Thieves, the blowing sand, only
> camel's milk to drink. Still, each
> pilgrim kisses the black stone there
> with pure longing, feeling in the
> surface, the taste of the lips he wants.

> —Jelaluddin Rumi (1207–1273)

Rocks

At the headquarters of Volcanoes National Park, rocks arrive every day. They arrive in the mail, in packages large and small, fifty or so in an average week. They come from New Jersey, from Florida, from Hong Kong, from L.A. and Dallas and Chicago. Some are black, porous chunks as large as a horse's head. Some are merely pebbles. Sometimes packets of black sand are sent, picked up years earlier at Kalapana's famous Black Sands Beach. They arrive in tiny cardboard boxes tightly wrapped, like jewelry. They arrive in padded mailing envelopes shipped UPS, or Air Express. The postal charges can run to twelve, fourteen, sixteen dollars— clear evidence that some souvenir had become more trouble than it was worth, and the time had come to get this out of the house.

Why are the rocks sent here, and sent to this particular building? According to local beliefs, if you pick up even one small shard of lava and slip it into your suitcase and carry it off, terrible things can happen. The word is *kapu*, a Hawaiian version of the more familiar Tongan word of warning, *tabu*.

Since Hawai'i is Pele's island, there is a *kapu* on everything
spewed up from the volcanoes that have formed it and
continue to form it; and Halema'uma'u, the pit crater said to
be her traditional home, happens to be inside the boundaries
of the park.

So the mysterious and the self-evident co-exist here at
park headquarters, which on one hand is very high-tech and
up-to-date, designed to service the multitudes of visitors. In
the reception lobby, smoothly narrated film loops run all day
long. The offices are equipped with word-processors and
satellite hook-ups. A couple of miles farther along the
perimeter road there is a new installation run by the U.S.
Geological Survey, where the earth's most active volcanic
region is wired to a wall of computerized dials and screens.
But when you descend the stairs to the Park Service
mailroom you leave the high-tech world behind and enter
another realm, where older forms of communication and
energy transfer prevail. Omens are in the air, signs and
portents, and luck both good and bad, along with the
unchartable magnetisms that have sent lava rocks on a
strange round-trip journey. They have traveled three and four
and five thousand miles, only to be called back to their
natural habitat.

I have come to this mailroom out of curiosity, but not as
a skeptic. The packages labelled Air Express convey an
urgency I recognize. I know it all too well, since I myself
have sent rocks back to this island, thinking, "It can't hurt.
And it just might make a difference." And I have often
wondered if those rocks arrived; and if so, what had become
of them? Now I know.

Some are addressed to "Superintendent." Or to "The
Director." Some are addressed to Pele herself. Her name will
appear on the envelope, as well as in the heading. The only
thing I can think of that might be remotely akin to this is the
annual blizzard of letters kids still send to Santa Claus. But

these letters are not from kids. They're from adults. They are usually typed, and rather formal. They are often detailed, full of the need to be understood, to be unburdened.

Pele is a very possessive woman. According to the numerous stories and legends about her, she is also fiery, jealous, unpredictable, passionate and vindictive. As I flip through this week's sheaf of letters, it occurs to me that Pele is also in a class by herself. Can there be another goddess, in the United States or elsewhere, with a zip code?

> *Dear Madame Pele:*
> *I am returning the lava I took from Black Sands Beach in 1969. I hope this pleases you, so my husband and I will have better luck on future trips....*
>
> *Dear Madame Pele:*
> *Your volcanic rock is enclosed. There is no return address on this because I don't want any return....*
> *I am sending by mail my shoes (writes a fellow from West Palm Beach) worn on my trip to Hawai'i. They are dirty from the mud, which was picked up on my trip. I feel foolish doing this, but with all the bad luck I have been hearing about since my trip, you and Hawai'i can have them. I have always considered myself a lucky person. But in the six to eight weeks after leaving Hawai'i I have heard over thirty separate incidents of bad luck. It's unreal. A former native of Hawai'i sincerely told me to send the shoes back.*

Occupied Territory

"I don't like to be out there at night," the geologist said.

"Out on the lava, you mean."

"Anywhere around the volcano. I have had to do that a couple of times, taking readings, you know, something we were monitoring on a twenty-four hour basis. But it was too uncomfortable."

"At this altitude the air cools down a lot. I've noticed that."

"I don't mind the air," he said. "And I don't mind the rocks. I can sleep almost anywhere. I mean, it is occupied territory. You always have the feeling somebody is right behind you, watching you. It's like being in a dark alley with the sense that someone is following you, even though you know you're alone and there is nobody else around for miles."

"Pele, perhaps."

"Okay. The Hawaiians will say it's Pele. Or they will say it's the spirit of somebody who might have got buried in a flow or something like that. Down towards Ka'u you can still see footprints of warriors who got caught there during an eruption two hundred years ago. A hard-nosed scientist would more likely attribute anything you think you are feeling to the electromagnetic field up there. I don't know. I don't necessarily put a name on it. Let's just say it's a presence you develop a respect for."

Sacred Places

No coco palms for shade, no white beaches, no condos overlooking a turquoise pool. The dirt road is iron red. It leads you through two miles of cane field to a broad clearing and a long rectangle of lichen-spotted chunks of lava. Inside the sloping walls there are pathways and restored stone platforms open to the sky.

It is said to be among the most venerable and sacred of all Hawaiian places—the walled worship site itself, which is nearly the size of a soccer field, as well as the surrounding terrain. Members of the Mo'okini family have been the appointed guardians of this site for over fifteen hundred years. According to their genealogical chant, the *heiau* dates back farther than Taos Pueblo, farther than the temples of the sun and moon at Teotihuacan.

It was first laid out in A.D. 480, under the direction of Kuamoʻo Moʻokini, the high priest from whom all guardians have been descended, down to the present day. The walls were originally six feet high. About a thousand years ago the temple was enlarged by a priest from Samoa, named Pāʻao. The walls were raised to their present height of thirty feet, without the use of mortar, and a unique scalloped altar was added inside. A family chant tells us the new stones came from Pololu Valley, fourteen miles down the coast toward Hilo. They were moved in a single night. Between sunset and sunrise, fifteen thousand men stood in a line and passed the stones by hand, from the deep valley to this windswept headland.

I have heard of Moʻokini for years. I have seen photos of the ancient stones where the birth of Kamehameha I was consecrated (he was born just a thousand yards away). I have read about the long stewardship of the Moʻokini family. But what I did not know, could never have grasped from afar, or by reading, or by studying all the photographs, was the impact of the location.

Moʻokini *heiau* is out there by itself, a mound of stone on a treeless point.

It occupies the very end of the Big Island's northernmost point, a peninsula that juts like a thumb, pointing across the channel toward Maui. Standing there you have behind you the green and rugged slopes of the Kohala Range and, in front of you, Maui's high shield-cone, Haleakalā, The House of the Sun. It is the world's largest dormant volcano. Viewed from the south, it is certainly as noble and blood-stirring as Fuji or Mount Shasta, with the added benefit that it comes rising straight out of the sea.

Wind through the channel is constant and as mysterious as the silence of the craters that made the islands, while the waters are spectacularly blue, a moving, shifting, current-driven blue. The point is empty. The sea is moving. Twenty-five miles across the channel the old volcano, in early afternoon, makes a dark cone against the sky.

Standing here, it isn't hard to imagine the first human who stopped and gazed toward the next island in the constant wind and felt an urge to consecrate the moment, to send a voice across the water, make a song or chant or gather a few stones in a heap. The place has a kind of power, which is to say, it releases something in those who experience it. And after enough people have visited the spot, to stand, to pray, to sing, to fast, to chant, century upon century, its original impact has been layered and amplified until the ancestral atmosphere around a site like Mo'okini is so rich with what Hawaiians call *mana,* you can feel it like a coating on your skin. Later, trying to explain this to myself, I begin to think of sacredness as a kind of dialogue between the human spirit and certain designated places. These sites that call forth reverence and awe and humility and wonder, we make them sacred. It is a way of honoring those feelings in ourselves.

And when we hear the songs the places sing, we are hearing our own most ancient voices.

Permissions

The Curriculum Research & Development Group has made every effort to trace the ownership of all selections in this book and to make full acknowledgment and compensation for their use. For selections whose authors we could not find, the copyrights remain with the owners of the works. We thank the following for permission to reprint.

Baber, Asa, "The Surfer," from *Hawaii Review East/West Issue #10* (Spring/Fall 1980). Reprinted by permission of Asa Baber.

Burgess, Puanani, "'Awapuhi," from *Hawaii Review #9* (Fall 1979). Reprinted by permission of Puanani Burgess.

Bushnell, O. A., "Malie," from *Moloka'i* © 1963 by O. A. Bushnell. Published by The World Publishing Company. Reprinted by permission of O. A. Bushnell.

Chock, Eric, "Ancestry" and "Papio," from *Ten Thousand Wishes*. Reprinted by permission of Eric Chock.

Doi, Marshall, "The Luna of the Landing," from *Bamboo Ridge* (December 1978). Reprinted by permission of Yutaka Doi.

Farmer, David C., "Summer's Day Hālau," from *Kani Lehua*. Reprinted by permission of David C. Farmer.

Hara, Marie M., "Old Kimono," from *Bananaheart & Other Stories* (Bamboo Ridge Press, 1994). Reprinted by permission of Marie M. Hara.

Harada, Gail, "New Year," from *Hawaii Review #8* (Fall 1978). Reprinted by permission of Gail Harada.

Harstad, James R., "A Haole Stops in Kaimuki," from *Bamboo Ridge, The Hawaii Writers' Quarterly #30* (Bamboo Ridge Press, 1986). Reprinted by permission of James R. Harstad.

Holt, John Dominis, "The Pool," from *Princess of the Night Rides.* Reprinted by permission of Allison Holt Gendreau.

Hongo, Garrett, "The Hongo Store, 29 Miles Volcano, Hilo, Hawaii," from *Talk Story: Big Island Anthology,* edited by Arnold Hiura, Stephen Sumida, and Martha Webb (Talk Story, Inc. and Bamboo Ridge Press, 1979). Reprinted by permission of Garrett Hongo.

Horiuchi, Lisa, "The Mystery Writer's Class Reunion," from *Keola* (University High School, 1986–87). Reprinted by permission of Lisa Horiuchi.

Houston, James D., "A Foreword," © 2001 by James D. Houston. Printed by permission of James D. Houston.

Houston, James D., "A Pilgrim's Kisses," from *Mānoa #1 - A Pacific Journal of International Writing* (University of Hawaii Press, 1989). Reprinted by permission of James D. Houston.

Kakugawa, Frances H., "Bonsai," from *The Path of Butterflies.* Published by The Naylor Company, San Antonio, Texas. Reprinted by permission of Frances H. Kakugawa.